Published by Autumn Day Publishing
Copyright 2024
Cover by Toby Gray
Edited By Cheryl Whittier
Other works by L.S. Gagnon,
Witch: A New Beginning
Witch: The Secret of the Leaves
Witch: The Final Chapter
Warlock: Descension into Darkness
Original release 2024
ISBN 978-0-9967707-8-1
All characters in this book are fiction
and figments of the author's imagination.

Warlock: Keeper of the Gates
Book Four
by L.S. Gagnon
Facebook/TheWitchSeries

I want to make a special dedication to two very special people in my life. Sean and Susan Gurry. Thank you for always being there for me. Sometimes a simple, 'Are you ok?' goes a long way. Thank you for your help, your friendship and your sincere concern.

I would also like to dedicate this book to you, the fans. I would be nothing if not for your love of my books. You keep my fingers tapping those keys. Ryan Peace, you will always be Netiri to me. You're a fan and a friend that turned into one of my favorite characters, and a friend. You hold a very special spot in my heart.

Cheryl Whittier, I cannot put a price on your friendship and help. Thank you for putting me at ease and helping me in any way you could. I've learned so much from you. It's not easy being an author when you have dyslexia. God bless you for making sense of my gibberish.

Paul Danforth, know that in every dark place we find ourselves in, there is always a ray of light that somehow gets through. Follow that light. The journey is what makes us stronger even when the goal seems impossible. The light never dies, it only dims a little sometimes. I love you. Kid.

Table of Contents

Prologue
Chapter One...Lois
Chapter Two...The Bank
Chapter Three...Stupid Questions
Chapter Four...First Contact
Chapter Five...Forgiveness
Chapter Six...Honor
Chapter Seven...River of Life
Chapter Eight...Splendor of Magia
Chapter Nine...Fish
Chapter Ten...Big Mouth
Chapter Eleven...Unbeknownst
Chapter Twelve...I'm Sorry
Chapter Thirteen...Kidding Around
Chapter Fourteen...Breathtaking
Chapter Fifteen...The Pit
Chapter Sixteen...Tree of Life
Chapter Seventeen...Torn Dress
Chapter Eighteen...Thoughts
Chapter Nineteen...Viola
Chapter Twenty...Morphine
Chapter Twenty-One...Explanation
Chapter Twenty-Two...Hardest Worker
Chapter Twenty-Three...I Do
Chapter Twenty-Four...The Banquet
Chapter Twenty-Five...Howl
Chapter Twenty-Six...Idiot
Chapter Twenty-Seven...Nor'easter
Chapter Twenty-Eight...Keeper of the Gates
Chapter Twenty-Nine...Dragon's Fire
Chapter Thirty...Black Witch
Epilogue

Prologue

It is said that evil walks the earth, looking for victims to fill its book of lost souls. Had evil touched my heart? Had it filled my head with lies? Would I be one of those pages in evil's book? I was turning into someone I no longer knew. The voices were getting louder and louder. The Tree of Life had shown me the future, written my name on its bark. There was so much riding on my shoulders. William had recruited warlocks to help us. I first believed they were here to fight evil. I never imagined they were here to kill *me*.

It was my dream all over again. I knew I was about to kill these men. I looked at Netiri as he pointed his sword at me. It was then I knew it would be his sword that I would use to decapitate him. All the characters of my dream were here, all ready to die at my hand.

Chapter One: Lois

    I tried to fix my tie as I stood in front of a mirror in the foyer. I'd never worn a tie before, nor had I any clue what a *tie* even was. James, my father, had to explain its purpose and why humans wore them. Apparently, there were many types of ties in many different colors. I still couldn't understand the point of them. Why did humans put them around their necks again?

    Today, I would be paying my respects, and my father was kind enough to assist me in looking like a gentleman. I just wish wearing a tie wasn't a requirement because I felt a bit foolish with a piece of rope hanging from my neck. Yes, I knew it was a tie, but it felt like a rope to me. I was dressed in slacks and a nice shirt my mother had picked out. My attire was all black, another requirement to attend a funeral. I didn't question their customs, I only wanted to make sure I didn't stand out like a sore thumb, as Fish would put it.

    This would be my first time going to a human funeral service. We didn't have these types of things in Magia, the magical land I came from. Wizards didn't bury their dead; in fact, we didn't have the ritual of burning them, either. I knew witches burned their dead to give them a sendoff, only they didn't burn them the same way the humans did. In the witch society, they built platforms to burn their dead, sending their spirit back to the earth. I was told that when the humans burned their dead; it was called, cremation.

    Today, the humans would be burying one of their deceased. Her name was Lois Marcia, and she was one of the three women I rescued from those three evil witches that had captured them. The three women had been kept in a dungeon, chained to a wall and starved so that the three witches could make themselves look and act just like them. Then they took their places in the women's lives and by using spells, the witches were also able to walk like them, and even talk like them. It was their way to get around Salem without getting noticed.

    I gave those three witches a horrible death, killed them for what they had done to Steven and Joshua. I did not go easy on them. I took pleasure in all the pain I caused them. My mind had gone dark, and I couldn't get enough of their pain. I could still hear their screams in my head, begging me to stop. As sick as it sounded, it actually made me smile whenever I thought of it. I don't know why it gave me such joy to recall how I killed them, I only knew it made me smile—a lot. Even now, as I struggled with this 'rope' around my neck, I smiled, thinking of their agony.

William, my grandfather and King of Magia, was not happy that I kept thinking about them, and how I killed them. He was constantly reading my thoughts and snapping me out of it. He was a great wizard king and had extraordinary powers; reading minds was one of his talents. I was still trying to perfect blocking my mind from him, but it still wasn't working. He would always remind me, "If it didn't work for your mother, it's not going to work for you."

I would have thought William would stay in Magia. He had already killed Wendell, a wizard who betrayed him, so why was he still in Salem? I didn't bother trying to put any of his puzzles together; they were too confusing. William was a very intelligent man. As a matter of fact, the word 'brilliant' wasn't enough to explain how intelligent he truly was.

Before William killed Wendell, he'd been in contact with Irene, who I always thought was the Black Witch. William explained how Irene was only a *prisoner* to the real Black Witch. William also said the real black witch I nicknamed, Creepella, lived in hell. That she was most likely a damned soul because she had made a deal with her master, the devil. Now she wanted out of hell, and she needed my mother to do that. Creepella tried using Irene, but Irene was too weak-minded and riddled with guilt for killing her children. It was a blood promise that changed Irene. My mother explained that when you make a blood promise, it always changes you.

It's a kind of deal you make with the darkness. You need something, so you make a promise to do something in return. The darkness grants that request, but makes you a prisoner to that promise. Well, Irene never kept her promise and the darkness claimed her anyway. William explained that by just making a blood promise, it changes you, even if you kept your end of the bargain. It's the price you pay for dancing with the devil.

My mother, on the other hand, made a blood promise, broke it, and yet it never changed her. When she got pulled into hell, she battled Creepella and won. The promise never changed my mother like it had Irene. When Creepella saw what my mother had pulled off, she realized there really was a way out of hell. By possessing my mother and using *her* strength to fight her way out, she realized she could walk the earth again. It's the main reason my father didn't want my mother to come to Salem. He wanted her to stay in Magia, where she would be safe. But if you knew my mother, she wasn't running from anyone.

Fish, Delia, and Cory were all still in Magia. They had taken the news about Joshua's death very badly. The mansion felt so empty without them. Only my parents, William and I were staying here. I knew they were keeping an eye on me, thinking I was turning into some dark lord. I had given up on trying to convince them I was fine. It didn't matter to me what they thought; I was stronger than they ever imagined. I just couldn't understand why they kept telling me I was becoming forgetful. What was I forgetting? I know one thing, I never forgot about the amount of pain I was always in.

You see, one of those witches I killed put a gypsy curse on me for killing their friend. She gave me something humans called the shingles. According to William, I had internal and external shingles. The blisters came first, then…nerve pain like I'd never felt before. Needle-like flames were sent through me and ripped me apart. At least, it felt that way. No spell can calm it, no chant or potion does anything to lessen the pain.

William had the bright idea of having Sean, my boss, beat me to a pulp. He said that it would make me stronger and not think of the pain so much. It worked, in a sense. I still feel the pain most days, but it's getting easier to ignore. On bad days, I go see Doctor Crowley, a pain specialist Sean recommended. He was giving me something called nerve blocks to ease the pain. I think Crowley is the only reason I haven't gone mad.

Then there was the White Witch, who was a pure entity needed to send a black book of spells *back* to hell and there was Creepella, the Black Witch, who was using that black book of spells to call demons from hell to help her. She wanted to walk the earth and rule the living. William said she was getting things ready for her master, the devil.

I still didn't know how a White Witch was called back. Vera, a witch who died years ago, was apparently the perfect candidate to be a White Witch. I didn't know where all that stood at the moment. William hadn't mentioned it again.

"Are you still trying to fix that thing," my mother said, pulling me from my thoughts.

"Do I really need to wear this?" I said, stepping away from the mirror. "I look ridiculous."

My mother walked over, stepped in front of me, and began to tug and pull at it. She smiled at me as she fixed the rope, I mean, tie.

The rays coming from the window hit her eyes, making the brown really stand out. My mother had matted, tangled hair that she refused to use a spell to change it. She called it a sign of love that she kept for my father.

"If his eyes are forever blue, then my hair will be forever messy," she said one day.

My mother looked into my eyes and smiled.

"Is going to her service really that important to you?" she asked.

She took a step back and looked at her handy work. I faced the mirror again to see how I looked.

"It is, Mother. I have to and I want to go."

"You didn't even know her, Ethan. Why does this mean so much to you?"

My mother didn't know this, but I had been keeping a watchful eye on all three of the humans. After I rescued them, I gave them all my word that I would protect them. I knew they would never remember that promise, seeing how my mother and William erased their memories. They would never remember all the horrible things those three witches did to them. Still, I didn't care, I looked after them anyway.

For some reason or another, I felt a connection to them. I think it was their faces when I rescued them. That desperate look, their screams of terror, I suppose I felt sorry for them. After William and my mother placed them back into their normal lives, I watched them, making sure they hadn't missed a thing. I looked for signs of any trauma, for anything that told me they remembered the past. William said it took him weeks to get their lives back in order. That still didn't stop me from checking on them. Judy, Sue and Lois were good people.

I was sad to learn about Lois. She was the spunkiest of the three. As I watched her live her life, I was able to see that she had a big heart. In fact, they all did. It pleased me to see them go to movies, parks, dinners, and walks along the lake again. I was happy they had all done well and moved on with their lives.

"Ethan? Didn't you hear me? Why does this mean so much to you?"

"It just does, Mother. Maybe I feel guilty for what they went through."

"But it wasn't *your* fault."

I didn't answer and reached for my jacket suit. I put it on and faced my mother again.

"How do I look?" I asked.

She smiled. I felt so bad for my mother. Before Wendell was killed, she had been switching places with Susan and whoever else would let her. She made herself look like them just so she could keep an eye on me. Her need to stop a vision she had about me was tormenting her. I always thought it was Viola sitting in front of the deli. It had been my mother the whole time.

"You look so much like your father," she said. "You have his brown eyes, his dark hair, and you're so tall," she said, running her fingers along my face. "You've turned into such a handsome young man."

"You're not still following me, are you Mother?"

"Ethan, you must continue to call me Thea, and your father, James. It's still dangerous."

I didn't see what the point was anymore. The whole town of Salem knew she was my mother, and that James was my father. I hated that the witches called me the prodigal son, especially when I found out what that meant.

"I'm going to be late," I said, turning and giving myself one last look.

"Is Netiri going with you?" she asked.

"No, I'm meeting him later. We have an errand to run for William."

I said goodbye to her and headed out the door. It was a bright, sunny day in Salem, and the streets were finally quiet. Tourist season is officially over. Now Salem was preparing for what the humans called *Christmas*. It was still mid-November, but Salem was already putting up decorations for the festivities. I was excited about it. My mother explained how there was a man named *Santa Claus*, who brought gifts to all the children of the world in one night. In fact, my mother was a personal friend of his. She said she met him when she was a child. He apologized to her for never realizing that witches were, in fact, real. After she learned about Santa, Christmas season is my mother's *second* favorite time of year, with autumn being the first.

She explained how the humans decorated trees with lights and trinkets. They gave gifts to their friends and loved ones. It was a time of giving and sharing. I was still confused and amazed about how someone could travel the world in one night to leave gifts under all those trees. I was really looking forward to meeting this, *Santa Claus*.

As for Irene, well, I still couldn't find her. I spent countless hours searching all over Salem, but she wouldn't come out. I really thought I had made a connection with her. I called out to her at night, hoping she still had trust in me.

I discovered that she wasn't the real Black Witch. The real one, Creepella, lived in hell, or her own version of it. William had tricked her and Wendell into believing they would win a battle; a battle I had no idea about. William brought a Trussel from Magia into Salem. A Trussel was a magical being that was known for only telling the truth. The Black Witch knew this so, the one question the Black Witch wanted to ask him was would she really win that battle. When the Trussel lied and gave her the answer *she* wanted, Wendell came out of hiding. It was a crafty plan William thought of so he could destroy Wendell once and for all.

Huck, who was the Trussel, died as a result of that lie. I was still confused about the whole thing. Apparently, Netiri and I were the only ones that didn't know what was going on. William and my mother had us all believing they were scared and nervous about the whole thing. I should have known better. William was a powerful wizard king, in fact. There wasn't a battle he wasn't prepared to fight.

"Why are you walking so fast?" I heard Netiri say. "Is there a fire somewhere?"

I stopped and faced him.

"What are you doing here?" I asked.

Netiri was my best friend, after Attor that is. I've known him since I was born. He used to live in Salem but lived in Magia since he found out he was half-wizard. I considered him more like a brother. He was a young-looking kid, but that was deceiving because he was actually much older, in fact, hundreds of years older.

He looked me over.

"I'm getting ready for our errand. I think you're a little overdressed."

"That's not till later," I informed him. "I have somewhere to be right now."

"Want some company?"

"Not really. I'll come look for you later."

He nodded and said he would meet me at the park when I was done. I continued walking until I reached the cemetery. There were cars parked everywhere. I spotted Judy, one of the women I rescued and headed that way. I stayed behind a tree and watched from far away. I saw Sue, the one I had sent running to the deli, sitting up front with Judy. I was surprised to see Renee, one of Viola's guardians, standing at a distance. What was *she* doing here?

I remained behind the tree as a man began reading something out of a book he was holding. Lois's remains had been placed in a large box. There were flowers on top of it, with silver and gold crosses along the side.

"It's called, a coffin," I heard from behind me.

I spun around, surprised to see William standing behind me. I never heard him coming. He also had a suit on, with a tie and all.

"And the book he's holding is called, a bible," he added. "You really should learn these things, Ethan."

I looked toward the crowd again; they were all crying. It was a sea of black, all here to honor Lois.

"Why are *you* here?" I asked, never looking at him.

"I'm paying my respects, like you."

"Why? *You* didn't know her."

I looked at Renee again; she had moved a bit closer. Was she crying?

"You must remember, Ethan. Renee and Cheryl have been in Salem for a very long time. They made friends here, close friends. I believe Renee became very close to Lois. She blames herself for not being able to heal her."

"Heal her? Was she poisoned?"

"She had cancer. As much as Renee wanted to use her magic to heal her friend, we do not interfere with things like that. It's not our place to say who dies and who does not."

"I don't understand. We heal ourselves, prolong *our* lives. Isn't that interfering?"

"We are magical beings, brought to life for a purpose. The Tree of Life will choose our fate, not us."

"What about the witches? They use potions to stay young, to extend their lives. Are *they* interfering?"

He looked at me from the corner of his eye.

"That is a very good question, Ethan."

I waited for an answer, but there was none. William only looked toward the crowd as they began to lower the coffin into the ground. Their sobs filled my head as a man began playing a violin. The sobs grew louder as Lois made it to her final resting place. Some people began throwing flowers into the grave.

"May she rest in peace," William muttered.

I turned to leave but William grabbed my arm.

"Fight against those bad moods, Ethan. There is a reason you feel that way sometimes."

I pulled my arm away.

"If you don't mind, I'd rather be alone right now."

"I see you are still angry with me," he said in such a calm tone. "I thought we were past that already?"

He was wrong about me being angry with him. I was hurt. I thought he trusted me and had faith in me. I couldn't have been more wrong. When I first arrived in Salem, he gave me this big speech about how only someone like *me* could fix the future. He lied and said how much he trusted me. What happened?

"Is that what you think?" he said, still looking toward the crowd.

"I really wish you would stop reading my thoughts," I growled at him. "You make me feel like I can't get a moment alone."

He finally faced me.

"Ethan, I had no choice in the matter; I had to

lie to everyone. Wendell was watching our every move. I needed to take him out of the shadows. It was the only way. The Trussel was the only person he would have believed. Never in a million years did Wendell think a Trussel would lie. He had no way of knowing that Aurelius wanted to die, wanted to lift the curse from his people. When I sent Wendell away, Trussels were still known for their greed. I used that to my advantage. I knew he was listening when the Black Witch asked that question."

"Everyone else knew your plan, William, but you kept *me* in the dark about everything."

He shook his head.

"If you think for one second that everyone knows my plan, then you haven't been paying attention, young man."

Ok, now I was angry.

"Why didn't you say that Irene had been in touch with you? Why didn't you tell me about the Trussel, and why he was here? I know why… because you don't trust me."

William looked deep into my eyes for several long moments. He finally looked away, shaking his head.

"This whole time, I *assumed* we understood each other. I do believe you are starting to turn into your mother."

"What is that supposed to mean?"

He only sighed.

"Netiri is looking for you. Please don't keep him waiting," he said, turning on his heels.

I wanted my answers, but as usual, I wasn't

getting any. I looked back at the crowd; it was thinning out. I waited until there was no one left. I wanted to say my goodbyes to Lois personally. I still didn't know why it mattered so much to me.

I walked over and took a seat under the empty tent. Only the groundskeepers were nearby. I tried to think of words to say but couldn't think of any.

"Ethan? What are you doing here?"

I quickly got to my feet. I was surprised to see Kelly Ohlson, a nurse from Doctor's Crowley's office. She didn't know this, but I thought very highly of her. She was always so kind, so helpful. She took the time and explained all about those nerve blocks I was getting. She was also very feisty. She made me laugh a few times when she put other patients in their place.

It just so happens that she was also a witch. She had long, red hair with beautiful hazel-like eyes. On some days, they looked green, but I noticed on cloudy days, they looked blue.

"*You* knew Lois?" she asked.

"No, not really. She came into the deli a few times."

It wasn't a lie.

"I was so sad to hear about her passing," she said. "She was a very nice woman."

Before she could strike up a conversation, I said I was late for an appointment. I wasn't trying to be rude, but I was in a weird mood today. She stayed behind, throwing some flowers into Lois' grave.

Chapter Two: The Bank

I quickly made my way back to the mansion. I desperately wanted to take this rope off my neck. I was hoping William, and my parents would *not* be there. I wasn't in the mood for anyone today. I wasn't sure why, but there was a certain numbness to me. I felt cold, weak and heavy, all at the same time. I was having mood swings and getting upset at the smallest things. Whatever it was, I didn't like it.

I made my way up the stairs and quickly changed my clothes. I threw on a pair of jeans, slipped on a t-shirt, and headed back out. I double-checked my back pocket for my wand before closing the door behind me. I wanted to hurry up and get this over with. I was seeing Viola tonight so I didn't want to be late.

Viola was the only good thing in my life right now. My mood always got better when I was around her. Any bad thought that lived in my head would fade away when she was in my arms. This is why I couldn't understand why both my parents were against me marrying her. Vera and Steven were going to have their wedding in Magia; why couldn't it be two weddings?

When I first told my parents that I had proposed to Viola, they didn't take the news very well. They kept telling me that I was too young and hadn't lived my life yet. I truly was not expecting that. I had hoped they would be happy for me and want a big celebration. What did 'sowing my wild oats' mean, anyway?

I thought about sneaking off and marrying her regardless, but I knew Viola deserved better. She was still getting over the news about her mother. William told her everything, even the part about her mother trying to kill her as a child. William was hoping that Viola would be the one thing that would help Irene pull herself out of the darkness.

I tried not to think about that as I was nearing the park. Netiri was already waiting for me. We had one quick stop to make before running William's errand. I was hoping Netiri would be in a better mood about it.

It was so weird seeing the park so empty. My mother's park was usually crowded with people walking on its grounds. The Witch Museum sat right across from here, with the Hawthorn Hotel next to the park. My mother's old apartment was nearby. These were her old stomping grounds. Ever since my parents had come back to Salem, I'd never seen them so happy. My mother couldn't wipe that smile from her face every time she walked the streets. She loved Salem and called it her palace. I had fallen in love with Salem as well. There was something about this charming town that stole people's hearts.

I breathed in the fresh air. The trees were holding onto their colored leaves. It would be the last of the autumn splendor before winter came.

"Thought you'd never get here," Netiri complained.

"Am I late?"

"No, but I just want to get this over with," Netiri said, making a face.

"I can go alone if you want?"

Netiri had already explained that he didn't want to run this errand for William. We had to go to some place called *Somerset Glass* and talk to some guy there. All we had to do was tell him that William needed to speak with him. It seemed simple enough. But for some reason, Netiri was not looking forward to it. He'd been complaining about it all week.

"What's the big deal, Netiri? Why don't you want to go?"

He shook his head.

"That guy can't stand me, Ethan."

"You know him?"

"Kinda-sorta."

"What do you mean? Who is this guy, and why does William need to speak with him?"

"I don't know why William needs him, but I do know that he hates me. He's old school and stuck in our old ways."

"Why do you say he hates you?"

"Can I tell you later? Let's go open up that account first."

Today, I would be opening my first bank account. I had no idea what that was, but apparently, I needed one. Netiri said it would be easier to get things that way. The witches taught him a spell they used to produce social security numbers, whatever that was, and open bank accounts. I didn't care about having a bank account, I was just excited about finally having a cell phone.

My bad mood quickly changed when we left for the bank. Netiri couldn't wait to show me all the different cell phones that were available. He reached into his pocket, then handed me a card that had my picture on it.

"Here, you'll need this."

"What's this?" I asked, looking down at it.

He rolled his eyes.

"I told you, it's called an I.D."

He came to a sudden stop.

"You know, you really should learn this stuff, Ethan. I had no idea you were this clueless. You don't live in Magia anymore, learn more about this world. You seem to have moments of clarity, but then seem so clueless the next day."

I started laughing. I couldn't help it, but I had to laugh—a lot.

"What so funny?" Netiri asked.

"You," I answered, pointing at him. "Look who's talking. I wasn't even born yet when you arrived in Magia. When I was growing up, I remember how you reacted every time you found something new or strange. I never teased you about that. Did I ever tell you what you just said to me?"

He bowed his head.

"I'm sorry, Ethan. I think I'm just on edge about seeing Rapoza again."

"What's a Rapoza?"

"It's not a what, it's a person. He's that guy William is sending us to. I'm not looking forward to seeing him again."

I knew Netiri didn't want to talk about it right now, so I suggested we leave for the bank. We passed the Hawthorn Hotel and when we got to the corner, Netiri looked down the street. I knew he was looking toward Witches' Brew. It was a restaurant where Brittany worked. She was a waitress Netiri was in love with.

"You apologize to her yet?" I asked, eyeing him.

"Ethan, why did you tell her I was going to ask her to the Halloween Ball?"

"I was just trying to give you a little push, that's all."

"You shouldn't have done that. I don't even go there anymore because of you."

"But why did you stand her up? I know she was waiting for you. Why don't you just apologize and maybe she'll understand?"

He didn't answer.

"You just can't ignore her, Netiri."

That seemed to upset him a little.

"Oh, looks who's talking?" he snapped at me.

"What do you mean?"

"*You* ignore Viola all the time."

"No, I don't."

"Really?" he answered, pulling out his phone. "Then why does she call *me* to ask about *you*? Why does she ask if you're okay?" he pointed out, showing me his phone.

"She calls *you*?"

"Yes. You stand her up all the time, Ethan. She gets worried that something happened to you, so she calls me. You have some nerve giving *me* advice."

"I didn't realize I was doing that," I sighed, looking away.

"Worry about your own relationships, Ethan. Don't worry about mine. The only one that needs to apologize to anyone, is you."

Was that true? Was I ignoring Viola like that? I mean, I knew I was forgetting things lately, but Viola? How could I possibly forget about her?

"Come on," Netiri said. "Let's just get to the bank."

We didn't talk much after that. I tried to put what Netiri said behind me. It was really bothering me that I was ignoring Viola that much. I honestly didn't realize it. I didn't realize a lot of things lately. My mind seemed to be taking little naps on me. If that wasn't bad enough, my constant mood swings didn't help matters.

"Good, it's not that busy," Netiri said, when we got to the bank. "We beat the afternoon rush."

I saw a sign that read, '*Please wait for the next cashier.*' I pulled out a pocket full of paychecks I got from Sean, the I.D., and other stuff Netiri said I needed. We got in line and waited for the next cashier. I looked around the bank and saw an older man in uniform, standing by the door. Some people were filling out papers, then getting in line. There were about six cashiers, all busy with customers.

"What kind of phone are you getting?" Netiri asked.

"I don't know, the kind I can talk into?"

Netiri just laughed. "I'll have to show you the different types of phones. Your father still has a flip phone. I think that's kinda funny."

"Why?"

Netiri only laughed.

As we waited, I noticed Netiri kept looking at some guy in the next line. The guy wore a black jacket with a hood on it. He would look all around the bank, then put his head down. It was then I noticed the man's hands were in his pockets and he was holding something.

"Oh, this isn't good," Netiri said, while looking around.

"What is it?"

"No matter what happens, stay out of it," Netiri whispered to me.

Netiri kept his eyes on the stranger that was in the line next to us.

"Why? What's going to happen?"

"Just don't use your magic, Ethan. There are cameras here. Those cameras will record everything you do."

"Use my magic on what?"

Just as I said those words, the man next to us quickly slipped on a mask and pulled a gun from his pocket. He began to point it around the bank.

"Everyone, put your hands up! Now!"

Another two masked men came running in, both pointing guns at everyone.

"On the floor, now!" they shouted.

Netiri pulled me down with him as he hit the floor. They had guns like our friend, Jason's, but I don't think they were magical guns like his. These men were human.

"What's going on?" I asked Netiri.

"They're robbing the place. Just stay down."

"Robbing? You mean, they are stealing?"

"Yes, Ethan. Just shut up and stay down."

"We have to stop them," I said, trying to get up.

"Get down," Netiri said, pulling my shirt. "I told you, there are cameras here. You can't use your magic. We don't get involved in things like this."

I almost lost it when one of the men put his gun to a cashier's head. He wrapped his arm around her neck and made her face everyone. He kept his gun to her head as he walked backwards with her.

"I need the manager!" the thief yelled.

A small, bald man slowly got up.

"Open the safe," the thief demanded. "You have one minute before I put a bullet through her head!"

The woman began to cry as the bald man made his way toward the back of the bank. Netiri had a good hold on me. "Stay down, Ethan," he kept instructing me.

There had to be something I could do. I didn't see why I couldn't use my magic without the cameras catching me. Suddenly, a red headed woman walked into the bank.

"Let me see your hands!" one of the thieves shouted.

I was shocked to see it was Kelly, the nurse from Doctor's Crowley's office. The thief yelled for her to get on the ground, but Kelly seemed too shocked to move.

"I said, get on the ground!" the thief commanded, striking her in the face with the gun.

Kelly fell to the ground, scattering the papers she was holding. Now I had no choice; I had to help.

"Let go of my shirt, Netiri."

"I don't think so, kid."

"Let go or I'll blast you across the bank."

"Dammit, Ethan."

He finally let me go and I jumped to my feet. I was about to send my magic toward the men when I noticed something. Kelly, who was still on the floor, was glaring at the man who struck her.

"You're going to regret that, scum," she hissed.

I was surprised when she began to mumble something. It didn't take me long to realize she was chanting a spell. I already had my arm up, ready to send my magic to the thief if he moved. When Kelly was done, a huge smile spread across her face.

"What are you smiling at?" the thief asked her.

Suddenly, the thief began to turn the gun on himself. He tried with all his might to stop it, but there was no stopping Kelly's spell.

"What are you doing!" one thief shouted at him. "Why are you pointing the gun at yourself!"

"I don't know, man!" the thief replied.

The thief that was holding the cashier pushed her aside, and also began to point the gun at himself. Kelly's smile grew wider as the two men pulled away their masks, revealing a look of terror of their faces.

"What the hell is going on?" the third thief yelled.

When he, too, began to turn the gun on himself, I had to stop myself from laughing. Kelly slowly got to her feet, picked up her scattered papers, and quietly walked out. The moment she was outside, she clapped her hands together making all three guns go off at once.

There was screaming and panic as the bodies fell to the floor. An alarm began sounding off as the humans stampeded out of the bank. I kept my eye on Kelly. She flipped her hair and made her way down the street.

"William is going to kill us," Netiri said, rising to his feet. "I told you not to use magic, Ethan."

"It wasn't me," I laughed.

I pointed outside, you could still see Kelly almost skipping away.

"I like her," I said, looking back at Netiri.

By now, there were sirens outside. Police officers, with guns drawn stormed in. It took a few hours before we were allowed to leave. Netiri was nervous about Kelly using a spell. I assured him there was no way the humans would have noticed what she'd done.

"She chanted a spell, Netiri. How could they possibly know that?"

"She clapped her hands, didn't she? What if they saw that?"

What was he so worried about? What was odd about a woman clapping her hands together? I didn't see a problem with what she did.

By the time we left the bank, we were late for our appointment. William wanted us to run an errand for him, but it had gotten late. The good news was, I opened a bank account. Finally, I could get me one of those cell phones.

Chapter Three: Stupid Questions

Netiri was explaining how cell phones worked on our way back to the mansion. We still had to tell William what happened at the bank. I didn't want to rat Kelly out, but I knew William would want to know.

As usual, William was in the kitchen cooking up some dinner. I missed Delia and Fish, but I sure didn't miss Delia's cooking. As it turns out, William was quite the chef. I loved his cooking. I tried not to miss a meal, no matter what it was. Yesterday he made something called shepherd's pie, and it was fantastic. I think I had three helpings.

William was King of Magia and the most powerful wizard I knew. He was my grandfather and mentor. He had salt and pepper hair with emerald-green eyes. He wore his wisdom like a badge of honor. Although I was hurt by his distrust, I still had immense respect for him.

"You're late, gentlemen," William said, as we walked into the kitchen.

Netiri was about to explain what happened when we both noticed a television in a corner of the kitchen. The news was on, and they were talking about a bank robbery that had gone wrong. William glanced at the television, then at us.

"Is there something you need to tell me?"

"It wasn't us," I quickly explained. "We didn't use our magic. There was a witch there, and she cast a spell. In her defense, she didn't have a choice."

"We always have choices," William said, shutting off the television. "I'll have to make sure she didn't leave behind any loose ends."

There was an awkward silence.

"How did it go with Raposa?" William finally asked.

I shrugged my shoulders.

"It got late, you know, because of the bank thing. We can go tomorrow."

William raised a brow.

"Did I ask you to go tomorrow?"

"You still want us to go *today*?" I complained.

I was really hoping he would say no. I told Viola I would come by and see her tonight. It was the only thing I was looking forward to.

"If you wouldn't mind," William said, in a not so happy tone.

Mind? Yes, I mind, but I wasn't telling him that.

"Good," William said, returning to the stove. "I'll keep dinner warm for you."

"Will he still be there?" Netiri asked. "Doesn't Somerset Glass close at five?"

William looked into the pot, took a whiff, and put a lid on it. "Listen gentlemen, you must make contact with Rapoza today, not tomorrow. I don't care if he doesn't want to speak with you, but you must make contact today, understand?"

Netiri cleared his throat.

"William, there's something you should know. Rapoza doesn't like me. In fact, he hates me. I don't think he'll give us a moment of his time."

William smiled.

"And that, dear boy, is the reason I'm sending *you*."

It was clear there was no changing his mind. We gave up and headed out the back door to the kitchen. I reached into my back pocket for my wand.

"Guess it's safe to fly now, isn't it?"

Netiri pulled his out as well.

"Yeah, it's pretty dark."

I commanded my wand to turn into a staff. I was about to mount it when William opened the kitchen door.

"You'll find Rapoza at a country club in Fall River. He's having dinner with his family and friends. Don't come back until you have contacted him."

He slammed the door behind him before we could answer. I wasn't happy about going, now I just wanted to get it over with. I could see that Netiri was still not happy about the matter either. I decided to ask him what the problem was.

"Ok, Netiri. Spit it out. What's your problem with this guy? I want to know before we leave."

Netiri made his staff hover, mounted it, and jumped on. Was he not going to answer me? He shook his head a few times before explaining.

"Before I tell you, don't judge me, okay?"

I mounted my staff.

"You have my word."

We were both hovering in the backyard. Netiri seemed reluctant to give me answers. I was about to insist when he finally started explaining.

"This was a long time ago, Ethan. You weren't even born; guess you were still stuck in that crystal your mother placed you in. Anyway, Simon had all the warlocks recruiting other warlocks to help him. We all thought your mother was our enemy and believed she wanted to get rid of all warlocks."

"Yeah, I know about all of that. You all believed Simon was some powerful wizard or something. My mother said you *all* were trying to kill her."

He nodded knowingly.

"Like I said to you a few weeks ago, I really hated your mother. I was willing to do anything Simon asked of me. When he sent me and a few other warlocks to recruit Raposa, it did not go well."

"What happened?"

"You must understand who Rapoza is first. Simon desperately wanted him because he saw what Rapoza was capable of. He thought if Rapoza helped him, he would be able to defeat Thea. Simon always called Rapoza a feather in his cap."

"But what's so special about Rapoza?" I prodded.

"He's old school, Ethan. Like I said before, he's stuck in our old ways."

"Netiri, you realize I have no idea what *old school* means, right?"

"It means Rapoza doesn't take shit from anyone, Ethan. He doesn't take orders either. No one tells him what to do, or how to do it. Just like the Santos brothers, Simon was never able to convince him to help. I'm lucky he didn't kill me when Simon sent *me* to recruit him."

"What happened?"

He sighed. "You promised not to judge, right?"

"I gave you my word, Netiri."

He sighed again, then continued.

"Back then, witches and warlocks didn't get along. Simon hated those witches for marrying humans. He called their children half-breeds; said they deserved death. When he learned that warlocks had also made it a practice to marry humans, he gave orders to kill the humans and recruit the warlocks. Some warlocks sent their partners away to protect them from Simon. They joined Simon out of fear, and believed if they helped Simon, their loved ones would be spared. Little did they know, Simon had already sent out death squads to find those humans."

Netiri put his head down. "I never *wanted* to do any of those things. It's just that my heart became hateful and evil when Simon told us all those lies. I began to hate humans as much as he did. I also hated the witch that protected them so much."

"My mother," I said, looking away.

"Yes, we all hated her for helping them. She was powerful and fearless, and not very kind to warlocks. It only gave us fuel to reinforce the lies Simon told us about her. When she lost her powers, we all thought Simon had done that. It only made us fear him more."

"What does that have to do with Raposa?"

When he bowed his head again, I think I understood. Netiri didn't want to see Rapoza because he was full of shame.

"Rapoza married a human, didn't he?"

Netiri shot his head up.

"How did you know that?"

"It's obvious. Rapoza thought you a death squad sent to kill his wife."

"I still don't know how I got away that day. Rapoza is such a skilled fighter. I think that's why Simon wanted him so badly. Rapoza called us idiots and morons for following Simon. He said he was embarrassed that we shared the same kind of blood. He even dared Simon to come find him, himself. They say he killed over twenty warlocks that dared come near his family. Each time, he sent Simon back a message."

"What message was that?"

"*You missed.*"

I smiled.

"You know what, Netiri? I think I like this guy."

"This isn't funny, Ethan."

As Netiri bowed his head again, I couldn't help but hear the remorse in his voice.

"Listen Netiri, I think I know why William sent you. You're not the same person anymore. I've told you a million times, you've changed. You're a good, decent man. I don't know why William wants to speak with Raposa, but he's sending the right person."

He looked at me. "We may get our asses kicked, Ethan."

"Stop it. You're making me like him even more," I teased.

I took to the sky with Netiri behind me. Fall River was a couple of hours' drive from here, but we were not driving, were we? I knew this town of Fall River. Delia had brought me food from that area once. I flew there often to get one of those chourico sandwiches I liked so much.

"He may attack us," Netiri warned, on the way there. "Just be prepared to fight and not cause damage."

"Don't worry, I won't hurt him."

"Hurt *him*? Boy, you're in for a surprise, kid."

It didn't take us long to arrive in Fall River. You could see the old mills and churches from where we were. Fall River was known for its Portuguese culture, the Lizzie Borden murders, textile mills and the largest collection of World War II naval vessels. *I only knew it for those wonderful chourico sandwiches.*

"Where is the country club?" I asked.

He shrugged his shoulders.

"I don't know, but how many country clubs can Fall River have?"

We ducked into a small cloud and hovered as Netiri pulled out his phone. He checked for something then quickly put it away.

"Come on, it's this way."

"The phone told you where it was?" I asked, in amazement.

Netiri shook his head.

"You really need to learn this stuff, Ethan. You ask a lot of stupid questions lately."

Well, that wasn't nice.

He led the way, leaving me shaking my head at his remark. Netiri had never spoken to me like that before. We joked around a lot, but never made a habit of insulting one another. This just showed me how much he didn't want to do this.

We flew for just a few minutes before we arrived at the country club. The property had a lot of land, with a large, gray and white house that was three stories high. The large windows looked like they surrounded each floor. We made sure no one was outside and landed in some nearby tree.

"Is this someone's house?" I asked, shrinking my wand.

Netiri gave me a sideways glance.

"It's the clubhouse, and that's the golf course," he said, pointing to a stretch of land.

Now, you know I wanted to ask what the heck a golf course was, but feared I would be called, *stupid again*. I think Netiri suspected it.

"Just so you know, a golf course is an area of land laid out for golf. Golf is a game humans play with a metal stick. They use it to hit a ball that they are trying to get into a hole that is far away."

"Who's asking," I answered.

I still had no idea what he was talking about.

"Lights are on," I said, pointing to the first floor.

Netiri put his wand away as we came out from the trees. The place looked busy. There were cars taking up all the parking spaces. One very small car came zooming by with metal sticks mounted on the back. Netiri must have known I was about to ask.

"Golf cart," he said, pointing with his head.

I nodded like I knew what he was talking about. We made our way to the side of the building. Another *golf cart* almost ran me over.

"Looks like a busy night," Netiri said. "This isn't good."

"Are we going in?"

"No, let's walk around and look inside first."

I could see people sitting at tables with plates of food in front of them. I understood that this was a restaurant. We began to sneak around a terrace, stopping when Netiri put his hand up.

"That's him," he said, ducking out of sight.

Netiri was squatting behind a big chair that was on the terrace. "Get down," he waved at me.

I ignored him and looked inside. I wasn't sure which one Rapoza was. It was a big table. They sat in front of a stone-covered fireplace with bookshelves on each side of it.

I looked back at Netiri.

"There's ten of them sitting down. Which one is Raposa?"

"He's sitting at the head of the table. He's the one wearing black, square-framed glasses, and has a blue shirt on."

I looked inside again. Rapoza had his back to me, but I could see he was an older man. He was dark-skinned with a horseshoe hairline, meaning, there was hair on the sides all around his head and bald on top. In fact, all the other men who were sitting with him were older, too.

"Ethan, this terrace isn't that big. They're going to see you."

"You sure that's him? I only see older men sitting in there with some women."

Netiri stretched his neck out and looked in.

"Yes, that's him," he said, returning to his place behind the chair. "The women are their wives."

I couldn't understand why Netiri was nervous about talking to this guy. He seemed harmless to me. Rapoza looked to be in his early sixties. He wasn't a big man, or full of muscles like Cory and the boys. To me, he looked normal and not intimidating at all.

"I'm going in," I said, making my way to the front doors.

"You're going to get us killed," Netiri said, trying to pull me back.

I pulled away from him.

"How are we supposed to talk with him if you won't go inside?"

"Ethan, there are a lot of humans in there. If Rapoza comes at us, there's going to be panic."

"Isn't that a good reason for him *not* to come at us?"

I turned and made my way to the front doors. There was a big mat that read Fall River Country Club at the entrance. I walked in and instantly heard music playing. I looked to my left. There was a young lady in front of a tall podium. She was smiling and looking right at us.

"Do you have a reservation?" she asked.

I heard the front doors open; I knew it was Netiri.

"Table for two?" I answered, making my way to her.

"What's your member number?" she asked, looking at her computer.

"We don't have a number," Netiri quickly informed her. "We're just checking out the club, to see if we want to join."

I glanced toward the room with a fireplace; Rapoza was still sitting. I could see his face now. He had dark brows over those glasses. His mustache was salt and pepper and he had chubby cheeks.

"Oh, I'm sorry," the young lady said. "We don't allow jeans."

Netiri and I both looked down at ourselves. We were both wearing jeans. So much for blending in.

"May I use your men's room?" I asked.

"Yes, down the hall and to the left."

"Thank you," I said, heading that way.

Netiri was right behind me.

"Now what? Should we wait outside?" he asked.

"Give me a minute, Netiri."

I was walking faster. I really did need to use

the men's room. Netiri waited for me just inside the men's room. I did my business and proceeded to wash my hands. I was about to rinse off the soap when I heard the distinct sound of a sword being pulled from its sheath. Seconds later, I felt something sharp pressed to the side of my head.

"Ethan, don't move," I heard Netiri say.

I slowly put my soapy hands up and faced whoever it was. Rapoza was holding a sword, and he was smiling. Netiri was being held by another man who was tall and gray-haired.

"Lima, seal that door shut," Rapoza ordered.

Rapoza took a step closer and put the tip if the sword to my neck.

"Come stand next to your friend," Rapoza said to Netiri.

When Netiri did what he was ordered, the man named Lima spit a spell into his palm. My mother always said that warlock spells sounded like matches being lit when they spat them out like that. Witches needed to chant their spells, but warlocks, they only needed to spit them out. The spell looked like an orb of fire that spun in their hands.

Lima faced the door as the spell spun around in his palm. He held it up to his mouth and blew it at the door. The spell spread like sparkles of light, covering the whole door. I saw a silver metal seal forming on the frame of the door. When the door was secure, Lima faced us again.

"I see the witch, Thea, never killed you," Rapoza said to Netiri. "I'm afraid your luck has run out today."

"We're just here to talk," Netiri nervously answered. "We didn't come to hurt anyone."

Rapoza's eyes slowly moved over to me. I managed to crack a smile.

"Hey, I'm a big fan of yours. He's telling the truth; we only want to talk to you."

With the sword steadily held to my neck, Rapoza spit a spell on it. The spell spun on the handle of the sword, but then slowly began traveling down the blade. I know this wasn't the time, but I couldn't help but admire his sword. It had a beautiful silver handle with two dragons on it. Their wings were spread and wrapped around the handle.

"When that spell touches your friend," Rapoza said to Netiri, "You'll have to pick him up in pieces."

I heard another spell spinning to one side of me. I looked over to where Lima was holding two of them.

"William sent us," Netiri tried to explain. "He wants to talk with you."

Rapoza moved the tip of the blade over to Netiri. I knew I could wave my hand and stop this, but I really wanted to see what this guy could do. Like I said, I was a fan.

"The wizard?" Rapoza immediately asked.

I was surprised he knew who William was.

"Yes," Netiri replied.

"William would never associate himself with the likes of you," Rapoza said, placing the tip of the sword right on Netiri's cheek. "You are scum, why would someone like a wizard send dirt like you?"

"He's not like that anymore," I tried to cut in.

Rapoza almost slapped me with the blade of the sword. It was more like a tap, but it was a hard tap.

"I don't think I was talking to you, scum."

I kept my eyes on his spell; it was still moving slowly down the blade.

"Why are you here?" Rapoza asked. "Simon has been dead for years. Is there someone new recruiting warlocks?"

I wouldn't look away from his spell as Netiri tried to explain why we were there.

"I'm not here to hurt or recruit anyone," Netiri said. "William sent me, he wants a word with you."

I looked into Rapoza's eyes. Behind those glasses was a fierce look. He was ready to defend himself and his family. As much as I wanted to see what he could do, I decided to help Netiri convince him.

"William is my grandfather," I explained. "He really did send us here. He said he just wants to talk with you."

"No one is asking you," Rapoza said, digging the tip of the sword to my neck. "Anyone that is friends with *this* scum, is no friend to me."

His spell was getting closer to my face. It was time to end this. I only intended to slightly push his sword away, but when I took a small step, I slipped on the soap that had dripped from my hands. Rapoza mistakenly thought I was making a move on him. In an instant, there was chaos.

"Get them!" Rapoza shouted at his friend.

I managed to push his sword away as I fell to

the floor. His spell fell next to me and exploded on the tile, leaving behind a burn mark. I was quickly met with a boot to the face before I could get up. Rapoza spun around and kicked Netiri in the chest, sending him flying into one of the three stalls. He turned and raised his sword with both hands, thrusting it down and into my leg. Netiri tried to help me, but he was struck by Lima's two spells, sending him crashing back into the stall.

Netiri began to twist and turn as the spell released small, tiny daggers. I could see his skin being torn apart.

"I'm not trying to hurt you!" Netiri shouted.

I finally waved my hand, causing Rapoza's sword to hover. I waved my hand again, making the sword shoot across the bathroom and pierce itself deep into the wall. As Rapoza tried pulling it out, I managed to get to my feet.

"I don't want to hurt you," I said, putting my hands out. "I just slipped, that's all."

The moment I put my hands out, Lima spit a spell at them. The instant his spell landed, my hands and arms were pushed together as new skin began to form over them.

"What the hell?" I said, when it looked like I only had one big arm.

"Try waving your hand now," Lima growled.

He kicked me hard in the chest, sending me right into Rapoza's waiting fist. I was hit hard, so hard that I bounced right back to Lima. I was like a ball, bouncing back and forth between them. They each took their turn, kicking and punching my face.

When it was Rapoza's turn to punch or kick me, he spat a spell onto my face. I felt when his spell began to grow another layer of skin over my lips. Seconds later, my mouth was sealed shut.

"Who sent you?" I heard Lima asking Netiri.

He already had another spell, spinning in his palm. He was holding it to Netiri's face as the poor kid was seething in pain.

"Make it stop!" Netiri pleaded.

I wasn't doing any better. Every time I moved even an inch, Rapoza would spit another spell at me and render me useless. He already had my arms *and* legs sealed together.

I didn't want to hurt them, but they were giving me no choice. If I didn't do something soon, these men were going to kill us. Just as I was preparing a command in my head, there was a knock at the door.

"Go away!" Rapoza yelled. "It's occupied."

When the seal they had put on the door began to disappear, they both spit spells into their palms, got into a stance, and faced the door. Lima tried another spell to keep the door shut, but it too began to disappear. Once the seal was gone, the door slowly swung opened. I was never so happy to see William walking in with a big smile on his face.

"Am I interrupting?" he asked.

Chapter Four: First Contact

William waved his hand, causing the spells they were holding to extinguish themselves. Lima tried spitting out another one.

"That won't be necessary," William said, waving his hand.

There was a look of shock on Lima's face when his spell came out looking like regular spit.

"Stop," Rapoza said, before Lima could try spitting out another spell. "I think it's the wizard."

I wanted to slap myself for not doing what William had just done. I never thought about extinguishing their spells. I have to say, I was totally impressed by these two men. Netiri was right about them; they were very skilled fighters.

William was dressed in his human clothes. I would have thought he was a member of this club if I hadn't known who he was. He was so calm, so collected. William looked at Netiri and me.

"I see you made contact."

He waved his hand, releasing both of us from their horrible magic. My leg was instantly healed;

Netiri stopped squirming in pain. Rapoza's sword took itself out of the wall.

"I believe this is yours," William said, sending him back the sword.

Rapoza reached for the sword and spat on it. The sword shook once, made that sound I'd heard earlier, then shrunk down into the size of a pocketknife. As he placed it in his pocket, I quickly went to help Netiri to his feet.

"You okay, partner?"

Netiri shook his head.

"I need a minute, kid. That spell really did a number on me."

"We got our asses handed to us," I said, grabbing my jaw.

"I told you, kid. These guys don't play."

"I apologize for sending these two," William began. "You see, I'm afraid I could not make first contact with you. It would appear you still have an old spell on you."

Rapoza seemed surprised.

"A spell? Cast on me?"

"Cast on both of you," William explained, looking at Lima. "I believe the spell is over a hundred years old. I'm certain that spell was meant to keep both me and my daughter away from you."

"Is that when everyone thought you were dead?" Rapoza asked.

William nodded.

Rapoza didn't seem happy about what William was telling them. He looked at Lima and made a motion for them to leave. Lima returned the nod and began to walk out.

"If I can just have a moment of your time," William said to them. "I can explain everything."

Rapoza gave him such a dirty look.

"Save your riddles, wizard. I have no interest in what you have to say. I suggest you leave me and my family alone. Take your two messengers with you and don't come back."

As Rapoza began to walk out, William put two fingers up, flicked them, and forced Rapoza to face him.

"Your world is in peril," William warned. "I assure you; it won't be me that comes after you or your family."

"Is that a threat?" Rapoza said, moving closer to William.

William took two steps back, as if he didn't want Rapoza to touch him.

"I don't do threats, Ron. If I wanted to hurt you, I could have killed you already."

Rapoza got right in William's face, and again, William took two steps back. Rapoza got closer, but William kept his distance.

"Don't ever call me by my first name again, wizard. You were never my enemy, but you were also never my friend. Don't think for one minute that I won't hurt you."

He motioned to Lima again, and they began making their way out.

"Before you leave," William said, facing them. "Thank you for going easy on these two."

Easy? What was he talking about? They didn't *go easy* on us. I know I hardly used my magic, but if I had, they still would have put up a good fight. Now, I understood why Simon wanted them on his side. Just as that thought went through my head, I began to understand everything. When William told them about an old spell, I got really confused. But now, seeing how useful these men could be, it made sense.

Simon tried to recruit them. When they said no, Simon made sure no one else would get to them. I just wasn't sure what kind of spell it was or why William couldn't be the one to make first contact and I had no idea that spells could last that long. I couldn't help but wonder what would have happened if William was the one who made first contact?

"They would have died," William said, reading my thoughts.

When Rapoza and Lima walked out, William said it was time to leave. He waved his hand and repaired the damage in the bathroom. I glanced over to the fireside room as we took our exit. Rapoza and Lima were sitting with their family again, smiling and talking as if nothing had happened.

I was surprised to see James, my father, waiting for us in his car. William got in the front seat and slammed his door shut. Was he angry? More importantly, was he angry at us? Netiri and I both looked at each other.

"Mind if we fly back?" I asked, peaking into the car.

"Get in," William growled.

I couldn't think of a single reason why he

would be angry with us. We did everything he asked us to. What was his problem? We both jumped in the back seat, confused by William's reaction.

"How did it go," James asked.

"Not very well," William answered.

"They didn't give us a chance to explain," Netiri cut in. "I tried to warn you about him. He hates me; why would he listen to what I had to say?"

James drove away as William let out a big sigh, sounding frustrated.

"It's not about what *you* did or did not do, Netiri. I'm disappointed in Ethan. I thought by now, he would have learned a few lessons. This meeting with them was of utmost importance. Failing was not an option."

I shot my head up.

"What did I do wrong!"

"Calm down, Ethan," James said. "Let William explain himself."

"I am calm! I'm only asking what it is that I've done."

William sighed again. We weren't even out of the parking lot yet when William said…

"James, can you stop the car, please? Ethan and Netiri will be flying home."

What? What did I do? Now he didn't even want to be in the car with us? You know what, that was fine by me. I didn't care to know what was bothering him. It seemed like nothing I ever did pleased him. The moment James stopped the car, I got out and slammed the door shut.

"You coming, Netiri" I asked, when he stayed in the car.

I could see my father saying something to William. He didn't seem happy about leaving us behind. I felt like a fool as I waited for Netiri to get out of the car. If my father was trying to convince William to let me back in the car, he shouldn't have bothered. There was no way I was getting back in.

Netiri finally got out and stood next to me. We both stood there, shocked as James drove away.

"What the hell just happened?" Netiri asked.

"The hell if I know."

"Why was William upset with you?"

"Didn't you just hear me? I have no idea."

I was about to pull out my wand when a set of lights hit us. We stepped to one side as the car drove by us. Moments later, another car started driving towards us.

"They're patrons of the restaurant," Netiri said. "Maybe we should get out of sight before flying out of here?"

"Good idea. I think I saw railroad tracks under that bridge we crossed."

We began walking down the long driveway. It was more like a road than a driveway. As we walked, Netiri explained the layout of the place.

"That's the ninth hole," he said, pointing. "This course has eighteen holes. Golf is actually a relaxing game. We should try it sometime."

I was hardly listening. I couldn't get William out of my head. What had I done wrong? Did I not handle the situation right? I never hurt them, something I could have done. Didn't he see how *they* hurt me; hurt both of us? I came to a sudden stop. Netiri was still jabbering about the golf course.

"I *know* why he's mad," I said, realizing my stupidity.

"Why?"

I looked back toward the clubhouse.

"We have to go back," I said, turning on my heels.

"Are you crazy?"

"We're going back," I said, over my shoulder.

"And do what?" Netiri asked, following behind me.

"I need to talk with Rapoza again."

"No way," Netiri said, stopping dead in his tracks. "I'm not going back there."

"Then I'll go alone."

Netiri caught up to me and tried to grab my arm, but I didn't stop.

"Ethan, you know what they'll do to us, right?"

"Stay here, if you want to. I'm talking to him."

Netiri finally gave up and followed me.

"You realize we'll have to hurt them this time, don't you? William left. There's no one here to stop them."

"Stop them from doing what, exactly?"

I was walking faster. Netiri was walking beside me, trying to talk me out of it.

"They're going to spit spells at us, Ethan. I don't want to hurt anyone."

I stopped and faced him.

"Did William hurt them?"

Netiri shook his head.

"No, but he's a wizard."

"What the hell are we, Netiri?"

I continued walking. I was so mad at myself. William didn't have to touch a hair on their head to get them to stop. He was wise and had control. It was something I always admired about him. He could've been facing death, and even then, he'd have stayed calm. He used his magic wisely, never doing the things I had. When I killed those witches, William told me I could have gotten what I wanted without killing them. I didn't agree. I felt they needed to die. But this, I could see where I went wrong. William sent us to convince them to help, and all we kept telling him was that William wanted a word with him.

"What are you going to say to him?" Netiri asked.

I stopped again and looked at my friend. Although Netiri was hundreds of years old, he looked like an eighteen-year-old. He was a thin kid but had the heart of a lion. I couldn't compare my life to his; he'd been through far more than I ever had. I didn't know much about his past, but I did know this; Netiri wasn't a good person back then. Fortunately, he felt regret for what he had done in those days. It was the one thing he never stopped talking about. He was riddled with remorse and shame about it. He never missed an opportunity to tell me about his ugly past, and I always reminded him he wasn't that person anymore.

"What would *you* say to him?" I asked.

"I don't know. Tell him that William wants a word with him?"

"Did it work the first time?"

"Then why are we going back?"

"Listen, Netiri, William sent us for a reason. Most of all, there's a reason he sent *you*. Rapoza hates you because you were one of Simon's men. Maybe he still thinks that? It's up to us to show him he's wrong."

He thought about it for a moment.

"Hope you know what you're doing, kid."

We walked back to the clubhouse, making sure we stayed out of sight. We thought it best to stay behind some trees until Rapoza and his friends were done eating. I spotted a small gazebo and headed that way. As it turns out, it gave us a perfect view of the fireside room.

They were all still there, still eating. I took a seat on the grass and waited patiently. Netiri still seemed nervous about it all.

"Relax, Netiri. Nothing is going to happen."

He took a seat next to me and sighed deeply.

"I don't know, Ethan. I have a bad feeling about this."

"What did this guy do to you?" I asked.

Netiri put his head down.

"It's not what he did, but what he said."

"What do you mean?"

"Ok, you know how I keep calling them, *old school*? Well, guys like them never fell for Simon and his lies. They couldn't believe so many warlocks feared Simon. Rapoza told me that I made him sick to his stomach for following Simon. He called me *blind* and *ignorant*. He said warlocks follow no man, especially one that was telling them who to love. He used to live in Salem, but moved away when he realized how many warlocks were following Simon."

Netiri looked toward the clubhouse. I felt he had a lot of admiration for these men.

"That other guy, his friend," he continued. "His name is Bob Lima. They used to call him *Protector of the North*. He's really quiet, but he's deadly. I was told he was a kind man and would do anything for anyone. He doesn't like getting credit for his good deeds. He used to watch out for others, *King of the Corner*, as other warlocks put it. He's a skilled fighter, like Rapoza. They took on many warlocks that Simon sent. Like I said before, no one tells them what to do. They don't make guys like them anymore. They live an honest life, work hard, and put their families first."

I looked toward the 'fireside' room as they finished their meal. I like them even more now. No wonder William wanted their help. I would see that he got it.

"Come on," I said, jumping to my feet. "I think they're done now."

Chapter Five: Forgiveness

We waited in the shadows until Rapoza and Lima came out. I wasn't sure how to approach them, but I had to be careful. Their wives were with them, and I didn't want Rapoza thinking that we wanted to hurt them in any way.

"They are leaving," Netiri said, panicking. "I thought you wanted to talk with them?"

"Be patient," I said, putting my hand up.

Rapoza's wife was the first to get in the car. Lima was parked next to them. A woman with salt and pepper hair got into that car. When Rapoza and Lima shook hands, I came out of the shadows.

"Good evening, gentlemen."

At once, both Rapoza and Lima spat a spell into their hands. Lima was quick to seal the doors on both cars, leaving the women inside. I could see the panic in their eyes as they both looked out the car windows.

"Lima, get them out of here!" Rapoza said.

"That won't be necessary," I assured him.

Rapoza slowly pulled out his pocketknife as Lima began removing his spell from the doors. He quickly got in the car with his wife. I knew what was coming next. I couldn't let him spit on that knife.

"Like I said, that won't be necessary," I said, commanding his knife to come flying into my waiting hand.

I heard an engine start, then another one. Rapoza's wife had jumped into the front seat. I waved my hand again, killing both engines. When Rapoza tried throwing his spell at me, I put my hand up, stopping his spell in mid-air. Rapoza got into a stance as his spell fell to the ground. I had to calm him down. It was time to have my say.

I waved my hand, causing Rapoza to float in the air. When Lima jumped out of the car, spell in hand, I waved my hand again. Both men were floating above me, both trying to fight my magic. Lima quickly threw another spell at the cars, sealing the doors shut again. I felt bad for the women when they kept screaming and pounding on the windows.

I looked at the cars, waved my hand, breaking the seal Lima had just placed on the doors.

"I'm going to cut out your heart!" Rapoza shouted at me.

I didn't expect them to get out, I only wanted to show these men that I could hurt them, if I wished to. I waved my hand one last time, making a bubble-like circle to form all around us. I knew other people would be walking out soon, and seeing two floating men would certainly scare them. Once the bubble formed, I looked up at the two men.

"No one can see or hear you," I began. "I only want a few moments of your time. After today, you never have to lay eyes on me again."

Rapoza gave me such a fierce look.

"After today, you won't live to see another day, scum," he shot back.

I couldn't help but admire them both. I had them in a helpless situation, and still, they stood their ground like warriors.

"Netiri, get out here," I said, over my shoulder.

I knew I had trapped him inside the bubble with us. He was listening to every word I said.

"Why is that scum with you?" Rapoza spat.

"He's not scum. He's a good man, a man of honor."

Rapoza laughed.

"Really? Where was his honor when he killed innocent people? Where was his honor when he became a puppet? You dare use the word *honor* when referring to him?"

Netiri took his place next to me, his head bowed in shame. It was time to release him from his torment. I thought of what William would say to these men and went with that.

"The man you met back in those days is not the same man that stands before you," I began. "He has saved my life more than once. He's changed, opened his eyes to the mistakes he made."

"Scum never changes!" Rapoza shouted.

Lima said nothing, he only glared at Netiri like he wanted to chew him up. I could see that Lima was the kind of man that didn't tell you he was going to kill you, but his eyes did. I wanted to tell Netiri to put his head up. I hated that he kept putting it lower and lower.

"They're right, Ethan," Netiri said, softly. "Scum like me never changes. I did horrible things to so many people. I don't deserve forgiveness."

"I don't remember asking them to forgive you," I pointed out.

"Maybe I need forgiveness? Maybe my soul needs to hear that? I have a price to pay for my past, and I don't deserve them holding back."

"Don't worry, we won't," Rapoza growled.

Netiri looked at me. He had tears streaming down his cheek.

"Put them down, Ethan. Get out of here and let them kill me. I deserve nothing less. He's right, I am a low life, a bottom feeder, heartless and evil."

"He never said that."

Netiri put his head down again.

"He didn't have to."

I looked up at them again. It was obvious Netiri didn't want to confront their judgmental eyes. I could feel Netiri's shame over his past. He hated who he once was. These men had never seen the good side of Netiri, only the evil in him. To be honest, I think Netiri blamed himself the most. That said a lot as to where his heart was now. He was kind, caring, and most of all, giving. I grew up with him in my life. Not once did I ever see any sign of evil in him. I needed to make these men see the same thing. I looked up at them again.

"Before I put you down, I want you to know something. I trust this man with my life, my family and my love. It doesn't matter to me who he once was. I can only speak to who he is now. I know you won't understand this, but he's literally traveled into hell with me, literally. If his heart was dark at one point, my mother realized it could be brought into the light. He helped her fight Simon, despite all the warlocks turning their backs on him. He's more special than you'll ever know. And as far as his evil heart, well, he could have killed you the moment we got here. You see, gentlemen, Netiri has wizard blood flowing through his veins. He can wave his hand and cause any kind of damage that he wants. It's because of him that I didn't hurt you. I don't know why William needs you, and I don't care. I only know that your world is in peril. There are forces of evil that want to walk this earth. If we could do it alone, trust me, we wouldn't be here."

I looked at Netiri, he still had his head down.

"Put your head up, Netiri. These men don't deserve your shame. They judge you as if perfection runs through their blood. That man was willing to kill me, wasn't he?" I asked, pointing at Rapoza. "What kind of person does that make him, make both of them? William can find someone else to help him. I thought he was sending us to noble men, not judges of other people. And to think, I actually admired them."

I pulled out my wand and commanded it to grow. When my staff was floating in front of me, I jumped on.

"Let's get out of here, Netiri. "You're not staying behind. I'm not going to let them kill you," I said, returning the dirty look right back at Rapoza.

Netiri looked up at them as his tears spilled over. Why couldn't they see his true heart?

"I'm sorry for everything I've done," Netiri cried. "I can't change the past. I can only move forward and be the best person possible. My words may not matter to you, but their lives should," he said, pointing to me. "If you think Simon was evil, you haven't seen anything yet. What's coming can't be stopped, not without your help. I'm ready to die for them, to stand in front of evil and offer myself up. Judge me all you want, but at least I'm not standing aside and doing nothing. Keep living your lives as if nothing is wrong. I just hope you don't live with regret, like me."

He pulled out his wand, commanded it to grow, and mounted his staff.

"I'm ready, Ethan," he said, looking straight ahead.

I waved my hand and let the men down. I removed the bubble as we flew away. There was nothing left to say. We tried everything we could to convince them. I only hoped that William would understand.

Netiri was quiet the whole way back to Salem. I have to say, I was very proud of him. He owned his mistakes and faced whatever life he thought he deserved. Deep in my heart, I knew Mother Earth had forgiven him.

All the lights were on when we arrived at the mansion. We landed in the back yard, shrunk our staffs, and headed for the kitchen door.

"Ethan, wait," Netiri said, stopping me.

"What is it?"

He swallowed thickly.

"I just want to say, thank you for saying those things about me."

"You don't have to thank me, friend. It's all true. I hope you can finally let the past go, for your sake."

"I love you, kid," he said, throwing his arms around me.

"We're *hugging* now? I didn't realize we did that."

He laughed. "You know, you're starting to sound like Fish."

We were still laughing when we walked through the kitchen door. I wasn't surprised to see William sitting at the table with a cup of coffee in front of him.

"You did that faster than I anticipated, gentlemen."

I smiled. "You knew I was going back, didn't you?"

He reached for his cup and took a sip.

"Why do you think I left you behind?"

"You think they'll help now? I asked.

He was thoughtful for a moment.

"We'll have to wait and see, won't we?"

I really wanted to know why it was so important they help us. Yes, they were skilled fighters, but there was no way to fight demons from hell. William said the Black Witch was looking for new soldiers, was Rapoza one of them?

"No," William said, reading my thoughts.

"May I ask why you need them so badly?"

He took another sip of coffee, looking at me the whole time.

"You should get some rest now," he said, putting down the cup. "James is in the study. He wants a word with you."

I knew he wasn't going to answer my question. I gave up trying and asked Netiri if he wanted to stay the night. We had become roommates for a short time. He was staying in my mother's old apartment. After William killed Wendell, he asked me to come back to the mansion. His concern for me was annoying sometimes. He made me feel like I was turning into some monster. Yes, it's true that I thought of the way I killed those witches—a lot. Gruesome, as William put it, but that didn't mean anything, did it?

Netiri headed up to one of the guest rooms as I said goodnight to William. I went to see what my father wanted to speak to me about. I was about to knock when I heard my mother's voice. It wasn't my intent to listen in, but they were talking about me. I made sure William was still in the kitchen then put my ear to the door. I remembered a story my mother once told me, about how she would send a command to be able to hear what people were saying. I thought I would give her technique a try. I thought of the command and began to listen in. To my delight, their conversation was flowing softly through my ears. It was my mother's voice I heard first.

"I only worry that we may push him away. He says she's the one. He really wants to marry this girl."

"No, Thea," my father answered. "He's too young, too inexperienced. We've kept him sheltered his whole life. We were overprotective and didn't prepare him for this world. I want him to live his life for a few more years. Don't forget, he thought Vera was the one as well."

"I always knew *you* were the one," my mother answered. "I didn't need years to realize that. Maybe this time, his love is real?"

"You're not a man, so you wouldn't understand this, but he's only sixteen, and a virgin. I had my fair share of women before I met you. I just want him to be certain, that's all. What's to say that later in life he'll realize he should have waited?"

"So, what you're saying is; you want him to bed down with a woman *before* he decides to marry?"

"You make it sound like a bad thing, Thea. Like I said, you're not a man, so you don't understand."

"Tell me, James. What would you have thought of *me* if I, as you put it, *lived my life*. What if I had more than one man in my bed before you? Would it be the same? Should I have done that to be certain?"

"You can't compare the two, Thea. Ethan is still a boy. Dating women at his age is almost a rite of passage. I don't want him to live with regrets."

"And men get these, *rites of passage?* Women are looked down on if they do the same? Why was it okay that I marry you when I had no other men in my past?"

"Did you forget about Cory?" my father asked, in an angry tone.

"I never dated him," my mother shouted at him. "Why do you always have to bring him up?"

I'd never heard my parents argue like this before. It was never my intention to cause a rift between them.

"And by the way," I heard my mother shout. "Your son just turned seventeen!"

"Are you saying we should just stand back and allow him to get married?" my father shot back. "He'll be throwing his life away, don't you understand?"

"Why? Why would he be throwing his life away? Is it really that important to you that he bed down with a woman, first? Are you serious, James?"

"I knew you wouldn't understand. You're as stubborn as ever, Thea!"

"You're the one who doesn't understand," my mother yelled. "He's old enough to kill someone, but he can't love who he chooses? Explain that, James?"

"He's too young, Thea. Don't you understand that? Kids his age fall in love every day with a different person. They think they've found true love, but later regret getting tied down. I don't want that for Ethan."

"We can't force him to do our will, James. If we expect him to face challenges that an adult would, then we should treat him like one."

I stepped away from the door feeling guilty. Why did I have the bright idea of having a double wedding? I had even asked Vera and Steven how they felt about it. They were fine about the whole thing. I never imagined my parents would be arguing about it like this. My intention was to knock, but I gave them their space and ran up the stairs to my room.

Chapter Six: Honor

    I couldn't stop thinking about what my father said as I lay in bed. I thought about going back downstairs and talking to him but changed my mind when I realized they may still be arguing.

    Was my father, right? Would I live with regrets later in life? I knew I loved Viola with all my heart, but truth was, I *did* look at other women with lust. I had made that confession out loud to no one. My desire to take a woman in my bed was all consuming sometimes. There were times when I thought I would rip Viola's clothes away. I became excited when I held her tight. Half the time I couldn't even remember what she'd said. All I could think about was her naked body lying next to mine. One time, in the shower, I thought about…

    "Ethan, you awake?"

    It was Netiri.

    "Come in," I said, sitting up.

    "Is that your parents, arguing?" he asked, closing the door behind him.

I sighed. "Yes. Apparently, I need to live my life before I get married."

"What are you talking about?"

"Come on, let's go into the sitting room," I said, jumping out of bed.

I was staying in my parents' old room. It was very large with its own sitting room area. The sitting room had an extra-large fireplace with two large seats that sat in front of it. We lit a fire before taking our seats.

"I thought you were sleeping already," I said, looking into the fire.

"I wanted to shower. I went to go ask William where the towels were that's when I heard your parents."

"They're still at it?"

Netiri nodded.

I began to tell him what my father said. I told him about all the desires I'd been having. Of all people, I knew *he* would understand.

"Is he right, Netiri?"

"About what, playing the field?"

"What does that mean?'

Netiri leaned forward.

"Listen, Ethan. When you said you wanted to marry Viola, I didn't say anything. I backed you up on your choice and gave you all the support I could. To be honest with you, I agree with James. You haven't been in the human world for long. As far as I know, you didn't date anyone in Magia, either. Vera was the first girl you had feelings for, and she didn't share those feelings. When you met Viola, you proclaimed your love for her in less than a week. A week after that, you wanted to marry her."

"What's wrong with that?"

"My point is, unlike me, you really are sixteen. You haven't lived your life."

"I just turned seventeen," I reminded him.

"No, kid. Mentally, you're still sixteen. I may look young, but I have hundreds of years under my belt."

I laughed.

"What's the big deal about being hundreds of years old? You're still a virgin, Netiri."

I stopped laughing when I noticed he wasn't laughing with me.

"Sorry, Netiri. I was only joking."

Netiri always had such a sad look about him. His green eyes would always change color when he was excited. Although he was much older than me, he looked a couple of years younger.

"Stop joking about that, Ethan. It's really getting annoying."

We both looked into the fire. There was a question I wanted to ask him, but wasn't sure if he would answer it. I decided to take a chance.

"Can I ask you something, Netiri?"

"Depends on what it is."

"It's personal."

He laughed.

"Of course it is."

"So, can I ask?"

"Go ahead, I think I know what it is."

"*Why* are you still a virgin?"

He shot his head up.

"I'm not trying to make a joke," I assured him. "I really do want to know."

He looked into the fire again with a faraway look in his eyes. I didn't mean to make him feel bad.

"I shouldn't have asked you that, sorry."

"It's okay, kid. I'm not sure about that answer myself. I guess I've always felt awkward around women. It's not for lack of wanting them, trust me. When I get lonely for a woman, I usually end up jerking off."

"What do you mean by that? You mean, kidding around with them?"

Netiri slowly looked at me. He stared at me for a short moment, then began laughing, hysterically. I couldn't understand what was so funny.

"Why are you laughing?"

He laughed even louder. What was his problem? I didn't get the joke.

"Ethan, please tell me you have done *that* before—please?"

"I kid around all the time, especially with Fish."

Netiri was almost on the floor laughing.

"Kid don't say it like that. You're killing me."

What was so funny? I couldn't understand it.

"Wait till I tell Fish about this one," Netiri laughed. "I can finally get payback for that, *throw it in her* thing."

He was trying very hard to compose himself, but when he looked at me, his laughter came back in full force. He kept trying to say something to me, but his laughter wouldn't let him.

"Y… y…you can s…skin someone a…alive, but you don't k…know what jerking off is?"

He kept shaking his head.

"Ethan, there's no way you should get married right now."

His laughter echoed off the walls. I was starting to get a little annoyed.

"I think you'd better go to your room," I said, heading toward my bed.

"Should I go get Fish? You know, so you can, *kid around* with him?" he laughed.

I wanted to go ask my father what that meant, but I didn't want him laughing at me. Netiri left for his room, still laughing, still shaking his head. By morning, I was hoping Netiri had gotten over his laughing spirt. I showered, got into some jeans, and headed down the stairs. I instantly smelled William's cooking on the way down.

When I walked into the kitchen, Netiri was whispering something into my father's ear. The moment they saw me, Netiri leaned back on his chair, trying not to laugh.

"Good morning, Ethan," my father said, turning the other way.

Were his shoulders bouncing up and down? My father was the last person I expected would laugh at me. I think Fish and his jokes had made my father a little too insensitive.

"Morning," I said, pulling out a chair.

"How would you like your eggs?" William asked, as he gave Netiri and my father a dirty look.

"I'm not very hungry," I lied. "I'll just have some toast."

My mother was next to walk in. She gave my father a disappointed look and headed to the stove. I assumed they were still angry at one another. It made me wonder what time they stopped arguing.

"Good morning," she said, flatly.

She poured herself some coffee but did not join us at the table. My father glanced her way, but did not try to speak with her. After she gave him a few dirty looks, he cleared his throat and got up.

"I think I need some air," he said, heading out the kitchen door.

William looked at my mother, then out the window at my father.

"Problems?" he asked, as he stirred some eggs.

My mother rolled her eyes.

"I don't know, Father. I'm not a man, so I don't understand."

William glanced at me.

"Speaking of that, Thea. You should go out there and speak to James. I believe there's a certain, *talk* he needs to have with Ethan."

"Why, what's going on?" she quickly asked.

William looked my way again. Netiri was on the verge of laughter. He got up, pushed his chair in, and joined my father outside.

"What's going on?" my mother asked again.

I'd never been so happy to hear the doorbell ring. "I'll get it," I said, leaving them to their laughter.

I had no doubt William was about to tell my mother whatever it was that Netiri found so funny. And what was this *talk* William was referring to? Why couldn't my mother tell me? They were all starting to make me feel really stupid.

The doorbell rang again.

"Coming," I called out.

I was stunned to see Rapoza when I opened the door. He stood, hands in his pockets, glaring into my eyes. I took a step back, prepared to use my magic if he came at me. To my surprise, he looked over his glasses and said...

"Is the wizard here?"

I looked behind him, he was not alone. There were three other men with him. One was much younger than the others. I couldn't help but notice how much he looked like Rapoza. Lima was there, and another older, bald man. They all had their hands in their pockets. Were they trying to show me that they came in peace?

"Please, come in," I said, opening the door even more.

"If you don't mind, we'll wait out here," Rapoza answered.

I turned to go get William, but he was already standing behind me.

"Good morning," William greeted them.

There was no friendly smile on Rapoza's face. He glared at William the same way he'd been glaring at me. The other men moved closer and stood right behind Rapoza.

"You have ten minutes of my time," Rapoza said to him. "Spit out what you need to say."

"Won't you come in?" William said, motioning with his arm. "I assure you; no harm will come to you."

Rapoza looked at his men. After a few moments, he nodded to them, and they walked in. They scanned the house as William closed the door behind them. They wouldn't take their hands out of their pockets as William took a few steps away from them. Why did he keep doing that?

"Thank you for coming," William said.

No one answered. They all kept staring at me as if I was about to attack them. I decided to do what they had and put my hands in my pocket. Of course, I didn't need my hands to use my magic, but they didn't know that. I think William noticed and followed suit. Now everyone had their hands in their pockets.

"This is my son, Brad," Rapoza said, motioning to the younger warlock. "You already know Bob Lima. This is Moe Berube, all men I can trust."

I felt so silly with my hands still in my pocket. None of them made an effort to shake hands with us. Then again, William didn't offer his, either.

"Thank you for coming," William said again.

"Ten minutes, wizard," Rapoza reminded him. "We didn't come here for a visit. What do you want from us?"

Brad, the younger warlock kept glaring at me with those dark eyes of his. He had a rounded nose and was muscular in build. He looked to be in his early thirties. Moe, the bald one looked to be the same age as Rapoza and Lima. I couldn't help but wonder, what could William possibly need these older men for?

My father and Netiri walked in before William could explain what he needed them for. The moment they saw Netiri, they pulled their hands from their pockets. They'd been holding spells this whole time. They spun in their hands as they held them up.

"Please, gentlemen. There's no need for that," William said.

"What is *he* doing here?" Rapoza asked.

My father was already holding his weapon, ready to attack if they threw their spells. William quickly tried to calm the situation.

"No one will be fighting today, understood? We are all here for the same reason. Please put out your spells so my family can be at ease."

William looked at my father.

"James, put your whip away, please."

"Maybe I should leave the room?" Netiri suggested.

"You will stay," William quickly shot back.

He looked at the warlocks and put both his hands up. The warlocks still had their spells, spinning in their palms.

"I only want to show you that no harm will come to you. There's no need for spells," William said, calmly.

"William," my father growled. "If *that one* throws his spell at Ethan, I'm going to kill him."

He was talking about Brad, the younger warlock. He wouldn't take his eyes off me. My father only made things worse when he said that. They all spat another spell into their free hand.

"I've had enough," William said, waving his hand.

Everyone was tossed across the room, including us. Their spells hit the floor and were instantly put out. We flew past the foyer and right into the living room. We were like decks of cards, being shuffled around and into our seats. The warlocks were on one side of the room, with us on the other. When Rapoza tried shouting something at William, he waved his hand, sealing their mouths shut. William calmly began pacing back and forth.

"Please forgive me for being a little rough," he began. "But I need you to hear me out with no interruptions. If you wish to leave this house when I am done, you will be free to do so."

I knew he was talking to the warlocks. The only reason he also sent us to a seat was because he didn't want the warlocks getting nervous about us.

"I'm afraid we are faced with a serious problem," William continued. "Your realm is in peril. There are forces of evil, desperate to get into your world. A woman we'll call, the Black Witch, has gotten her hands on a black book of spells. Within that book are spells and potions, unknown to this world. The pages hold secrets from Satan himself. It is my job to ensure that she never opens the gates of hell for him and his underlings."

He paused for a moment as they absorbed what

he was telling them. Rapoza shook his head, as if to tell William that he wanted to say something. William waved his hand, releasing him from his magic.

"What does that have to do with us?" Rapoza asked.

William waved his hand again, releasing everyone and giving them back their voices. No one got up or tried to leave.

"May I continue?" William asked.

Rapoza nodded.

"I know the Black Witch is looking for soldiers, an army that can't be killed. She had resorted to using humans that were dying, but quickly learned they were of no use to her. As you know, warlocks were Simon's choice of men. The Black Witch tried to do the same and recruited them with spells and potions. But now, she is looking for a stronger army, one that I cannot destroy alone."

Rapoza started laughing.

"You're a wizard," he said to William. "If you can't kill them, what do you expect us to do?"

William raised one brow.

"You can start by allowing me to remove a spell that was cast on you."

"What is he talking about?" Brad asked.

Rapoza put his hand up, silencing Brad.

"Explain yourself, wizard."

"When I was rendered with no powers, Thea, my daughter, was the only one left here to fight Simon. If you know the story, she stored her powers in a crystal, along with other things. A wizard from my realm was helping Simon, sharing spells from my world so he could use them here, in yours. When Simon tried recruiting you, and you denied him, he cast a wizard spell on you; one that would kill you if I or Thea ever came calling. That's why I couldn't make first contact with you. You would have died, instantly."

"Why is it safe to break it now?" Rapoza asked.

William smiled.

"Because you came to me, willingly."

Rapoza looked at his son and friends.

"Yes," William said, reading his thoughts. "They, too, have that spell on them."

"Can you break it?"

"I can."

"What are you waiting for, wizard?"

"I'm afraid it's not that easy. You see, you must trust me first. I cannot put my hands on you without your consent. If I try to remove it with force, you will die."

"It's a trick," the one named, Moe spat. "You can't trust these beings. They're wizards, from another realm. There's no telling what he'll do to you."

Rapoza looked at William, then at his friends again. I could see he was really thinking about it.

"What if I don't let you break it?" Rapoza asked.

"Then you are free to go."

"That's it? You'll just allow us to leave? Just like that?"

"Just like that," William answered.

"What about the Black Witch?"

"She will no longer be your concern, will she?'

Rapoza was thoughtful for several long moments. I don't know what he was thinking about, but it changed his mind.

"Break the spell, wizard. If this is a trick, my men won't stop until you are dead."

I was surprised when William turned his back on them. "You are free to go, gentlemen. My apologies for wasting your time."

Rapoza rose to his feet.

"What about the spell?"

William looked over his shoulder.

"I can't break it. You are free to go."

"But you said you *could* break it?"

William faced him.

"I also said you needed to trust me. There is no other way to break it."

"That's a tall order, wizard."

As they were talking, I couldn't help but notice how my father was staring at Brad. He wouldn't take his eyes off him. He would tilt his head and squint his eyes, as if he was looking at something odd.

"As I said, you are free to go," William said again.

My father leaned forward, squinting his eyes as he looked at Brad.

"Brad, is that you?"

Chapter Seven: River of Life

Brad looked at my father and did the same thing with his eyes. Both of them had their heads tilted, like they were trying to solve a puzzle.

"James?" Brad finally said.

William didn't seem to know what to say. Rapoza had the same reaction. In fact, we all did.

"It can't be," my father said, getting to his feet. "You had hair the last time I saw you."

Brad laughed and ran his hand over his bald head. "I shaved that fro."

They shook hands.

"I can't believe this," Brad said. "I was so worried about the wizard, I hardly gave you a second look, James."

"Same goes for me," my father laughed. "I wanted to kill you for a minute there. It's been years, Brad."

William and Rapoza still had that dumbfounded look on their face.

"How is Ciro?" my father asked. "I haven't seen him in years. Not since he was last here, in Salem. He said he would pay us a visit soon."

"The Spanish warlocks?" Rapoza asked my father. "You know them?"

My father nodded. "We consider him family."

"I had no idea," William said.

That was a first. William knew everything about everyone. This had truly caught him off guard.

"How do you all know each other?" Rapoza asked.

"It was years ago, before William and I returned to Salem. I'd been traveling around Mexico when I met Ciro and his family. Brad was there visiting him, but he didn't look like this," James said, pointing to Brad's bald head.

"You never told me that," William said to him.

James nodded knowingly.

"It was when you were weak and couldn't go outside, William. Brad never came to our home. My encounters with him were always brief, and always when I saw Ciro. I think that's why I didn't recognize him."

"Did you ever find your wife?" Brad asked.

James laughed. "Yes, that's why I came back to Salem. Her name is, Thea."

I thought Brad's eyes were going to pop out of his head when James said my mother's name.

"The witch is your wife?"

"You know her?" James asked.

"Know *of* her," Brad answered.

Just then, my mother came out from the kitchen. She looked surprised to see that we had guests.

"Speak of the devil," my father said, motioning with his arm.

"This is Thea, my wife."

When Brad put his hand out to shake my mother's, William quickly grabbed my mother's shoulders and pulled her back.

"Don't touch him, or his father," he warned.

"What?" my mother asked, confused.

"I wouldn't hurt a woman," Rapoza said, offended.

Before William could explain what was going on, Rapoza tapped my mother's shoulder.

"My apologies if I scared…"

The moment he touched her, there was a flash of light that sent my mother flying across the room.

"Thea!" my father shouted.

She crashed into a wall and began squirming on the floor. My father instantly pulled out his ring.

"You can't take her yet!" William shouted at him.

I knew my father wanted to take her into Magia and straight into the River of Life so she could heal.

"She's dying, William," my father shot back.

"Not yet!" William ordered.

Netiri and I already had our swords out.

"Do not touch or hurt them," William instructed. "It's the spell."

When I faced Rapoza and the others, I was shocked to see their eyes were dark as the night. There was no life in them, no anything. They all had spells they were getting ready to throw. Suddenly, Brad and Lima began to grab at their chest. Moe and Rapoza were next. They fell to their knees as they dropped their spells, leaving holes in the floor.

"James, Netiri, grab them and take them to Magia," William yelled. "We'll be right behind you."

"What about Thea?" my father asked. "I'm not leaving her here."

"*I* can take her!" William answered. "Don't you see, I can't touch them!"

William closed his eyes and began to move his arms in a circle. A string of light began forming when he did that. When the ring was nice and thick, William waved it towards Lima and Brad. He did it again then sent it to Rapoza and Moe.

"Netiri, grab this rope and get out of here!" William shouted. "You must hurry, before they die!"

My father ran and grabbed the other rope of light from William. Within seconds, they all disappeared into a vortex. I picked my mother up in my arms, waiting for William to form a vortex.

"I've got her!" I said to William.

He had his back to me. He kept shaking his head. Why wouldn't he turn around?

"William?"

He slowly turned to face me when an evil smile spread across his face. I almost dropped my mother. I took a few steps back, with my mother still in my arms. William approached us, his eyes had turned dark like the others. There was no sign of the William I knew and loved. He was coming at me like he was getting ready to kill me.

"William, it's me!" I yelled, in hopes he would snap out of it.

He made a fist as he stopped dead in his tracks. I could see there was a struggle going on in his head. He shook his head again, then came at me with evil in his eyes. I wanted to put my mother down so I could pull out my ring. I had to get her out of here. I could see she was in a lot of pain.

"Dammit, William! Snap out of it!" I shouted.

When he raised his hand to wave it, he was tackled to the floor by someone. It took me a few seconds to realize it was Renee, Viola's guardian. William tossed her a few feet, then tried coming at me again. Renee kicked him in the stomach, sending him tumbling to the ground. When he tried waving his hand at her, she kicked him across the face and jumped on top of him. She quickly pulled out her ring, slipped it on, and disappeared into a vortex with William.

I breathed in a sigh of relief and put my mother down. I reached into my pocket, slipped on my own ring, and was pulled into a vortex with my mother. I didn't know what to do as we traveled into Magia. My mother wouldn't stop squirming in pain.

"We're almost there, Mother," I said, holding her tight.

I began to smell Magia's flowers. We were almost there. When the vortex faded away, my father was there waiting. He took my mother from me as I scanned around to look for William. Netiri and one of the guards were trying to hold him down. Renee was helping them. I could see that William was trying to fight the spell. He would pound his fist on the ground as horrible, deep grunts escaped his lips. By now, everyone could clearly see that William wasn't himself. I think we all knew what would happen if William decided to use his magic on us. He didn't even need to wave his hand; he could just *wish* us dead.

"It's a spell," Netiri told the guard. "Go get the wizards!"

My instinct was to heal everyone, but I had a feeling that it was too dangerous. I ran to William's side, pushing Netiri and the others out of the way. I grabbed Williams face and made him look at me.

"William, it's a spell. You have to fight it. I don't know anyone stronger than you. You're a powerful wizard, king of this realm. If you don't fight this spell, your daughter is going to die."

William pushed me away, let out a horrible grunt, and looked at my mother. She was starting to turn blue. My poor father looked so desperate.

"Please, William," my father cried. "She's dying."

There was a horrible sound surrounding us. It was the sound of people gasping for air. My mother, Rapoza and his men, all stretched their necks upward in a desperate attempt to get air. It was taking everything I had *not* to fly everyone to the river. William would have done that if it were that easy.

"William!" my father shouted. "She's dying!"

As William staggered to his feet, you could see the veins on his face were turning black. He would take a deep breath, look at my mother, and let out a roar like a lion. Renee was in position in case William lost his battle. I think she knew that none of us could ever hurt him.

"You can do it, William!" Netiri yelled at him.

I heard something above us and looked up. It was a sea of wizards coming to help their king. They flew down and made a circle around William.

"N…n…no!" William said to them.

His voice was raspy and deep. I wanted to help him, but knew this was a battle he had to fight on his own. William looked at Rapoza and the others. They had all turned blue and were moments from death. William dropped to his knees and dragged himself toward Rapoza.

"Say it!" he growled.

Rapoza was gasping for air as he tried to sit up.

"Say it!" William said again.

"I…I trust you," Rapoza finally answered.

William quickly put his hands over Rapoza's head. He let out a loud grunt as streams of dark smoke began coming out of Rapoza's head. The dark smoke spiraled for several moments, then began to get absorbed into William's head. William pushed Rapoza back and grabbed his head.

"Now!" he shouted, just before he fell back.

The wizards picked up one body after another. I already had William on my staff, and I was flying us to the River of Life. My father passed us like a bullet. He flew my mother into the water before we could even get there.

"Fly faster!" Netiri said, from behind me.

Rapoza was draping off his staff like a rug. There was no sign of life in him. We flew our staffs right into the water. I released William and allowed the river to work its magic. I closed my eyes and hoped it wouldn't be too late.

I knew the River of Life had magic powers no one understood. Wizards only knew that this river gave them life, energy and powers. William told me the story of this river as a child. This is where the roots of the Tree of Life ended. It was the same tree that created wizards to fight evil. William explained that thousands of years ago, evil walked the earth. Innocent people were slaughtered or taken as slaves. Many realms were destroyed. It was then the gods decided to create a Tree of Life, one that would be the source of life. A force that connects all lives, or the cycle of life and death itself. William called it a bridge between heaven and earth.

"This tree is not God," William explained. "The tree does not change what God has decided."

I opened my eyes to find the dragons swimming around William. They spread their wings and made a protective wall around him. William still had his eyes closed as the current moved him back and forth. The guards surrounded Rapoza and his men, swords drawn and ready. Their owl heads scanned the area, looking for more danger. I knew they were only protecting William. I had to warn them not to hurt the warlocks.

Netiri made the motion for us to swim up. I

nodded no and pointed at my mother. She was still in my father's arms, still not responding. Netiri left Rapoza drifting in the current and swam up. He wasn't going up for air, there was no need for that. The river gave life, it didn't take it. You could stay down here for hours and not die. Then it hit me, my own thoughts reassured me that everything was going to be fine. The river *gave* life, it didn't *take* it.

    I could see more guards and wizards diving into the river. They all tried to surround William, but the dragons wouldn't let them. They wanted the honor of protecting him. William had always been friends with the dragons, even though wizards used to hunt them down. Wizards didn't understand the dragons at one time and saw them as enemies. William changed all that when he came back to Magia. He made Attor, my favorite dragon, head of his army. Since then, dragons and wizards have been living in harmony.

    The dragons blew fire around William when he began to move. It was the most beautiful thing I'd ever seen. The fire turned a bright blue as the flames moved through the current. The moment William opened his eyes, Attor took him in his mouth and swam up and out of the river. I quickly looked over at my mother, my father was already swimming up with her. Rapoza and his men also began to open their eyes. One by one, the guards took hold of them and swam up.

    I was about to swim back up when I began to feel something inside of me tingle. I looked at my hands when they wouldn't stop shaking. What was happening to me? The current picked up and began to swarm around me, forming something similar to a cone. My heart began racing at the thought of what it could be. Was it possible that the river broke that gypsy curse? I smiled at the thought of it.

    I had wanted to come here when that gypsy curse was cast on me, but William wouldn't allow it. He said the pain I was in would make me stronger. Although he was right, I hated the agonizing pain it still caused me. Doctor Crowley called it *nerve pain*, damage left behind from the shingles. The pain tortured me, gave me the sensation of being burned alive with hot needles. It was a pain I wished on no one. But now, the river was healing me. I can't even describe how happy that was making me. William would have to forgive me for this one. I was in this river to save *him*, not to heal myself. This was just an added plus in my eyes.

    I began to swim up when the current died down and released me. I hadn't been in this much of a good mood in weeks. And to think, William was waiting for me to turn into some dark lord. Well, at least we didn't have to worry about that anymore. And with that thought, I broke the surface and took a deep breath of relief.

Chapter Eight: Splendor of Magia

I almost burst out laughing when I walked out of the water to find Rapoza and his men looking absolutely terrified at the sight of the guards. There were about fifteen of them. The guards stood over seven feet tall. They had owl-like heads and leathery tails like an alligator. Every time one of the guards would spin his head to look behind him, the warlocks would gasp and step back.

"They can turn it all the way around," Moe gasped.

"They can do much more than that," I replied.

I almost skipped my way over to William when I saw him. I couldn't get over my good mood. William was still catching his breath as he checked on my mother. She was on her feet and looking much better. Netiri was by Rapoza's side, asking him if he was okay. Rapoza was not answering him. His eyes were glued to the dragons, the guards, and the wizards. He and his men kept looking all around the land, then back at the dragons. This would have been a good time to have one of those cameras. The look on their faces was priceless. I had to ask myself again; did I look like that when I got to Salem?

The wizards placed their staffs beside them, awaiting their king's orders. It was a sea of velvet robes and golden threads. When William gave them the signal to leave, they bowed to him before mounting their staffs. Rapoza and his men gasped at the sight of it all. Their mouths were still agape when the dragons began blowing fire to celebrate that their king was alive. It only made me wonder how they'll react when they see that dragons in Magia can *talk?*

It didn't take long to answer that question.

"Long live the king!" Attor cheered.

Jaws were on the ground as Rapoza and his men took two steps back in disbelief. Some of them were still looking up at the wizards who had just left. Then they spotted Magia's sun. Its beautiful rays beamed down and spread all over the land. Unlike a regular sun, you could look at the sun here and not hurt your eyes. Something I learned the hard way in the human world. My mother said when she first came here, she thought we were on the other side of the sun.

"Is that a backwards sun?" Moe asked, in amazement.

"Dragons, they have dragons," Brad kept saying.

"Talking dragons," Lima added.

Magia's flowers began to open up, releasing speckles of light into the air. Lima reached out and touched one of the flowers. He drew breath when the speckles of light stuck to his fingers. They all began to touch the flowers.

"I think we're dreaming," Brad said, looking at his fingers.

They gasped several times as they took in my home. Every time they spotted something new, they drew breath and pointed. When the nearby forest began to move, I thought Rapoza would pass out.

"The trees, they moved," he gasped.

They had no way of understanding this, but Magia was overjoyed that their king was safe. Here, even the forest celebrated our king. The Tree of Life had given its magic to all who lived here, even plant life. This was my home, the place I was born. And according to William, it would be the kingdom I would rule one day.

Netiri was smiling as he watched Rapoza and his men react to Magia. When Rapoza realized Netiri was watching him, he approached.

"Obrigado," Rapoza said, offering Netiri his hand.

"You're welcome," Netiri said, shaking it.

I was pleased to see the other men also shook Netiri's hand. I was enjoying the moment when I felt an arm on my shoulder. It was William. His emerald-green eyes were sparkling.

"Thank you, son."

I chuckled.

"I knew you would do it, William."

He raised a brow.

"No doubts?"

I shook my head.

"None."

"Will *they* be okay?" I asked, looking at the warlocks. "I think they're stunned, but there's no sign of the spell you absorbed."

"How did you know I absorbed it?"

I looked into his green eyes.

"I don't know, it was the way you reacted. I saw the dark smoke, entering your body. Back in Salem, when Rapoza touched my mother, I knew that it made the spell come alive. It was killing them, but it was changing *you*."

"Indeed, it did, Ethan. I had hoped to break it before that happened."

"How were you going to break it?"

"They needed to trust me first. After that, I would have asked Netiri to remove his spell."

Did he just say, Netiri?

"Wait, Netiri cast that spell?"

"Unknowingly, yes. He had no idea what kind of spell Simon had given him. When the spell came alive, it was too late for Netiri to break it. I had to absorb it."

"Wait, but Netiri touched them and nothing happened."

"That's because the spell was cast to keep away your mother and me. It was Simon's way of making sure they would never help your mother."

"Does Netiri know about this?"

"No, and there's no need to tell him. All is well now."

"Can I ask you something, William?"

"You may."

"What's so special about these men? Why did Simon need them so badly? Why do *you* need them?"

"You haven't figured that out yet?"

"No, I have no idea. Is it because they're good fighters?"

"Ethan, ask yourself one question: what battles evil? If you know the answer, then you'll understand why I need them."

William looked over at Rapoza and his men.

"I think we'd better get them out of here, before they become enchanted with Magia."

It was the one thing about Magia. If you weren't from here, you became enchanted with it and not want to leave. Fish, Delia and Cory had been here several times, so they were used to it.

"Can we show them around really quick?" I asked hopefully.

I was proud that I came from this magical place. The splendor of Magia left a mark in your heart. I would never love Salem as much as I did Magia, but it was pretty close. I loved Salem for different reasons. It's where my mother grew up, fought her battles and fell in love.

"I suppose we can make time for that," William replied.

He was about to turn away when he gave me a second look. It was more like a double take.

"What is it?" I asked. "Do I have something on my face?"

He eyed me intensely. There was a look of disappointment in his eyes as he looked away.

"I'm sorry, Ethan," he murmured.

"Sorry about what?"

He looked at me from the corner of his eye.

"Why don't we show them around first? We can talk later."

He walked away leaving me a little nervous. What had he seen in me? You know what? I didn't care right now. I was in a very good mood, and I wanted to enjoy showing Rapoza and the others around Magia. My mother was standing next to them, asking if everyone was okay.

"Mother," I said, giving her a hug.

My father wouldn't let go of her hand. I knew this had scared him. It didn't help they had argued just before this happened.

"I think your father is in shock," she whispered in my ear.

I smiled as she pulled away. My father kept kissing her hand and placing it over his heart.

"Welcome to Magia," William said to Rapoza and his men. "Land of wizards and wonder. It's a realm not known to humans."

"What is this place, wizard?" Rapoza asked, gazing around.

"It's my home, Mr. Rapoza."

"Please, call me, Ron."

"William," he said, extending his hand.

The two shook hands, sealing the beginning of a long friendship. William gave Attor a signal.

"Care to take flight?" William asked the men.

Ron's eyes grew wide.

"On a dragon?"

"A talking dragon," Lima added.

William smiled.

"They are harmless, I assure you."

I wanted to ride my favorite dragon, but I knew this was a once in a lifetime for these men. I pulled out my wand, commanded it to grow, and then made it hover in front of me.

"Where are we going first?" I asked, mounting it.

Netiri was quick to hover next to me.

"Does everyone have the ability to fly in this place?" Lima asked.

William thought it over for a moment.

"Ah, yes. The trees…they can't fly. The flowers can drift, but I supposed that may be considered flying."

Netiri and I wanted to laugh at his answer. But I think William was right. The guards flew, we flew, the fairies flew, the dragons, and even certain types of fish flew. Yeah, it was just the trees.

"Father let's go see Fish, Cory and Delia," my mother suggested.

I knew my mother missed them. They had been staying here in Magia for their safety. The Black Witch had been taking people my mother loved and replacing them with imposters. They were still getting over the death of poor Joshua. Those witches I killed had tortured had killed him in the most horrible way. I was happy we were going there. I wanted to see how Fish and the others were making out living here. Had they adjusted? There were no cars in Magia, no phones, radio, television, fast food, or even alcohol; not that any of them drank. We also had no plumbing here. There was no such thing as showers or bathtubs. We had lakes and rivers for that.

There were also no stoves or refrigerators, no air conditioning, fans, washing machines or dryers. It was a different world here. You lived off the land and grew your own food. Here, there was no need for roads. We all flew to where we needed to be. I know what you're thinking…where do they relieve themselves? You'll have to wait and see, won't you?

"Your Highness," Renee said, bowing at William. "May I leave now?"

"You may rise," William answered.

He put his hand on Renee's shoulder and thanked her for her bravery.

"It's not every wizard who would have dared do what you did. You have shown Magia and the other wizards that women are as brave as they, if not more."

"Thank you, My Liege."

"What brought you to the mansion?" William asked.

Renee glanced at me before answering.

"Viola was worried when Ethan never showed up the night before. She asked me to check on him."

My heart sank. I forgot all about going to see her. Why did I keep doing that to her? I didn't mean to place her on the back burner like that. I loved Viola, but I couldn't understand why I kept forgetting about her.

"Please tell her he's fine and will see her today."

Renee bowed to William before pulling off her ring. She disappeared into a vortex, but not before giving me a dirty look.

"What are they doing?" I heard from behind us.

I looked over my shoulder, it was the dragons. They had laid down with their talons in front of the warlocks. It was their way of telling you it was safe to mount them.

"Shall we?" William said, leading the way.

William instructed Rapoza and his men to mount the dragons. They looked too terrified to move. The dragons huffed and moved closer to them.

"They will not harm you," William assured them.

The men looked at one another.

"You go first," Lima said to Rapoza.

Rapoza's eyes grew wide.

"No, after you," he answered.

William rolled his eyes. He waved his hand, lifted the men, and placed them each safely on a dragon. They didn't know what to do.

"What do we hold onto?" Brad asked.

"The dragons will hold onto *you*," William said, mounting Attor.

The dragons rose to their feet. All you could hear were gasps. We took to the sky with loud, thunder-like screams coming from our new friends. Netiri couldn't stop laughing.

"What are you laughing at?" I asked. "That's how you sounded your first time."

"Shut up, jerk off," Netiri said, flying away from me.

I could see his shoulders bouncing up and down as he flew ahead of us. What the hell did those words mean?

"Virgin!" I yelled out.

Chapter Nine: Fish

William was in the lead as we flew over Magia. The waterfall would be coming into view soon, and I knew these men would be amazed by it. Magia had several waterfalls, but this one was my favorite. That's where my father built our home. He said he made it an exact model of my mother's home that she had as a child. My mother always said she had lived the happiest days of her life there. The small cottage where she grew up was in Salem, but our cottage was a replica of it.

I spread my arms as I let the air hit my face. I didn't realize how homesick I truly was. My happy moment didn't last very long. I heard horrible screams coming from behind me. I circled around and flew right next to Rapoza.

"Enjoying the ride?" I asked.

The look on his face was priceless. He was absolutely terrified. I think he was having trouble breathing. "I'm going to fall!" he yelled.

"As long as you're touching the dragon, you're not going anywhere," I assured him.

I decided to cast a calming spell at them. I really wanted him to enjoy this experience. I waved my hand, sending calming magic at him and the other warlocks. As my magic took effect, they dropped their shoulders, and actually smiled.

They all began to look down at the land. It was green as far as the eye could see. We didn't need rain to keep our forest and grass green. Magia just took care of itself. The fairies that came out of the waterfall spread their energy to all plant life that lived here. Magia was always lush, always green. It really was like a magical garden. I couldn't wait to show them the whistling ivy that draped off some of the trees. It was a sound I never grew tired of.

"What do you think?" I asked, Rapoza.

He was still looking down.

"I don't know. I'll tell you when I wake up," he said, shaking his head. "I never imagined a place like this could be real. It truly feels like we're dreaming."

"That's how I felt when I first arrived in Salem," I answered. "I think I'm still getting used to it all."

Rapoza shook his head again. "How can you compare Salem to *this*?" he said, looking around.

When William's castle came into view, I heard more gasps from the warlocks. They didn't know this, but William hated living there. He always opted to stay in our little cottage. He'd been in the human world for so long that he became accustomed to living a simple life. Well, compared to living in a castle it was. The only reason William lived in the mansion in Salem was because that's the house my father had built for my mother. It's a long story, but she didn't like living like that either. When I arrived in Salem, I couldn't get over how fancy they lived. It took me a while to get used to all of it.

"Is that a castle?" Rapoza asked in awe.

He squinted his eyes to get a better look.

"Is it made of glass?"

"It's made of crystal," I informed him. "Those stones in the battlements are gems from the river."

"Of course, they are," he said, shaking his head again.

"Look at that waterfall!" Brad yelled.

The fall was one of Magia's most beautiful accomplishments. It came down from Magia's tallest mountain. There were greenery and ivy draped along the mountain the fall came from. Flowers, of all colors grew around it. The water at the bottom of the fall was crystal clear. My mother always talked about how it looked like glass. The fish here were not like the fish in the human world. Here, there were fish of colors never seen by humans. Shapes that you could never imagine gave the fish their unique form.

We flew past it and over the mountain. When the Onfroi forest came into view, I think the warlocks stopped breathing. The Onfroi were tree-like people that lived in Magia. If you walked by one, you would never know it was a breathing being. Especially if they were standing still. They were massive in size, with arms that could reach the sky.

The warlocks couldn't take their eyes off them as they waved hello. William returned the wave as we passed them. We were about to pass the home of the pismas. They were dog-like animals that loved to gossip. Just imagine if a talking dog had pups with a lion; well, that would be a pisma.

We began to fly lower as our destination approached. I was preparing myself for their reaction when they heard a pisma talking.

"Did you see that, Manso? The king brought humans again," I heard one pisma say.

As I expected, the warlocks had a look of shock on their faces. Did I look like that when I first arrived in the *human* world? I remember being confused by their stone-covered ground, which I later learned were roads. There were many things that confused me when I first arrived in Salem and well, some things still did.

"No one is going to believe this," Lima said, gazing around. "This is absolutely incredible."

"Look at that mountain," Moe said, pointing.

It was a mountain called Talum, and it was one of the smallest mountains in Magia. What made it unusual was that it was full of holes. Well, not really holes, but rather tunnels. For reasons we still didn't know, it was always cold in those tunnels. If you crawled through the tunnels, you would find cold, clear water inside the heart of the mountain.

As we flew over Talum, the Fairy River came into view. Not far from here was the Tree of Life and its mighty forest. The Fairy River was a bright blue in color, with streams of purple and orange. If there was one thing I knew about the fairies, they needed water to survive.

"What are those lights flying around?" Rapoza asked.

"Those are fairies," I answered. "The red ones are soldiers, the purple are guards, and the yellow ones are the queen's court. The Queen is the bigger one with all the colors combined. Her name is Levora. She's not always that small."

"Simply amazing," Rapoza said, in wonder.

The dragon that Rapoza was riding on looked over his shoulder.

"You must bow to her when you are in her presence," the dragon said.

Rapoza drew breath at the sound of the dragon's voice. He shook his head and laughed.

"Is still can't get used to that."

We flew lower and lower. I could already see my mother's lake ahead. My father had created this lake with William when they moved to Magia. Since my mother took it very hard when she had to leave Salem, he wanted to bring a little piece of it here, to Magia. William didn't want Fish, Cory and Delia to miss it, either. So, he also had their cottages built near this lake when they had to bring them here.

Fish came running out of one of the cottages when he saw us coming. His face was one of joy.

"Delia, I think it's Thea!" he yelled, pointing up.

A huge smile spread across my mother's face when she saw him. Delia was next to run out. Cory came out from the cottage next to them. I had to take a closer look when I noticed there were small, blue orbs of light, following them around. I'd never seen that in Magia before. What were they? I knew of the white ones, but I had never seen the blue ones.

The dragons landed next to the lake. They lowered themselves so the warlocks could climb down. My mother ran to her friends the moment her feet hit the ground. Delia was already in tears.

"Thea," she cried, as she threw her arms around her.

Cory put his arms around both of them. Fish was next to join the circle. They were my mother's loves, her protectors at one time, and the only family she'd known. They grew up together. They shared a bond that only *they* understood. Even my father knew their relationship was special. He stood back and allowed my mother to have her moment with them.

"Why haven't you come to visit?" Delia cried.

"It's almost over," my mother said, squeezing her tight. "We'll all be able to go home soon."

Her words surprised me. She said that soon, they would *all* be able to go home. Did that mean she was going back to Salem?

Fish and my father embraced in what Fish called *a bro hug*. My father loved Fish. He was always funny, always in a good mood. Although Fish looked to be about seventeen years old, he was really over three hundred. In fact, they all were. I didn't know much about their back story, but I knew they took a potion to stay young back then to help my mother. As a matter of fact, I think they still took it.

Delia had long, dark hair and an angry-looking face. Don't get me wrong, she was pretty, but always looked mad. Cory was tall, muscular and very handsome. A lot of women came into his bakery just to look at him. My mother always called him, *pretty*. I knew Cory had loved my mother before he married. My mother said she would have married him if not for meeting my father. By the time Cory wanted to confess to my mother that he was I love her, it was too late.

"You're early," Fish said. "The wedding isn't for another couple of days."

William quickly cleared his throat. I knew he didn't want them to know about what was going on.

"May I introduce our new friends," William said, gesturing to the warlocks. "They came for a short visit. We won't be staying long."

Rapoza was staring at the blue orb over Fish's head. Fish held his arm out.

"They call me, Fish," he said, shaking hands with him. "And that *thing* over my head, I call it *Charles*."

"Charles? It's a person?" Rapoza asked, confused.

Fish laughed.

"He wishes."

I noticed that Delia and Cory also had a blue orb following them. When they would stop, so would the orb. What was the purpose of it? When Viola and Steven came out, they too had one following them. I just couldn't understand it.

After all the introductions were made, the dragons took flight and disappeared around the mountain. Six guards stayed behind and spread out throughout the small village. It was normal for them to do that. Since Wendell and his betrayal, it was a written rule that the king must always has guards near him.

"Staying for dinner?" Fish asked. "Charles makes quite the feast."

We all looked up at the orb again. When the warlocks looked at me to explain, I could only shrug my shoulders.

"That light can cook?" Moe asked, looking up at it.

"It does much more than that," Fish answered.

He moved a few feet away from us and tapped his chin, as if he was thinking something over.

"Let's see, what do I need right now?"

Fish snapped his fingers.

"Got it!"

Fish bent down and grabbed a handful of dirt. He sprinkled it over his head and looked up at the orb.

"Charles, I'm feeling *really* dirty right now. I think I need a shower."

The orb began to glow and released tiny speckles of light. The speckles came down and spread throughout Fish's body. It almost appeared as if Fish was getting rained on. When the speckles disappeared, the dirt was gone.

"All clean," Fish said, with his arms out.

Delia rolled her eyes and looked at my mother.

"He's been doing that since William sent those orbs to us. He said he wanted us to feel like we were home. I think Fish has been in heaven since then."

"Watch this," Fish continued. "Charles, I would like to wear one of those robes all the wizards wear, and I want it made of gold."

"Fish, don…" William tried to say.

It was too late. The orb covered Fish with its speckles and gave him what he wanted. The moment the robe made of gold was on his frame, Fish was like a statue. He couldn't move an inch. The robe was in fact, made of gold, *solid gold*.

William shook his head.

"I warned you, Fish. Be careful what you wish for."

William waved his hand and made the robe disappear. He stepped away and asked the warlocks to come with him. The warlocks followed William as they all looked up at the orbs.

"So, who are they?" Fish asked.

"It's a long story," my mother answered.

I made my way over to Vera and Steven as my parents went into one of the cottages with their friends. Vera was the spitting image of her mother. Same long, black hair, same angry look. Steven was a bit older than her. He had olive skin and very sad, droopy eyes. I looked for any signs of trauma in Steven's eyes. He looked utterly and completely happy.

"Excited about the big day?" I asked.

"I was about to ask you the same question," Steven answered.

I still hadn't told them we wouldn't be having a double wedding.

"Well, I've been doing some thinking about the matter," I lied. "It's your big day, and I don't want to take anything away from that. Viola and I are going to wait a few weeks."

That was also a lie. I hadn't even talked to Viola about the changes. I still felt bad that I forgot all about my visit with her. I tried not to worry about it. Besides, Viola was a very understanding person.

"Don't be silly," Vera said. "It can be a big day for all of us. We don't mind, Ethan."

"No, really. We want to wait a few weeks."

I said goodbye and told them I'd be seeing them at their wedding. On my way to find my parents, I heard voices coming from the nearby trees. I stopped when I heard my name. I took soft steps as I approached and hid behind one of the trees. It was William and the warlocks.

"We'll have to set up a meeting so we can talk freely," William was saying. "I'm afraid Magia is distracting you at the moment."

"There's just too much to take in," Rapoza answered. "I've never seen anything like this place before."

"My point exactly," William answered.

"Why us?" Lima asked. "What kind of help can we possibly give you that will help Ethan? We're not wizards."

"No," William answered. "You may not be wizards, but you are noble. Nobility means graciousness, decency, dignity and so much more. All the qualities that are required."

"Required for what?" Moe asked.

"Sounds like you want us to kill something evil," Rapoza said.

"Precisely," William answered. "You've taken no life or committed any crimes. Only someone like you can face the unknown."

"You make us sound like we're perfect," Brad said. "There's nothing perfect about us. I've told lies before."

"A lie I can live with," William answered. "Had you taken a life before, we wouldn't be standing here."

I jumped back when something poked me in the back. I spun around, it was Fish.

"Are you being nosey?" he whispered.

He had a stick in his hand, and he was trying to poke me again.

"Fish, go away," I said, waving him off.

"Is it a meeting of the minds?" he asked, getting behind the tree with me.

"Will you get out of here," I said, giving him a nudge.

"What's going on? Who are those guys?"

"I'll tell you later. Just get out of here."

"Why does William keep bringing warlocks here?" he asked. "This is the third time."

"What?

"Yeah, he brought Jason, the cop a few days ago and there was some guy with him I didn't know. I saw them when Charles and I were exploring Magia. William doesn't like us going too far away from this camp, but I was bored. Anyway, I saw them doing weird stuff with the dragons. Jason would disappear into one of those spinning cones, then come right back as the dragons blew fire at him. It didn't kill or burn him. I think they were practicing."

"Spinning cones? You mean, a vortex?"

"Yeah, the ones we need to get in and out of this place."

I looked back toward William; what was he up to? Why was nobility such an important thing to him? And what were the dragons being used for?

"Come on, Fish. Let's get out of here."

When we came out of the trees, Fish said something that changed everything.

"Why don't you ask Charles what William is up to? He has to do whatever we ask of him."

My heart started racing. That was a brilliant idea. I quickly grabbed Fish by the arm, and we headed to his cottage.

"Oh no, what did I just do?" Fish said, as I pulled him away.

Chapter Ten: Big mouth

Fish kept trying to pull away from me as I almost dragged him toward the cottages.

"I have such a big mouth," Fish kept saying.

"Which one is your cottage," I asked, grabbing his arm tighter.

He pointed to a cottage that was nearest to the lake. Once inside, I had to do a double take. The room was filled with flowers and fountains. I could hear the sound of a stream that wasn't there. I looked up when I heard the sound of birds chirping. There was even a big oak tree in the corner of the room.

As I let Fish go, the room began to change what it looked like. I got confused when steel bars began to form on the walls. A single light dropped down from above. I looked at Fish, hoping he would explain.

"Charles makes the room look like whatever I need it to," he said. "I think your about to interrogate me, so I guess I thought of an interrogation room. It was a garden before because I was in here with Delia. We were, well, you know."

"Know what? What were you doing?"

"It was Hide the Sausage time, Ethan."

"What the hell are you talking about, Fish?"

Just then, Netiri walked in. He looked confused as he took in the room.

"Are we taking the warlocks *prisoners*?" he asked.

The room began to change. It started looking more like a log cabin. Netiri looked at Fish, then at me.

"What's going on?"

When we didn't answer, a huge smile spread across Netiri's face.

"Were you guys jerking off?" he asked.

"What?" Fish yelled.

Netiri motioned for Fish to come closer to him. He whispered something in Fish's ear, pumped his fist, then began to chuckle. Fish's eyes lit up.

"Really?" he said, looking back at me. "You don't think he's ever done it, huh?"

"I don't think so," Netiri laughed. "He thinks it means, *kidding around*."

"What the hell are you two talking about?"

Fish put his hand up.

"Relax, Ethan. We're just *kidding around*."

Netiri's shoulders were bouncing up and down. He was trying to laugh silently but was having a hard time composing himself. Their laughter at my expense was beginning to irritate me. Why wouldn't they just tell me what the hell that meant? I was obviously missing the joke.

"Stop laughing at me," I said, as my temper began to rise.

Their laughter echoed like exploding bombs in my ear. It filled my heart with rage as they pointed and laughed at me. I began to imagine myself killing them. The thought of that was making me smile. That's when I knew it was time for me to get out of here.

"The hell with you," I said, storming out.

"Ethan, come back!" Fish yelled. "You know how I am; I *kid around* all the time."

I felt like an idiot as I walked out of their little camp. What was so funny? I was so angry with Netiri for making a fool out of me. I know I had joked around with him about what he'd said, but he knew what I was talking about. I certainly didn't want to come off as sensitive. I just wanted to know what they found so funny. Netiri knew how my state of mind was lately. Why couldn't he just tell me instead of laughing at me?

My mood was quickly changing as I mounted my staff. I took to the sky as thoughts of how I killed those witches, filled my head. I imagined myself skinning Netiri as he begged for his life. The thought of his bloodied body made me happy. I felt out of breath as I imagined other ways I could kill and destroy him. I began to think of Fish. I could still hear his mocking laughter in my head. Just thinking about the way his face looked as he laughed at me was making me seethe with anger.

I tried with all my might to shake the thoughts I was having. I felt my mind getting foggy as the sound of their laughter almost made my ears explode. Before I knew it, I was turning and heading back to their camp. My hands were shaking as I gripped my staff and flew faster. I would make them pay for laughing at my ignorance. I closed my eyes as dark thoughts of them dying engulfed my very being. I was seeing red. All I could think of was their dead, mutilated bodies lying before me. That thought made me smile. I had an amazing feeling of elation spreading throughout my soul. I flew even faster, desperate to end their lives.

I landed near the lake and shook my staff, commanding my sword to appear. My heart was full of rage as I marched toward the cottage. I could still hear them laughing inside as I neared.

"We should tell him to *kid around* with Delia," Fish was saying.

"She'll kill you, Fish," Netiri laughed.

Their laughter felt like poison bombs going off in my head. The louder they laughed, the more incensed I felt. My pride was hurt, so was my manhood. They were making a fool out of me and laughing at my expense. They were about to die for that. I would kill Fish slowly; use his own weapon to skin him alive.

I raised my sword, determined to strike them. Just as I was about to be near the entrance, I flew back and was tossed across the camp. My sword went flying out of my hands. I quickly jumped to my feet; William was standing in front of the cottage; the warlocks were next to him. William had a look on his face I'd never seen before. He looked at me as if I were a stranger. My anger rose even more. If I had to kill *him* to get to my targets, so be it. He wasn't going to stand in the way of my vengeance.

"You know what to do, gentlemen," William said to the warlocks.

I glared at the warlocks as they walked around William and faced me. Rapoza pulled out his knife, spat on it, and smiled as his knife grew into his sword. Brad was holding what looked like a machete. Lima had two blades, each strapped to his wrist. Moe just smiled as he put his hand up to his mouth. He spit up a spell and got into a stance.

I looked at William.

"Traitor!" I shouted.

I held out my hand, commanding my sword to come to me. I would save William for last. His death would not be merciful. His mistrust in me was going to make this easy. I was tired of his puzzles that never made any sense. I would silence him forever.

"Father, what's going on?" I heard my mother say.

"James, grab her!" William shouted. "Do not allow her to interfere. Remember what I told you."

"I have her, William," my father answered.

My mother tried to push my father away, but he pulled her back and made her look at him.

"We knew this day would come, Thea. You must stay out of this. William knows what's he's doing."

"It's too soon," she cried.

My father pulled her in and wrapped his arms around her. "Don't watch this," he said, turning the other way with her.

William waved his hand toward the cottages. He placed a seal on the doors so no one else could get out. When he signaled the guards, they came and made a circle around me and the warlocks. One guard took his place next to my parents.

"It's too soon," my mother kept saying.

William ignored my mother as he gave a nod to the warlocks. They swallowed thickly and all glared intently at me.

"It's a good day to die, isn't it?" I asked, in a mocking tone.

Rapoza held up his sword with both hands.

"It's also a good day to taste my blade," he shot back.

Moe began spitting spells on the ground in front of him. When he kicked one of the spells at me, the other warlocks attacked. I didn't even see it coming; Brad jumped over me as he slammed me across the face with his machete. Before I could shake it off, I was hit with a spell in the chest that sent me to my knees. His spell sent vibrating, electric shocks all over my body. I was met with a foot to the face that knocked me backwards.

When another spell hit my back, it felt like I was being dragged over a bed of coal. I closed my eyes as I felt something inside of me explode. It was like I had been put in a tub of boiling water. My temper rose to levels I didn't even know I had. As I got to my feet, I could feel spells bouncing off my body. I was vibrating with anger, causing waves of energy to surround me. I held out my hand, demanding my sword to come flying into it. I still had my eyes closed when I felt the sword slam into my waiting hand. I slowly wrapped my fingers around the handle, opened my eyes and smiled at the mayhem in front of me.

"Now!" William shouted.

Rapoza was the first to attack. He swung his sword toward my head, but I held mine up as if it were a feather. You could hear the blades clanging as I pushed Rapoza's sword away. He swung again, and again I stopped it with ease. Brad was next to try my patience. When he swung his machete at me, I only had to slightly move my head to one side in order to avoid it. Rapoza and Brad were both swinging their weapons at me. I moved and dodged them every time.

I could feel a force deep in my soul, guiding me which way to move. Every spell Moe threw at me, my body knew what to do. When they all attacked, I was like a bolt of lightning, a blur to the men I was battling.

"Ethan, come back to us!" I heard my mother scream.

I lifted my sword with both hands, leaning the blade against my forehead. It was time to kill these men and end this. I swung the sword hard at Rapoza. When the blade of my sword bent in two, I got confused. I was shocked when I pulled the sword back and the blade straightened itself out. I swung again, this time at Lima. I grunted when the blade refused to pierce his heart. It bent again, as if it were made of plastic or something.

I threw down the sword and tried waving my hand, but there was no magic to be found. I glared at William; I knew he was responsible for this. Before I could wave it again, Lima spit a spell on my face. It instantly made my knees bend. I began to get hit with one spell after another. Each one brought a whole new level of pain. The pain surged through me like a wild animal. I started rolling in the dirt as if I were on fire. I was trying to put out their spells. It was too agonizing, too much for me to endure. When my nerve pain flared up, I knew I had lost the battle.

I finally stopped fighting. I just lay there and waited for them to kill me. I couldn't even remember why I was angry; I only felt horrible and monstrous pain. Something inside of me had taken over who I was. I felt when it began possessing and changing my spirit. Evil had come alive inside of me, and now it was burning me alive. It would be my punishment for not staying strong.

"Kill me," I begged.

I felt the pressure of Rapoza's blade on my neck. I sighed as I welcomed my demise.

"Thank you," I said, slipping into darkness.

I felt I was falling into a pit of lava as all voices around me faded away. I heard the distant cries of my mother as she begged William to help me. I wanted to tell her not to bother with me anymore. I didn't deserve William's help. He tried to warn me about this and I didn't listen.

Whatever it was that made me change, I had no control over it. Anger had consumed me, made me thirst for blood. Why? Netiri and Fish were just joking; I knew that. Why couldn't I see that before? I seemed to be reasoning with myself right now; why not then? Is this what William was waiting for? It certainly felt that way.

What about the warlocks? What was their role in all of this? My sword had avoided hurting or killing them. How did that happen? Was William making it do that? So many questions were racing through my head. I couldn't make sense out of anything. Where was I now? Was I dead? Was I still burning? Had Rapoza killed me? Is that why I was able to reason with myself right now?

I felt as if I were floating in a dream. The burning sensation was still there, but the rage was gone. Something was touching my face. It felt like a feather, or maybe someone's fingers. All I knew was that it felt gentle and soft. I wanted to open my eyes, but feared I would go into another rage.

"Did you see his eyes? They were so red," I heard a voice say.

"I warned you about this, Thea. I tried to prepare you. There's no changing your vision."

Was that William? I decided to keep my eyes closed and listen in. I needed to make sense of it all.

"Why did it happen so soon?"

I slowly began to recognize the voices. My mother was saying something about it being too soon. Too soon for what?

"We didn't mean to upset him, Thea," Fish said. "I was only joking with him."

"It's my fault," Netiri chimed in. "I should have known it would make him feel foolish. I mean, I never imagined he would be *that* innocent. I assumed he knew a little when he teased me about what I'd said. You know, about 'throwing it in' someone before? He laughed about *that*."

"What did you expect?" William asked. "He's been living in Magia his whole life. His best friend is a dragon. If there is any blame to place, it should be with me. I should have prepared him for the world he would be facing."

"Geeze, William," Fish said. "No one had *that* talk with me. My body started doing things it never had. I just figured it out by myself."

"Can we *please* change the subject," my mother hissed. "It doesn't matter why he got upset. The point is, there will always be something that triggers him. We just need to figure out how to avoid that."

"You can't avoid it, Thea," William answered. "He will have to learn how to bring himself back. He's a wizard, there are strengths in us that we don't even realize."

"May I ask you something, William?"

It was my father.

"You may."

"Why didn't you stop that witch from making my son swallow that pit? If you knew it was going to happen, why didn't you stop it? Why did you allow Ethan to swallow pure evil?"

I almost opened my eyes and gave myself away. I knew what day my father was referring to.

It's the day one of those witches made herself look like Viola. She came to the mansion to look for me. I remember when they placed that pit in my mouth then taped it shut. That meant William lied to me when he said it was another curse. I thought it was more of those shingles, at least, that's what he said. Now I want to know what that witch *really* gave me.

There was a long pause before William answered.

"I'm going to say this loud and clear, so there's no misunderstandings. I didn't *allow* Ethan to swallow that pit. It would have happened regardless. I can't change what is already written for the future. What I've done is prepare Ethan, try to make him stronger. I have unwavering faith in him. I know he can fight what grows within him. We all must have faith in him. I remember a time when some of you were frustrated with Thea. She was impulsive and bad-tempered. I never lost faith in her; the same way I will never lose faith in Ethan. He will be up against the forces of evil. If there is anyone who can do it, it will be him. Some of you may find his ignorance funny at times, but it's that same ignorance that will help him in the end. He needs to find the true wizard inside himself. None of you can do that for him. The most we can hope for the most is that he realizes that *love* is the most powerful tool he will ever need. I know of no other tool that will help him more. Allow him to make his mistakes. They will only make him stronger; the same way they made Thea stronger."

"Why don't you tell him?" Netiri asked. "I know Ethan, and he can take the truth. Tell him he's becoming some evil guy that's going to try to kill us all then rule the human world."

"He knows as much as he needs to," William answered.

So, I really *was* turning into some dark lord. Why wasn't I surprised?

I felt someone touching me again, probably my mother.

"I can't let the darkness take him, Father."

"Only *he* can stop it, Thea."

"Will the warlocks help?" my father asked.

"Today was a good test for them," William answered. "I think they will help more than we expected."

"Why them?" Netiri asked. "Why can't *we* help Ethan?"

"Who said you wouldn't be helping?" William shot back.

"I think what I'm trying to ask is; what's so special about these warlocks? Why did we go through all this trouble *for them*?"

I heard William sigh.

"There is only one way to fight evil. It's the only tool that has ever defeated it. Good must triumph over evil. When I used that white book of spells, I did something that none of you will ever remember. I brought two people back, using that book of spells. They were only allowed to fight the dead, not the living. Once the dead were gone, so were they. That probably does not make sense to you, but that's because you don't remember it. You're not supposed to."

I knew what he was talking about. Why did I remember it? He was talking about Sammy and Javier.

"I began to read that white book of spells," William continued. "There it was, plain as day. Good will *always* triumph over evil. It was then I realized what I needed to do."

"What are you saying that the warlocks are *good*?" Netiri asked.

"Don't you see?" William answered. "They are men of honor. They protect lives, not take them. Only someone like them can face evil and not be tormented by their past. Those men have nothing to be ashamed of. They have lived honest lives, honorable ones. The spell I cast can only work on someone with those qualities."

"Yes, I saw the way Ethan's sword avoided hurting them," my father said.

"If I had placed that spell on any of you, Ethan's sword would have found its mark."

"So, we're not honorable?" Fish asked, sounding offended.

"Have you killed?" William asked him. "Have you *not* skinned people alive?"

"Well, yeah, but it was to help Thea."

"You've killed out of vengeance, Fish," William reminded him. "Do you not remember the warlock that struck Delia and Steven? Didn't you kill him out of anger because he hurt Delia?"

"That was years ago," Fish answered. "I thought he had raped her."

"None the less, your reasons for killing him were the same. You have all taken a life in one way or another. Those men are free of that sin."

"That's not true," Netiri cut in. "I heard the stories about these warlocks. They've killed plenty of men."

"The stories are lies," William answered. "Those men have never taken a life. There has never been a need for it. They fight with their skills, not their tempers. Unlike you, they spared the lives of the men they fought."

"May I ask you something?"

It was Fish.

"You may."

"You're a wizard, a powerful one. Why can't you just use your magic to fight whatever it is that's coming? Can't you just wave your hand and make the evil go away?"

"It doesn't work that way, Fish. Honor must fight evil. There can be no taking of lives in their past. I am not free of that sin."

There was silence for several moments.

"Why did those witches pick Ethan to swallow that pit?" Fish asked.

"They didn't choose him, the Black Witch did. She's using Ethan to get to Thea. If she can turn Ethan evil, then she wins. She'll have the perfect soldier for her mission."

"What's her mission?" Fish asked.

"She wants to force Thea to switch places with her" William answered.

There was another pause.

"William, when can we go home?" Fish asked. "Don't get me wrong, Charles is wonderful and all, but I miss Salem. I miss the bakery, the deli, well, everything."

"I'm working on it, Fish," William answered. "You may be returning sooner than expected."

I didn't want to hear anymore. I wish I could jump up and fly out of here. It was almost at the point where I couldn't stop myself.

"I think he's waking up," I heard my father say.

Chapter Eleven: Unbeknownst

I opened my eyes and looked around. I was in our cottage, in my own bed in Magia. Everyone rose to their feet and gathered around me. They seemed tense and nervous as I slowly sat up. I almost got the sense that they were scared of me. That didn't make me feel any better.

I felt horrible for putting them all through this. I felt shame and disgrace. I couldn't face them. I was weak and powerless against what was inside of me. How could I possibly give them hope? I was about to tell them how sorry I was when…

"*Are you done having your pity party?*" I heard in my head.

It was William.

"*What?*" I answered, in my head.

"*Tell them you feel fine.*"

"How do you feel?" my mother asked.

I wanted to tell her that it still felt like I was burning alive; that I had so much pain, vibrating throughout my body.

"I feel fine," I lied.

"Tell her you're just tired."

"I think I'm just tired," I said, looking at William.

"We should let him rest," William said to them.

"Where are the warlocks?" I asked William.

"I took them home."

"Are they okay?"

"Don't look at me, Ethan. Your mother will know we're talking."

I looked at my mother.

"I feel fine, Mother. I'm just really tired."

"Come, Thea," my father said, grabbing her by the arm. "Let him get some rest. We'll come later and check on him."

I could see my mother had been crying. It only made me feel worse about myself. Netiri moved closer and tried to say something to me, but William told him it wasn't the time.

"I'll see you back in Salem," William said to him.

Netiri nodded and looked at me from the corner of his eye. I knew he felt guilty for teasing me earlier. I wanted to tell him that we were fine, but William softly pushed him out the door.

"I'll come back later," Fish said, following Netiri out.

"Lay down, so your parents can leave."

I did what William instructed and laid back down. I pretended to close my eyes as my mother gave me a kiss on the head.

"I love you, Ethan."

The moment she walked out, I sat back up and looked at William.

"What's going on?"

"*Talk only with your mind,*" he answered.

"Why? There's no one here, right?"

He raised a brow and gave me a look.

"*I'm sorry, William.*"

He nodded knowingly and looked away from me. I know this may sound strange, but he was acting like I was still asleep.

"*How do you feel?*" he asked, not looking at me.

"*Like I'm on fire.*"

"*I'm sorry the river didn't do what you expected. I truly feel bad about that.*"

"*It didn't cure me, did it?*"

He walked over to the wall, tilted his head, and began to dust it with his hand. Why was he doing that?

"*A gypsy curse must be broken, not cured.*"

Again, he wouldn't look at me as he answered my questions. It was like I wasn't even here. He was answering my questions but wouldn't acknowledge me.

"*I don't care about the curse right now, William. What the hell happened to me? I heard everything you said before.*"

With his back to me, he said…

"*Yes, I know.*"

"*You knew I was listening?*"

"*Isn't it obvious?*"

"Can you look at me, please?"

"No."

"William, what was the point? If you knew I was listening, then why wouldn't you just tell me the truth from the beginning?"

He began to look pointlessly around the room. He walked over to a shelf and just stared at it.

"I don't understand. I told you the truth about something?" he asked.

"Yes, I heard you."

"Was I talking to you?"

"No, but I heard you."

"I see," he said, fiddling with a candle.

"Wait, what are you talking about? You're confusing me, William."

"What are you confused about? Was I or was I not talking to you?"

"Well, no."

"Then I don't see what truth you are talking about, Ethan. I don't remember telling you anything. As far as I know, I was talking to your loved ones."

He still wouldn't make eye contact with me.

"I know you didn't tell me anything. You were talking loudly; I heard all the information you gave them."

"What information?"

"When you were talking to them."

"What did I say?"

"William, I just told you, I heard everything."

"Was I talking to you?"

"Why do you keep repeating yourself?" I asked frustrated.

"Why do you keep insisting that I gave you information?"

"You didn't give it to me, you gave it to…"

I froze when I realized what he was doing.

"You knew I was listening, didn't you?"

"I thought we already established that?"

I sat back, trying to figure this one out. If he knew I was listening, what did he want me to hear? I tried to think back and remember every word he'd said. It had to be something he couldn't say out loud.

"May I sit while you figure things out?" he asked.

I nodded and he took a seat. He crossed his legs and reached for a book that sat near my bed. He looked calm as he flipped through the pages.

"I don't think I've read this book before," he said, mostly to himself.

I ignored him and thought back to what he'd said. He spoke about the warlocks, and how they were honorable men. Is that what he wanted me to know?"

"No, I don't think I've read it."

I glanced at him, wishing he would stop talking. I returned to my thinking. Ok, what did he say that is so important? What part of his speech does he want me to think of?

"Oh, I like what this author wrote," William said, turning a page. *"He wrote it loud and clear, so there would be no misunderstandings."*

Why did he keep interrupting me? I needed to concentrate. I thought about his words again. Could it be the part about the spell he cast on the warlocks?

Did he want me to know that I couldn't kill them?

"*No, I don't like this part,*" he rambled on.

I gave him a dirty look. Why wouldn't he let me concentrate? I went back to my thinking. What else did he say when he was talking to everyone?

"*I like this book,*" William said, flipping another page. "*The author uses love, as a powerful tool. I have to agree with him. What better way to fight evil?*"

"*William, I'm trying to recall what you said. I can't think straight with you talking about love and…*"

I just sat there with a stupid look on my face. It finally sunk in. He wanted me to know what he's always said to me. Love is the most powerful spell he knew. The key word was *love*. Love was good, love was noble. Evil wasn't capable of loving anything.

"*Good will always triumph over evil,*" I said, looking away.

"*The end,*" William said, closing the book.

"*Can we talk normal now?*" I asked.

William tilted his head to one side.

"I wasn't aware we were talking. I was just sitting here, watching you get some rest. It must have been a dream, perhaps?"

I looked deep into his eyes, trying desperately to understand. William was never one to just hand me the answers; I had to figure it out. He made sure every word he said to me was a lesson. When I was a child, he would encourage me to play with the dragons. He called them *majestic creatures* that had many lessons to teach us. I think that's when I began my friendship with Attor, my favorite dragon. I learned so much from him. He taught me things about myself that I didn't realize were in me. It was no wonder Attor was William's favorite dragon as well. I always knew when they were talking with their minds. As a matter of fact, they too, would not look at each other when they did that.

"Are you ready to face the world?" he asked.

I was still trying to figure out why he couldn't tell me things out loud.

"Can I ask you a question, first?" I asked through my thoughts.

William rose to his feet.

"Choose your question wisely."

"You were talking loud enough so I would hear you. It's obvious you couldn't just tell me. You once said that if I figured things out, it wouldn't change the future."

"Is that the question?"

"No. You're giving me clues, aren't you? You can't tell me, so you're guiding me; maybe to help me change the future?"

He raised both brows this time.

"I don't remember giving you clues, Ethan. That would be cheating and would upset the rules of life. I think what you are trying to say is, you were reading my thoughts; unbeknownst to me."

I shook my head. I was in awe of him. I wanted to say thank you for saying he had so much faith in me. I didn't know what the future held, or what that pit was doing to me, but I was ready to face it all.

"Can I ask you one more question? It has nothing to do about what happened today."

"Very well."

"What does, *jerk off* mean?"

He smiled and looked down. I think he was trying not to laugh.

"Go home, Ethan. Look for Netiri and buy that phone the two of you want. I think you will find your answers there. I'll have James give you some money."

I jumped out of bed.

"I have money. I opened a bank account, remember?"

He nodded.

"I'll see you back in Salem in a few days. I'm helping Delia with the wedding preparations."

He turned to leave.

"William."

"Yes?"

I didn't want to cry, but I was getting choked up as I thought of the words, I wanted to say to him. I looked into his emerald-green eyes. His salt and pepper hair were strands of wisdom. I could see the knowledge just oozing out of him. He was the wisest wizard I knew. The Tree of Life had chosen him to be king for a reason. How could you say *thank you* to someone like him?

"Before you thank me," he said, moving closer, I wasn't always this wise. It took years before I realized what kind of wizard Magia needed. I made many mistakes, some that couldn't be fixed. Believe it or not, I was worse than your mother. I was quick to jump to conclusions, impulsive and hot tempered. I wasn't always the wizard you see before you. It took me hundreds of years to find myself."

"You? Impulsive?"

He chuckled.

"Someday, Ethan, I will tell you *The Story of William*. It was *Before the Beginning*. You remind me of that young wizard. The human world was new to me. I had never been out of this realm when I was your age. I had no idea that witches even existed, much less expected I would fall in love with one. I went through many sorrows, but it made me the wizard I am today."

"I would be honored if you told me your story one day, William."

He smiled widely.

"Soon, my boy."

I tried to hold back my tears, but it was pointless. I threw my arms around him as I finally broke down.

"I won't let evil change me," I cried. "I swear it, I will fight it till death."

I felt William's soft touch on my back.

"I know you will. And do you know how I know that?"

I pulled away from him as I wiped my tears.

"How?"

"Because you are just like your mother. You are stronger than you know. You're brave, like she is. You would face an army alone, if it was necessary. You would step up to the devil himself and offer him your life, if it meant saving others. You and your mother share those qualities. Don't tell her I said this, but I admire her. She was much stronger than I at her age."

"It will be our secret," I smiled.

"Remember one thing, Ethan. To have what you've never had, you must do what you've never done."

He excused himself and walked out.

Chapter Twelve: I'm Sorry

No one was home when I got back to Salem. I wanted to shower then go and see Viola. I needed to apologize for missing our date. I just wanted to get my mind straight and think things over first. My need to see her was being replaced by my fear of hurting her. I hadn't forgotten about William's vision. In his vision, I killed Viola and my son. William was trying desperately to change the outcome of that vision. I assured him that I would never hurt Viola like that. Now, I wasn't so sure.

When I was fighting those warlocks today, all I could think of was their blood. I thought of the agony I could cause them. Any other thought was quickly pushed aside. It wasn't until they got the best of me that I was able to reason with myself. I remember giving up and excepting death. After that, I don't remember much.

"Who's there?" a voice called.

I was heading into the kitchen but stopped when I heard the voice. Was my father back?

"It's Ethan!" I answered.

"I thought someone was robbing the place."
I realized it was Netiri.
"Where are you?" I asked, looking around.
"I'll be right out. I'm using the guest bathroom."

Guest bathroom? We had a bathroom for guests? What was the difference? I knew each bedroom had its own bathroom in this massive house. But a guest bathroom? Wow, humans really did spoil themselves, didn't they?

"I'll be in the kitchen," I said, heading that way.

I was so used to smelling coffee when I walked into this room. It felt odd to see the kitchen so empty. I walked over to the machine that made coffee and tried to figure it out. I tried to picture William and the steps he took. Nothing was coming to me.

"You know how to make coffee?" I yelled out.

"Why are you yelling?" Netiri asked, as he walked in.

"Oh, sorry. I thought you were still "guesting" in the bathroom."

Netiri laughed.

"What?"

"Nothing. You know how to use this thing?" I asked, holding up the pot.

"Yeah, let me show you."

It felt a little awkward between us. I wasn't sure what to say to him or how to put it. I think he was thinking the same thing. He didn't say much as he placed some coffee in a container, then slipped the container into the machine. We both looked like fools as we watched the machine brew the coffee. I reached for two cups.

"Having some?" I asked, holding up the cup.

"Yeah, I'll get the cream."

I was tapping the counter as I watched the coffee pour from the machine to the pot. Then I started watching an ant crawling on the counter.

"Sugar?"

I looked up.

"What?"

"You want some sugar in your coffee?"

"Yeah, that would be nice."

He picked up the sugar container from the table and placed it next to the machine. Then we both started watching the ant, now crawling near the stove.

"Oh, look, an ant," Netiri said, pointing.

"Yeah, he's a determined little guy, isn't he?"

Netiri started tapping his fingers on the counter. I hadn't realized I was now tapping my foot.

"Must be an old coffee machine," Netiri said. "They don't usually take this long."

"Oh really? Yeah, you're probably right."

We were both looking around the kitchen like fools. Why couldn't I just tell him I was sorry I had overreacted? Wait, he could read my mind. Why wasn't he doing that right now? It certainly would save us a lot of trouble.

"Sprinklers are on," Netiri said, looking out the sliding doors to the kitchen.

"Oh, yeah," I said, looking over my shoulder.

"Does the yard need watering this time of year?" he asked.

"*Are you reading my thoughts right now?*" I asked.

When he kept looking outside, I knew he wasn't. I started looking at the ant again. I felt so foolish.

"The pot is almost full," I pointed out.

"Oh, good. I could really use some coffee right now."

"Will you two just make out already?"

We both looked up, it was Fish and William. What were *they* doing here? Netiri never looked so happy to see someone walk in.

"Hey!" he said, as if he hadn't seen them in years.

I was one to talk; I did the same thing.

"We're making coffee," I said, holding up the pot. "Would anyone like some?"

William rolled his eyes.

"Yeah, I'll have some," Fish said, walking over to us. "William brought me so I could pick up clothes for Delia."

"I'll be in my room," William said, leaving the kitchen.

That awkward tension was back. Fish poured himself a cup and kept stirring it over and over again.

"Gotta make sure the sugar gets dissolved," Netiri said, watching him.

"Oh yeah, nothing worse than sugar granules," Fish answered. "Cold coffee is the worst, too."

"Iced coffee isn't bad," Netiri said.

"Yeah, yeah, I like iced coffee," Fish answered.

I looked back and forth at them.

"How about the weather? Should we talk about that?" I snapped at them.

I grabbed my coffee and headed out the back sliding door to the kitchen. I walked over to my mother's garden and took a seat on her bench. Why was it so hard for us to talk about what happened? Did they think I was upset with them? I was more upset at myself for overreacting. This awkward feeling was new to me. Why couldn't I just tell them how sorry I was? I didn't want to talk about the teasing, it didn't matter anymore.

I heard the sliding door open, then close. I knew they were both coming out. After a few moments, I heard their footsteps.

"Um, mind if we talk to you?" Netiri asked, nervously.

It suddenly occurred to me that they didn't want to upset me. After what happened, who could blame them?

"Sure," I said, taking a sip of my coffee.

I didn't get up, so they walked around me and looked at each other. Yup, they were nervous. Fish was first to talk.

"Listen, Ethan, about the teasing…"

"I don't want to talk about that," I quickly answered. "It doesn't matter anymore."

"William told us that our teasing is what upset you so much," Fish informed me. "You know what an ass I can be sometimes. Delia gets mad at me *all the time*. I realize that I just don't know when to stop."

"I'm sorry, too," Netiri said, putting his head down." I thought I was getting payback because you had teased me so much about the, *throwing it in someone*, comment. I didn't mean to make you feel like a fool."

I rose to my feet, feeling even worse than before.

"Are you done yet?" I asked.

A look of terror washed over them.

"I'm not mad," I quickly assured them. "I like our relationship. I don't mind the teasing and the joking. I never want that to change. No one can make me laugh the way you do, both of you. I don't know why I got so upset. I think it's because I wasn't in on the joke. Netiri, I knew what you meant by saying you had, *threw it in someone* before. I may not know much about being with a woman, but I knew enough to put that one together."

"You knew that, and you don't know what *jerking off* means?" Fish asked.

"It doesn't matter anymore," I snapped. "I don't care what it means. I'm just trying to say that I'm sorry. I don't want things to change between us. Don't treat me like a kid. Don't hold back on the teasing because you feel I can't take it. I didn't mean to make you feel that way. All I know is, it would really hurt me if you started treating me with kid gloves. I know what happened made you both nervous about being around me. I hope I'm able to show you that I can bring myself back. All I ask is, please don't change how you act around me."

"We can start off by telling you what those words means," Fish suggested.

I laughed. "Really, Fish, it doesn't matter to me anymore. The two of you can laugh at that. I promise it won't upset me."

I looked at Netiri.

"Are we good? No changing or anything?"

Netiri smiled and offered me his hand.

"Same as always, kid."

"Thanks, virgin," I said, slapping his hand to one side and pulling him into my arms.

My relationship with him was the one I was most worried about. I didn't want to lose what we had. Besides Attor, there wasn't anyone I felt so close to. If he changed, it would break my heart.

"Is everything resolved?" William asked.

I didn't even hear his footsteps. I was shaking Fish's hand when he arrived.

"All is well," Fish answered.

William nodded knowingly.

"Then I suggest we get back now," he said to Fish.

I smiled at William. I knew he brought Fish here on purpose.

"*Thank you, William,*" I said, in my head.

Again, he nodded.

"Shall we?" he said to Fish. "I think Ethan and Netiri want to go buy new phones. I took the liberty of packing Delia some clothes."

"Oh yeah, the clothes," Fish said, winking at William.

I pretended not to notice as Fish took his place next to William. They both nodded, then William placed his ring on. The wind picked up, spun around them, and they disappeared into a vortex.

After they left, I told Netiri I wanted to take a quick shower. It didn't take me long to head back downstairs. Netiri was waiting by the door.

"I think you should get an iPhone," he suggested, as we walked out.

"Is that a good one?" I asked.

"I think it's the easiest to use."

After a few blocks, Netiri asked me about work. "So, when do Susan and Sean get back from vacation?"

"Next week," I answered. "I have a few more days off until I have to go clean the deli. Sean wants it ready for business by the time he gets back."

I was waiting for Netiri to ask me about the fight with the warlocks, but that question never came. I was happy about that. I still didn't know the answer.

We talked all the way into town. It was a beautiful, cool day. New aromas I'd never smelled before filled the air. Netiri said it was apple cider. I had to make it a point of trying it. That wasn't the only aroma this time of year. Cinnamon, pumpkin and vanilla seemed to be very popular. The humans put it in their coffee.

When we arrived at the phone store, Netiri reminded me about my energy.

"Don't forget to re-direct it," he explained. "We'll blow up all the phones they have in there."

Since I arrived in Salem, it always bothered me that I didn't have a cell phone. As far as I knew, I wasn't able to. My mother explained that our wizard energy was too strong. I would never be able to use computers, phones, and things like that. Netiri was surprised to hear that. He said he'd been using a spell to re-direct his energy so it wouldn't do that. He taught me the spell which I made use of when I encountered Simon.

After casting the spell, we made our way into the store. The place was busy. They had phones of all types, placed along the walls. Netiri began showing me the one he had.

"This is the one I have," he said, showing me the phone on display. "It has voice command. I think you'll like that feature. Remember when we were looking for the country club?"

"Yes."

"Well, you can ask it for directions or ask questions, and it will give you the best answer possible. You just talk into it right here."

I was looking down at the phone when I saw Kelly Ohlson, the nurse from Crowley's office. She made her way to one of the walls and began to look at phones.

"I'm going to go ask someone if there's any deals available," Netiri said, stepping away.

I was checking out the phone when I felt a soft touch on my shoulder.

"Hello, Ethan. Buying a new phone?"

It was Kelly.

"Hello," I greeted her. "Yes, hoping to pick one up today."

I noticed the phone she was holding was broken; not into pieces, but rather, the face of the phone looked cracked.

"Me, too," she said, holding up the broken phone. "Had a little trouble at the bank. My phone was in my back pocket, and it broke when some jerk off threw me to the ground."

There was that word again.

"Anyways, I'm fine and now I just need another phone."

I couldn't stop staring at her. She had her red hair pinned up, with small strands of hair, softly falling along her face. Her eyes were her best quality. You never knew if they were going to look blue or green. I had already determined that a cloudy day made the difference.

"I'm glad to hear you weren't hurt," I answered.

"Can't say the same for them," she smiled wickedly.

I looked away as to not laugh. It was obvious she didn't know I was there that day.

"You missed your appointment," she continued. "Do you want me to reschedule it?"

I smacked my head. I forgot all about that.

"I'm so very sorry. Yes, please, if it's not too much trouble."

"I'll take care of it when I get back from lunch. I'm using my hour to get a new phone, as you can see."

"Thank you, Kelly."

As she walked away, I couldn't help but wonder about those words she'd said. She called the bank robber a *jerk off*. Now I had to know what those words meant.

"Kelly," I called.

Chapter Thirteen: Kidding Around

She spun around as I made my way to her. I don't know why I felt comfortable asking her this, but I did. I was just hoping it wasn't something that would embarrass me any further.

"Yes, Ethan?"

Her friendly smile made me feel like I was making the right choice. Besides, William said I would find my answers here.

"May I ask you a question?" I said, nervously.

I glanced over my shoulder to see if Netiri was nearby. I didn't want him to know I was asking about *those words*. Thankfully, he was still with a salesperson.

"Of course," she replied.

"Well, I haven't been in Salem for very long. There are things I still don't understand about this place."

"What do you mean? Do you need directions?"

I shook my head and checked for Netiri again. It was driving me crazy that I couldn't just spit it out.

"Ethan, do you mean about *our* world? I know you're a wizard and not from this realm."

I sighed. I had forgotten she knew all about where I came from. Melanie told Doctor Crowley about it when I first went to see him. I was glad for that, now it would make it easier.

"Well, you see, there are words used in this realm that I don't understand. I feel foolish constantly asking what things mean."

"I can understand that sweetie. What word are you inquiring about?"

I looked over my shoulder again. I know I told Netiri I didn't care about the teasing. But the truth was, it *did* bother me that I had no idea what those words meant. What had they found so funny?

"Do you want to go outside?" Kelly asked, when she saw I kept looking over my shoulder.

I quickly agreed.

"Let me just go tell my friend that I'll be right back."

"Sure."

I lied and told Netiri that Kelly was angry at me for missing my appointment.

"I'll be outside, talking to her."

"Okay," Netiri said, returning to the salesperson.

I hurried outside to join Kelly. She was sitting on a bench near the coffee shop next door. I sat next to her, began to fidget, and asked my question.

"What do those words mean? The ones you said in the store. You called the guy something."

She laughed.

"Oh, you mean what I called that guy who broke my phone? Well, it basically means he's not a very nice guy."

I couldn't believe my ears. What was so funny about that? Seemed harmless enough. I just couldn't understand why Netiri said he turned into *not a nice guy* when he was lonely for a woman.

"That's it? That's what it means?"

Kelly squinted her eyes.

"Why? What did you think it meant?"

"Well, my friend in there said that when he's lonely for a woman, he ends up doing that. But it doesn't sound so bad the way you put it."

She looked at me for several moments, then started laughing. She put her hand up, trying to say she was sorry."

"I'm not laughing at you," she said, trying to restrain her laughter. "I just wasn't expecting you to say *that*."

"Expecting what? That my friend turns into that word you said?"

She looked into my eyes, then stopped laughing. I think she saw how serious I was.

"Oh, okay," she said, nodding her head.

She scooted closer to me and leaned in.

"I'm going to ask you a very personal question. Do you mind?"

I gave it some thought. How personal could it be? Besides, I felt at ease with her.

"No, I don't mind."

"Have you ever been with a woman before?"

That question wasn't so bad.

"No. I mean, I have a girlfriend, if that's what you mean?"

"No, have you been intimate with her? I guess what I'm asking is, are you a virgin?"

"Oh, that," I chuckled. "Yes, I've never *thrown it in* anyone."

I made myself laugh at that one.

"Sorry," I said, putting my hand up. "It's an inside joke between my buddy and me. That's what he said about being with a woman."

"Lucky girl," Kelly laughed.

"To answer your question, no, I have never been with a woman."

"How about urges? Do you have the urge to be with a woman?"

"God, yes," I quickly answered.

"Ok, and what does your body do when you get those, *urges*?"

I looked away. I was embarrassed to tell her. What did my question have to do with any of this?

"Ethan don't be embarrassed. I'm a nurse, and I deal with people's bodies all the time. This will stay between you and me."

"I just don't understand why that has anything to do with my question. What do those words mean?

"Why didn't you ask your father?"

I didn't want to tell her that I was too embarrassed to ask him. I knew Netiri had told him something, and he was smiling. The last person I needed laughing at me was my father.

Just then, Doctor Crowley came out of the coffee shop. He was holding a tray of iced coffees in his hand. I thought Kelly was going to jump out of her skin when she saw him.

"Doctor Crowley!" she said, seeming relieved about something.

"Hey, what's going on?' Crowley said, eyeing me. "How are you doing, Ethan?"

"Hello, Doctor Crowley," I said, rising to my feet.

I wanted to shake his hand, but he was holding the tray of coffees. Doctor Crowley was a tall, athletic-looking man. He had brown hair and a friendly face. He reminded me of Sean, my boss.

"Ethan, can you excuse me for a moment," Kelly said, pulling him off to one side.

"Yeah, no problem," I said, sitting back down.

I don't know what Kelly said to him, but he looked surprised as he glanced my way.

"I got this," he said, stepping away from her.

"So, what's up, Ethan?" he said, taking a seat next to me.

"Sorry I missed my appointment," I said to him. "I've been very distracted lately."

That wasn't a lie.

He nodded, something he did a lot.

"Yeah, Kelly will schedule another one. How's the pain level?"

He always wanted to know what number my pain level was. He measured it from one to a ten.

"I'm at a nine today."

"I think I can squeeze you in later today."

"Okay."

"Listen, lean closer to me so I can whisper something in your ear."

Um, ok."

As Doctor Crowley began to whisper in my ear, I had to pull away from him when it got very personal.

"Oh. My. God," I heard Netiri say.

I looked up, he was standing next to Kelly. She pinched him.

"Why hadn't you told him that before?"

I sat, looking at all of them. When it finally hit me, I bent over and put my head in my hands.

"Someone kill me, please," I said, completely and utterly humiliated.

Doctor Crowley looked at Kelly.

"Ok, I think he's got it," he said, rising to his feet. "Sometimes you have to be direct."

As they walked away, I heard Doctor Crowley say… "I bet he can't wait to get home now."

The two laughed as I kept my face buried in my hands. I was *never* going to hear the end of *this*. How could I have been so stupid?

I heard Netiri sit next to me.

"I'm so sorry, kid. I wanted to tell you. I wish I knew you were going to ask them about that. I would have stopped you."

I still had my head buried in my hands.

"I asked a woman about something personal, Netiri. A woman!" I said, shaking my head.

"Ethan, don't wizards, well, you know?"

"Yes!" I said, hitting myself in the head. "But they don't call it that!"

"What do they call it?"

I shook my head over and over.

"I should have figured this out when you talked about being lonely for a woman. Why didn't I put it together? I feel like a complete imbecile. I'm coming off like a naïve nut case. I just want to shoot myself right now."

"Ethan, what do wizards call it?" he asked again.

Why wasn't the ground opening up right now? This would be the perfect time to get swallowed down to hell. Why did I just do that?

"I'm such an idiot," I said, wishing I could erase my *own* memory.

I looked at Netiri, his shoulders were also bouncing up and down. His laugh was silent, but I knew he was laughing.

"Did she give you any good advice?" Netiri asked.

I couldn't help it; laughter so hard came out of me. What else could I do but laugh at myself.

"Yeah, she said maybe I should hold it with both hands?" I shot back.

We laughed some more.

"Did you tell her you would only be using two fingers?" Netiri shot back.

That only made me laugh even harder.

"I should have, but then she would have thought I was talking about you," I said, pointing at him.

We must have looked like two drunk fools the way we were laughing. I couldn't stop shaking my head.

"So, have you?" Netiri asked. "You know, yanked on it?"

"I've said hello, but nothing more. I have to be honest with you; I think I was scared to do it."

"Why?"

"I don't know. I think because I thought it would make it grow."

Netiri was almost on the floor with laughter.

"If that were true, mine would be ten feet long by now," he laughed.

"No, I'm serious, Netiri. It's pretty big already."

"Stop it, Ethan. You're killing me."

"I can't believe I asked her about jerking off," I said, slapping my hand on my head.

I took a deep breath, wishing the air would choke me. I wanted to crawl into a hole and never come out. What must Kelly and Doctor Crowley think of me? I'll tell you what they thought…this dumb kid is so naive.

We must have laughed for another twenty minutes before going into the store again. I finally got my phone and Netiri spent the rest of the afternoon teaching me how to use it. He got a new one as well. He said it was a new model. There were so many features I was impressed by. I could give it commands, ask for directions, and look up words I didn't know the meaning of. That feature was my favorite; a little too late, but still helpful. By the time we finally put our phones down, it was dark outside.

"Later, I'll show you some cool games I play," Netiri said, as we walked out of my room.

"I'm starving," I said, realizing we hadn't eaten.

"Weren't you supposed to go see Crowley?"

"Ugh, yes. I forgot all about it. What time is it?"

I hated that I repeatedly forgot things. For instance, normally, I would have made sense of those words when Netiri talked about being lonely for a woman. It wasn't that complicated. It was like my brain was taking a lot of naps these days. I forgot things, couldn't make sense of things, so on and so on.

"It's five," Netiri answered. "He may still be there. Hey, why don't you call him?"

"Good idea. Show me how to do that?"

Moments later, Kelly answered the call. I explained about the phones and apologized for not coming in to see Crowley.

"Doctor Crowley said he could squeeze me in today," I informed her. "I think tomorrow will be better for me."

She said she'd put me down for a morning visit and hung up. I think I heard her laughing before the call ended.

I put my phone in my front pocket.

"Come on, let's go get something to eat," I said, heading for the stairs.

I knew we had some sandwich meat in the cooler. I could probably eat two sandwiches right now. Too bad the deli was closed. I could really go for one of those grinders.

"I think we have roast beef and turkey," I said, over my shoulder. "What kind of sandwich do you want?"

When Netiri didn't answer, I stopped halfway down the stairs and looked behind me. Where had he gone?

"Netiri? Did you go back in my room?"

There was no answer, so I called out again.

"Netiri!"

I began to feel a soft breeze brushing across my face. Did I leave a window open? I started ascending the stairs to check on Netiri. When I reached the top, he was on the floor, leaning against one of the bedroom doors.

"Netiri!" I said, running to him.

He didn't seem to be hurt. He looked like he was just sleeping.

"Netiri, are you okay?"

I shook him, but there was no response. I began to look up and down the hallway, there was nothing there. And again, I began to feel a cool breeze all around me. Within seconds, the cool breeze turned into a frigid cold. I began to shiver as small icicles began forming on my eyelids and inside my nose. I tried to bend down and wake Netiri, but it was getting to the point where I couldn't move. I felt stiff as a board as I tried to open the door behind Netiri and escape the cold.

My teeth were chattering as I tried to breath in some air. When I looked down at Netiri, there weren't any sings of him shivering or being cold. I managed to bend my knees, shocked to feel Netiri warm to the touch.

"N...Netiri," I said, between the chattering.

My muscles were aching from the shivering. I began to feel sleepy and tired.

"Ethan," a soft voice called.

I couldn't move or turn my head to see who it was. The voice was clear but distant. It was like they were saying my name from miles away.

"Ethan," I heard again.

I needed Netiri to wake up. If he didn't wake up soon, I was going to freeze to death.

"Ethan."

"N...no," I managed to say.

As my mind began to faze in and out, I started to feel a warm stream of energy going up my legs and spine. The warmth soon turned into horrible heat. I stopped shaking as the floor under me began to crack and release the smell of sulfur. I knew who it was, and she was about to pull me into hell.

Chapter Fourteen: Breathtaking

I could feel the sensation of needles crawling and tearing through my body. Immense pain started to vibrate through me, causing me to start shaking again.

"N…Netiri," I said again.

A feeling of sadness began to wash over me. I knew that despair and sorrow were coming next. My tears were already spilling over, destroying my earlier good mood. It felt like I was melting, sinking into a pool of lava. The burning sensation grew as my feet began to sink into the cracks.

"Netiri," I cried.

There was such a feeling of loss within me; so great that I believed everything I loved was dead. I felt I had nothing to live for, nothing to fight for. I wanted to die and leave this anguish behind me. My surroundings began to change the further I got pulled down. I began to hear the sound of tortured souls as they cried out for help.

"Think of love," a voice said.

My lips were quivering as I tried to hold in my sobs. I took short, labored breaths as darkness surrounded me. I could no longer see Netiri, or the mansion. I looked up as I heard the sound the cracks made as they sealed themselves up, trapping me this wretched place. Bone-like hands came out from the depths of hell and grabbed me by the ankles. I couldn't move, couldn't think straight.

"N...no." I wept.

"Please, let him go," I heard a voice beg. "I'll stay with you forever but let him go."

I knew that voice, it was Irene.

"You are useless to me, witch," a raspy voice answered. "Why would I settle for *you*, when I can have *him*? Besides, you will never be able to convince that witch to trade places with you. He will be the perfect bargaining tool. That witch would never leave her son here, like your sister left *you*."

I tried to look at my surroundings, but all I could make out was a dark cloud of smoke, floating in front of me. What part of hell was I in? The dark cloud floated closer to me; that seemed to make Irene nervous.

"Ethan, think of love."

"Shut up, witch! Get away from him or I will bring your daughter here."

"No, please don't. Forgive me, mistress. I never meant to upset you."

I didn't know who was talking to Irene, but whenever the one called mistress spoke, the dark cloud would vibrate. Was the voice coming from the cloud?

I turned my head as a rancid odor began to burn my nose. My feet felt as though I was standing on hot coals. I sobbed as the sound of tortured souls began to get louder and louder. Then, someone touched my face.

"Isn't agony exhilarating?" the raspy voice said. "You'll get used to it, my sweet boy. It will become part of you. It will free you and make you feel invincible. You'll experience pleasures you never thought were possible. Just open your mind and let me in."

I tried to focus my eyes on who it was. Slowly, the dark clouds began to fade away. Two piercing, red eyes came into view first, then her face. It was the Black Witch, the real Black Witch. She had spoken through Irene in the past, but I could see this was the real one. She had silky, long black hair that moved like flames of a fire. Her skin was like porcelain, her frame was tall and slender. She was beyond beauty; she was breathtaking.

My heart began racing as I looked into her eyes. I was mesmerized by her beauty. Any kind of pain I had been feeling quickly went away when she got near me. She made me feel like I wouldn't be able to breathe without her. I didn't want to. I wanted to breathe the same air she did; wanted our hearts to beat like one.

"Come closer," I murmured.

I wanted to touch her; hold her so tight that she became part of me. I breathed in her sweet scent, allowing it deep into my lungs. I don't know why it made me want to vomit.

"I'm here, my lord," a raspy voice said.

Where was that raspy voice coming from? It couldn't be this beautiful creature that stood in front of me. She was too beautiful; too memorizing to have a voice like that.

"I will never leave you, if you wish it so," the raspy voice said.

Why didn't her voice sound like an angel? I couldn't understand it. There should be nothing but musical notes coming from those lips.

"My love," I whispered.

"No!" Irene cried.

The sound of her cries made me angry. Why was she yelling no? She should be happy I was falling in love with her mistress. I turned away from my queen to address Irene. She looked just like she had the last time I saw her. There were only strands of hair, hanging from her scabbed head. Her nails were full of soot and grime. Her cracked skin looked as if it would fall off her frame at any minute.

"Leave us," I growled.

I felt the gentle touch of my empress. I smiled as I turned back and got lost in her beautiful red eyes. My heart beat faster as I fell completely and utterly in love with her. She put her lips to mine, opened her mouth, and slipped her tongue in my mouth. I returned the gesture and kissed her back. I felt my life made sense when our lips met. I became excited about spending the rest of my life by her side. I kissed her again. It was the most passionate kiss I'd ever had.

"Tell her to leave," I said, between kisses.

"You heard what he said," the Black Witch said, caressing my face. "Go back to your dwelling, witch. He doesn't want to hear about Viola anymore."

I felt a spark of light flashing through my eyes when she said Viola's name. I think Irene noticed because she moved closer to us. With her hands nervously held up, she said…

"Viola loves you, Ethan."

William's voice began ringing in my head. I heard him reminding me about *love*. It was the one thing Irene told me to think of. I tried to fight the force inside of me. It was making me think of only the Black Witch.

"Viola," I forced myself to say.

I began to see my surroundings clearly. I could see a wall of rusty cages, with dammed souls reaching out for help. A fire roared all around us like a waterfall. Sound waves I'd never heard before began coursing through the fire. With every wave came a new sound of agony. I looked at the Black Witch, she was no longer the beauty she was before. She was only rotting bones with maggots crawling all over her. She smelled of rot and sewage. Only her red eyes where still there. She slowly began to disintegrate as the dark cloud of smoke covered her bones. It took me a moment to realize that she had been the dark cloud this whole time. The beautiful woman was an illusion, a trick of the mind.

The dark cloud began moving towards Irene. When it touched her, Irene was thrown with force to the ground. I was surprised when Irene glared at the cloud, then started laughing. There was a look of determination in Irene's eyes as she got to her feet. Irene took one step forward and stepped into the dark cloud.

Irene screamed as her body began to absorb the dark cloud. It was a battle between good and evil as Irene tried to fight off the Black Witch. I could see the dark cloud leave Irene's body at times, but then would be absorbed again.

"Think of your daughter," I shouted.

I wanted to jump in and help her, but I knew this was her battle to fight. I was fighting my own battle. My mind kept drifting to the beautiful woman that had captured my heart. Although I knew she wasn't real, my heart was refusing to believe it.

I closed my eyes, and I thought of Viola again. How could I think of her when all my heart wanted was the Black Witch? I shook my head, refusing to believe I no longer loved Viola. I feared my heart had already chosen who it loved.

Hell cried out louder and louder as Irene battled the Black Witch. The fire around us began to burn red as it roared loudly. I could see it was giving strength to the evil that lived here. I honestly felt I had opened an oven door and walked in. I looked over at Irene as she struggled with the dark cloud. She was trying to cast the Black Witch out, but the evil force that lived here wouldn't allow it.

Irene turned to me and reached out her hand.

"Help me," she begged.

I closed my eyes as I began to sob. I knew helping her wasn't possible. If I helped her, the darkness would only take her back. Even William held back on helping her at the mansion. He said she had to pull *herself* out of this hell.

My heart was breaking as I heard the struggle between them. Suddenly, it stopped. The fire that once roared was now tamed and quiet. I knew Irene had lost her battle. Was I about to lose mine?

I hung my head as the Black Witch approached. I didn't want to look into her eyes and see that beautiful creature again. I knew I wasn't strong enough to deny her anything. When I heard the raspy voice in my ear, I knew she was back.

"That is the first time she has given me so much trouble. Didn't know she had it in her," the Black Witch laughed.

I lifted my head up, as expected, Irene's eyes were red. I knew it wasn't Irene looking back into my eyes. Before I could say a word, the Black Witch began making an awful face. She twisted her neck and placed her hands on her head. The dark cloud slowly began to stream out of her. For the tiniest moment, I saw the real Irene.

"Abrir," Irene yelled, as she looked up.

I began to hear the sound of cracks, opening the ground above me. The bone-like hands released me and disappeared into the earth. A bright light came shining down into this darkness. I tried running towards Irene, but stopped myself when I realized she was giving me a way out. Irene fell to the ground, reaching her hand out to me.

"Abrir," she yelled again.

The cracks got thicker and wider. Soon after, I heard voices coming from above. Before I could think of jumping out, the Black Witch called to me.

"Don't leave me, my lord."

I looked over at Irene, the beautiful creature was back. Her beauty was so great that it made me draw breath just by looking at her. My heart jumped for joy at the fact that she didn't want me to leave her. I took a step forward, intending to take her into my arms. Before I could take a second step, someone jumped in from above and blocked my way. A second person jumped in, then a third. Their presence seemed to upset my queen. She growled at them as if they were her enemies. I heard swords being drawn as my blood began to boil with anger. How dare they keep me from my true love? They would pay dearly for this.

The three men had their backs to me, but I could see who they were. It was the warlocks, Rapoza, Lima and Moe, all with swords in their hands. They would die for daring to hold a sword to my queen. I slowly reached into my pocket, searching for my wand.

"Yell to her, now!" someone shouted from above.

"Mother, it's me, your daughter."

The Black Witch's head instantly shot up. Her red eyes were full of fury as she desperately tried to keep Irene in. Then, Viola called out again.

"Mother!"

"No!" the Black Witch screamed, as the dark cloud began to leave Irene's body.

I grabbed at my chest, aching from the feeling of loss when the Black Witch left. I began to sob and dropped onto my knees. The warlocks surrounded me but kept their eyes on Irene. She was still on the ground, trying with all her might to keep the Black Witch away.

"Get out, before she comes back," Irene said, looking up.

The fire began to roar and turn red. The warlocks kept looking in every direction, their swords at the ready. They flinched when the lost souls began to cry out for help.

"We have to get him out of here," Rapoza said, trying to help me up.

My first reaction was to push him away. I wanted to go with my queen, live with her forever and be happy. I knew these feelings of love weren't real, but I was having a hard time shaking them off.

"Viola," I whispered, trying to bring myself back.

The rusty cages began to rattle. The cries for help echoed louder and closer. If the warlocks were scared, they didn't show it.

"She's coming back," Irene warned us. "She's not alone."

The warlocks forced me to my feet and put my arms around their shoulders. Rapoza looked up and yelled to whoever was up there.

"We got him!"

"Netiri, hurry!"

It was William's voice.

Netiri flew down on his staff and stopped right in front of us. The warlocks draped me over his staff and gave Netiri the signal. Netiri flew up, dropped me on the ground, and returned for the warlocks. Once everyone was out, I heard Irene cry out for help.

"We have to help her!" I said, dragging myself toward the cracks.

"Ethan, no!" William said, pulling me back.

I was able to see a pair of red eyes as the Black Witch smiled because she was back inside of Irene. I drew breath, realizing it was my queen. I never felt my heartbeat so fast before. I wanted to jump back in and be with her. I can't explain it, but I felt a love that caused me pain. It hurt to love her so much.

I pushed William back and tried jumping back into hell. The distance between me and my queen was suffocating me. I felt I would die at any moment. Being away from her was making me go insane.

"Ethan, No!" William said, waving his hand.

He sent me flying across the hall and into a door. I quickly jumped to my feet, pulled out my wand, and aimed it at William.

"Let me go back to her," I growled.

The warlocks stepped in front of William, but he slowly put his arm out and pushed them back.

"Ethan, what are you doing?"

It was Viola. Just the sound of her voice annoyed me to no end. Why was she here? There was nothing here that belonged to her anymore.

"Ethan?" she said, coming out from behind William. "It's me, Viola."

I closed my eyes as her voice pierced through my ears like a knife. It was torture, pure and horrible torture. I opened my eyes and glared at her.

"Get the hell out of here, witch," I hissed.

She took a small step forward.

"Ethan, I love you," she said, as tears streamed down her cheeks.

I don't know if it was her tears, or the heartbreak in her eyes made something inside of me snap. I looked at William and my father, I knew what they were hoping would happen. It was the same reason they brought Viola here. They knew if Irene heard her voice, it would help bring her back. Were they expecting the same results with me? I had news for them; it didn't work. I *still* wanted to be with my queen. I had to play it smart, pretend their old Ethan was back. It would give me time to get back to the woman I *really* loved. It was time to do a little pretending.

I forced a smile and tried to look at Viola with love in my eyes. I felt disgusted just at the thought of having to touch her. When she tried walking toward me, William put his hand out and stopped her.

"Let me go to him," she begged him.

William didn't answer and kept his eyes on me. He slowly began making his way down the hall. Viola didn't follow him. She was in tears as William got closer to me. I smiled as I thought of what a fool he was. His little plan didn't work. I could care less if Viola was here, or that she was crying. After putting on my little act for him, I would quickly go looking for my queen. I smiled again at the thought of seeing her again.

I readied myself as William approached. I planned on telling him that I wasn't feeling myself, but that I would be fine. I would even hug Viola, if needed. I smiled widely at my plan. When he stopped right in front of me, I almost burst out laughing. What a fool he was. He and my parents, all ignorant and useless. Perhaps I should get rid of....

Slap!

It was a slap heard around the world. William slapped me across the face so hard that I thought my head had spun all the way around. I was so busy rambling on in my head, that I didn't notice when he raised his hand up to strike me. Let me tell you, he didn't slap me softly, either. He must have used all the energy he possibly could.

I held my cheek as I looked back at him. His eyes were full of disappointment and fury. The warlocks looked away as the situation became awkward. I didn't know what to say as William put his face right up to mine.

"If you *ever* have thoughts about hurting your own mother again, I will kill you myself," he said, moving even closer. "Let me make this clear; I am *not* one of your underlings. I am your grandfather, and you *will* respect me as such."

I hung my head as he turned away. He descended the stars without saying another word to me. The warlocks soon followed him, never giving me a second glance. I still had my hand over my cheek. I could feel the stinging that his slap left behind. I was too embarrassed to look at Viola. How could I? Those were horrible things I thought about her. What the hell had gotten into me? Was I wrong about being able to bring myself back? I assured William that I wouldn't let evil change me but look at what happened. What was I going to do?

"Ethan?" a soft voice said.

I couldn't bring myself to look up. I knew it was Viola. It was breaking my heart to hear her cry. I wasn't worth it; I wasn't deserving of her love. Like a coward, I slowly walked away and headed to my room.

"Ethan, please," I heard her say, as I closed the door behind me.

I leaned against the door as I heard Viola crying. I was so mad at myself. I was making all the wrong choices. Even now, I was having what William would call a pity party. I needed to speak with a friend, and I knew of only one that would give it to me straight. I quickly pulled my ring out to slip it on, but the sound of Viola crying made me stop. I couldn't leave her this way. I had to apologize for my actions.

When I opened the door to look for her, she was not alone. Renee and Cheryl were with her, both with glaring stares at me. I could take the dirty looks from them, but it was the look from my mother that shocked me. My mother had never looked at me that way. She was angry, no, she was pissed.

"Come, Viola," my mother said, pulling her away. "We have to talk."

They all gave me the dirtiest looks before walking into one of the bedrooms. My mother slammed the door so hard that it made the hallway shake. I went back into my room and pulled out my ring. It was time to talk to a friend. I let out a sigh and slipped it on. Moments later, I disappeared into a vortex.

Chapter Fifteen: The Pit

My self-esteem was very low as I spun into my world. I was disappointed in myself for falling for the Black Witch's tricks. I still couldn't believe I could be that ignorant and clueless. That seemed to be my mindset lately…clueless. I don't even know if Magia could help me right now. That's not the worst of it. I hated that I couldn't stop thinking of that beautiful woman. My heart ached for her, caused me physical pain to think of her. I couldn't make sense of it. I knew she didn't look like that; why did I still love her. Yes, I said *love*. As horrible as that sounded, I felt I would stop breathing without her. I shook my head, trying to think of something else.

As the vortex disappeared, I breathed in Magia's air. I was hoping to feel reborn or maybe rejuvenated but I really don't know what I was expecting. I only knew that I felt so lost. This wasn't the Ethan I knew I could be. I usually had a knack for figuring things out right away. Take the *jerking off* thing; how did I *not* know what he was talking about? It was plain as day to me, now.

I shook off the thoughts I was having and mounted my staff. I took to the sky in search of Attor. I really needed his wisdom. Attor never spared my feelings, he always gave it to me straight. The best part about him was that he didn't talk in riddles, like William. He also never judged me or gave me special treatment because of who I was.

I remember sleeping in his cave as a young boy. I was so attached to him. I would use his cave to escape the nonsense of Magia. I hated always being told that I would be king one day. I hated the bowing and the respect the other wizards *thought* they owed me. They didn't know this, but I *hated* saying anything around them. When I would speak, they'd look at me as though I was about to share some kind of wisdom. I was just a kid, what the hell could I share at nine years old?

Most wizards would follow and watch me throughout my day. If I did the simplest thing that impressed them, they would make such a fuss about it. Their cheers always sounded so insincere to me. I never missed the looks they gave each other when I turned away. I knew the only reason they praised me so much was because William was their king. Those wizards knew I had done nothing to deserve the title of *future king*. I never wanted or asked for that title. I had no interest in being their king. That's one of the reasons I couldn't wait to leave and discover Salem. I wanted the adventures my mother had experienced. My reasons started off with Vera, but all that was behind me now.

I flew high into the mountains as I looked for Attor. It was midday and I knew he would be searching for food right now. Attor loved figs, which was also a favorite fruit of the guards. The big figs grew in a dense part of Magia. The guards hated going there, which left more for the dragons. They ate so many figs that it gave the dragons a sweet scent. I remember partaking in eating figs with Attor. I ate them for so long, now I couldn't stand the sight of them.

I slowed down and stopped when I spotted the dragons. As I hovered nearby, I watched them in the trees. The sight of them would surely have impressed the warlocks. The dragons looked like birds perched on the trees, as they ate their food. The dragons were a spectrum of earth tones in color. Attor, on the other hand, was black as the night. He had bright yellow eyes with red circles around the irises. He was also the largest of all the dragons.

I stayed a good distance away to allow the dragons to feast. There must have been at least twenty of them, ripping branches away. They would hold down the branch with their talons, then use their them to strip away the figs. Once the branch was free of figs, the dragons would flap their wings and send the signal to the fig tree. Wherever the branch had been torn from, the tree would grow new roots and wait for the dragon to place it back on. It was an unspoken respect between the dragons and the trees. The trees would never die, and the dragons would always have food.

When I saw the dragons stretching out their necks, I knew what smell would be coming next. Their droppings were also a bonus for the trees. It was the reason these trees grew the largest figs in Magia. I quickly flew away, knowing that smell would stay with me for days. I remember bathing in the waterfall as a child, trying desperately to wash off the stench. It was so strong, so pungent. The wizards were grateful the fig trees were so far away.

I landed in an open field and tossed my staff aside. I lay on the grass and looked up at the sun. Its rays beamed like stars in the night. It truly was a beautiful sight to see.

"I thought I sensed you," a voice said.

It was Attor. I smiled as I jumped to my feet. When he stretched out his neck, I quickly put my hands up in protest.

"Don't do that here!" I barked.

Attor looked down at me with those bright, yellow eyes. He spread his wings and lowered his head down to me.

"Do what, exactly?"

"You know what I'm talking about," I said, looking around for my wand.

He laughed, then began to spin around. My mother always said that dragons spun around like a dog would before laying down. I breathed in a sigh of relief when Attor tucked his wings in and made himself comfortable.

"I thought you were angry with me?" he said, looking away. "I don't think we spoke two words when you were here."

"Why would I be angry?" I said, taking a seat next to him. "You've done nothing to anger me."

He looked down at me.

"As I said, you didn't speak to me."

I had no idea I had hurt his feelings.

"Forgive me, Attor. I've had a lot on my mind."

"Yes, I see you are troubled."

"I don't know what's wrong with me, old friend. I haven't been myself since I left Magia. My whole purpose for coming here today is to seek you out. I'm truly sorry for not acknowledging you before. It was not my intention."

"All is forgiven, Ethan."

One of Attor's talons was close to my leg. I noticed it was covered in Fig juice, so I began to wipe it away. His talons were like polished steel. They could easily rip you to shreds in a split second.

"Is that why you came, to clean my talons?" he asked.

I let out a long sigh. I laid myself next to him, put both hands behind my head, and looked at the sun again.

"I've made a mess of things, Attor. I don't know what to do. Something is wrong with me."

"I see."

"William struck me today," I continued. "I never thought he would lift a hand to me. I mean, I don't blame him. I was having awful thoughts about him and my mother."

"Already?"

"Yes, they were horri…"

I sat up, looked into his yellow eyes, and got to my feet.

"What do you mean, *already?*"

He looked away from me, but I walked around until I was in his view again. Only his eyes moved down to look at me.

"Attor, you have always been truthful with me. Please, don't lie to me now."

I could feel the heat from his breath as he looked down at me.

"Dragons do *not* lie," he hissed.

"Don't start now. Okay?"

"You don't understand, Ethan. Dragons are incapable of lying."

"You mean, like a Trussel?"

"No, a Trussel can lie, but he will find death for that lie. Dragons are just not capable of telling a lie."

"Why didn't you ever tell me that?"

"There was never a reason."

This was an unexpected surprise. I quickly started thinking of questions to ask him. He was William's headguard and friend; that meant he had a lot of information.

"Do you know why I'm changing?" was the first thing I asked.

"Yes."

"So, you know about the pit the witches made me swallow?"

"Pit? I don't understand?"

"I thought you said you knew why I was changing?"

"Yes, but a pit? What does that have to do with anything?"

"They made me swallow it."

"And?"

"Well, you know, it's changing me."

"Into a tree?"

"What?"

Just then, Katu, one of the dragons, landed a few yards away from us. Attor began to chuckle.

"I believe I am having DeJa'Vu," he said, as Katu came closer.

"What are you talking about?" I asked.

He glanced at me.

"Nothing, I was just thinking of your mother."

"Young prince, I wasn't aware you were here," Katu said, as he began to spin around.

"You were saying?" Attor said, looking back at me.

"I'm changing, Attor. William says it's because of the pit I swallowed."

As fast as Ketu sat, he got right back up when I said that.

"Not again," he said, taking to the sky.

The ground shook as Ketu launched himself into the air. I couldn't help but think, what did he mean by that?

"I'm sorry, can you repeat that?" Attor asked.

"I'm changing, Attor."

"Because of a pit?"

"Yes!"

"I don't understand. Why would a *pit* change you?"

"Wait, you said you knew why I was changing, didn't you?"

"Yes, but it has nothing to do with a *pit*."

"Yes, it does. Those witches forced me to swallow it. I heard William telling the others that it was pure…."

I stopped talking when Attor burst out in laughter. It was pretty funny to see. Small flames of fire would come out of his mouth as he breathed in and out with laughter.

"What's so funny?" I asked.

Attor still had a little bit of smoke coming from his mouth when he stopped laughing.

"Dragons cannot lie, but the same cannot be said for wizards," Attor said, shaking his head.

"William lied to me, again?"

"There is no such thing as an evil pit, Ethan. Evil cannot be contained in something as meagre as a pit."

"What was it, then?"

"As far as I know, only a love spell requires the victim to swallow it. Unlike a spell that is cast, a love spell that is eaten or swallowed, will last forever."

"A love spell? To love what?"

"Or who," he corrected me.

Why would the witches need me to swallow a love spell? What purpose could that serve?

"You really are changing, aren't you? The Ethan I know would have figured this out by now."

I looked into his yellow eyes.

"Attor, before Katu got here, I was telling you about the horrible thoughts I was having. You said, *already*? What did you mean by that? Did you know this would happen to me?"

"I did."

"Did you know I would change?"

"Yes."

"And, you know why?"

"I do."

"Are you going to tell me?"

"I am not."

"Why!" I shouted.

It was quite a sight to see a dragon sigh. I'm surprised he didn't burn his eyes out when flames came out both sides of his mouth.

"Ethan, your grandfather, king of this realm, went through extraordinary efforts to put things in place for you. His efforts started hundreds of years ago. I haven't always agreed with the way William deals with things, but then again, I'm not a wizard. I will not ruin what he has laid out for the future. The map he built for you took thousands of hours to create. Every step he took was to ensure that you and your mother would live. William does not take a single step without it having a purpose. Perhaps your being here is part of his plan?"

I became frustrated. Of all my friends, I never thought Attor would speak to me in riddles.

"I wasted my time coming here," I said, turning on my heels.

"Ethan, wait."

When I didn't stop, Attor blew fire into the air.

"What?" I snapped at him. "What do you want to say to me that's going to help? Speak your mind, so that I may leave."

Attor leaned his head down, almost touching my face with his nose. I had to take a step back when the heat from his mouth became too much for me.

"Although I do not agree with William's tactics, I will help you none the less."

"That's all I ask, old friend."

"Climb on," he said, rising to his talons.

I grabbed my wand, jumped on his back, and he took to the sky. When we got close to the village where Fish and the others lived, Attor landed on a massive oak tree. Why did he bring us here? Attor curled his talons on a branch and sat back like a bird.

"Sit next to me," he instructed.

I jumped off and sat on a branch across from him. I looked down at the village and watched my friends decorating the surrounding trees.

"They're getting ready for the wedding," I said, watching Fish cut down some branches.

"I believe they are making an arbor."

"Why doesn't Fish use Walter for that?"

"Who?"

"Oh, sorry. That's what Fish calls the orb."

If you could envision a dragon smiling, that's what Attor was doing right now. I could see he liked Fish, and Attor didn't like very many people.

"Perhaps the young man wants to put his own work into the preparations?" Attor suggested.

I think Attor was right; none of them were using the orbs. Delia and Vera were decorating the branches that Fish was cutting down. Cory was busy building the frame of the altar near the water. I smiled as I watched Steven gathering as many flowers as he could hold. He had a good pile going next to the altar.

"He's come a long way," Attor said, as we watched Steven. "I think *love* healed him more than this land did."

I nodded.

"William says it's the most powerful spell he knows."

I watched as Vera gave Steven a kiss when he brought her flowers for her approval. She would smile, smell the flowers, and nod yes to him. Vera didn't take her eyes off him as he walked away.

"They look so happy, don't they?" I said, watching them.

"The love between them is powerful," Attor answered. "I noticed the changes in Vera when she came here with him. She was no longer the bitter girl she once was."

"Yes, she was spoiled and rude at one time."

"Love changed them both," Attor said. "It's a funny thing that word. *Love* can make you do things you never imagined. It can also change you in ways you never expected. I have no doubt that Steven would trade places with Vera, if death wanted to take her. He would offer his own soul, if it were possible."

"I agree with you, Attor. He wouldn't think twice about it."

"Do you think he would *still* love her if she were evil?"

That answer was easy. Steven wouldn't care if Vera was the devil himself. He would love her regardless of who she was.

"Without a doubt," I answered.

"Would he fight for her? Would he betray the world in order to please her?"

I thought of my mother and all the things she went through to save me. From placing me in a crystal to making a blood promise, she suffered and fought for my life. There wasn't one thing she wouldn't do over again, if she had to. I began to think of my father. He waited hundreds of years to come back to my mother. She sent him away, and he never stopped loving her. He always had faith in their love and knew they would be together one day. Even my mother's friends had loved her enough to spend their lives protecting her. They shared an unbreakable bond between them. Love had done all of that.

"I think he would," I answered.

"Wow, *love* really is a powerful spell, isn't it?" Attor said, looking down at my friends.

I looked up at Attor, he was giving me side eye, as Fish would put it. What was he trying to tell me?

"Some would say," he continued. "Love can also control a man, couldn't it? If they are willing to die for you, imagine who they would be willing to kill in order to save you."

It felt as if Attor had placed his talon inside my head and flipped a switch on. I sat there, my mouth agape and stared at him. I can't explain the feeling of stupidity that was growing inside me. I leaned forward, placing my hands over my head.

"Why do I keep doing this? I'm such an idiot!"
"I don't understand?"

I threw my hands up.

"It really was a love spell, wasn't it? I didn't swallow pure evil; it was a powerful love spell."

"Wouldn't you call that kind of love, *evil*?"

"Yes!" I said, hitting myself on the head. "And the worst thing is, I can't stop thinking about her. What the hell is wrong with me?"

I repeatedly hit myself over the head. I don't know if I was trying to beat some sense into myself, or if I was trying to slap stupidity out.

"I'm so broken, Attor," I said, shaking my head. "I'm getting worse by the minute. I can't even make sense of easy things like knowing I'm in love with evil."

"You love that creature?"

"Yes!" I said, giving myself one more smack in the head. "How does that make any sense? She's crawling with maggots and yet, I still want her."

I pulled out my wand and commanded my staff to appear. I took to the sky, leaving Attor behind. I needed to clear my head; shuffle out all the bad thoughts I was having. Why was this happening to me? What the hell did I do to deserve this? All I ever wanted was to visit the human world. Was I being punished for that? I shook that thought away. The negativity inside of me was starting to piss me off. I was a wizard, dammit. Why couldn't I act like one?

I flew pointlessly around Magia as my pity party continued. I thought of all the signs I had missed when I was in a stupidity coma. I became more angry and bitter about it. Even now, as I was making sense of things, I was still carrying on with a pity party. How could William ever think I would make a good king?

    The minute that thought crossed my mind; I knew where to go. There was only one place to find my answers. It was the one place where Magia chose its king. It was time to ask why it had chosen me.

Chapter Sixteen: Tree of Life

I flew up and around the mountains, traveling to a place I didn't know very well. It was a sacred place to wizards, and they did not like visitors going there. It was the home of the Tree of Life. A magical tree created by the gods. The wizards cherished these grounds. It was said that this tree had punished all the wizards when Wendell tried to rule them. William took their powers and allowed the tree to determine when to give them back. The wizards had to prove themselves again. I heard it took many years before the tree thought them worthy of restoring those powers.

I was in awe as I was nearing the forest. It was a magnificent sea of massive oak trees, all standing taller than a house. The massive trees covered miles of land with their beauty. One tree stood out from the rest. It was by far the tallest, and the most impressive. The massive oak tree looked majestic and alive. Its branches were twisted and curved like a ribbon. Many of the branches grew so large that they lay on the forest floor. It was like an arm, welcoming you to climb it. I threw my staff to one side as I looked up at the majestic oak tree. I was surprised to see orbs flying all around it. They were just like Charles, the orb that followed Fish. I took a closer look and realized the orbs were fairies. I'd never seen the fairies take that form before.

They gracefully flew around the tree as to protect it. Seeing fairies wasn't new to me, but they usually looked like sparkles of light, not an orb. I moved closer, taking in the beauty of the tree. I placed my hand on one of the branches. I could have sworn I felt a heartbeat. The branch was warm to the touch. It sent a feeling of peace all over my body. I wanted to cry, and I wasn't sure why.

The fairies began to fly all around me, guiding me toward the entrance of the tree. I would call it a burrow, but it was larger than that. I slowly took a few steps, hoping I wasn't disrespecting the tree. Did it want me to enter? Would the wizards be angry if I did? The fairies didn't seem to think so. The closer I got to the entrance, the more compelled I felt to go inside. I thought my heart would be racing. Instead, I felt a calmness I hadn't felt in months. I can't explain it, but I felt an utter peace flowing through me.

I walked inside, amazed at what my eyes beheld. The inside of the tree was hollow. There were gel-like beads coming from its walls. The beads shimmered and called to me. I reached out and touched one. It rolled onto my fingers and wet my palm. Were the beads made of water? One fairy landed on my hand. She smiled at me before taking the bead from my palm. I watched as the fairy left the tree and flew away, carrying the bead. I had to know where she was going. I quickly walked out and saw her placing the bead of water on one of the flowers. The flower opened its petals, absorbed the water, and then began sparkling.

"They are spreading Magia's magic," I said to myself.

A stream of fairies began entering the tree. I followed them in again and looked all around me. There were beads coming out of every inch of the tree. I was amazed at how far up the tree these beads were. That's when I noticed what the fairies were doing. When a new strand of beads came out from the tree, they would take them and fly away. Each fairy took a different route, spreading the magic all over Magia. It was a beautiful thing to see. The tree kept its workers busy. With every new strand of beads that grew, the more fairies would come into the tree.

I began to look around at my surroundings. I noticed a part of the tree where the bark had been removed. When I stepped closer, I noticed someone had carved names into the smooth surface. The penmanship was perfect and beautiful. William's name was there, with a few dark spots under it. It almost looked as if the names had been removed. Perhaps it was the names of kings from the past?

Then I saw it, letters from another name began to carve itself into the tree. I drew breath, realizing it was the tree that was doing the writing. I took a step back when I saw it was *my* name, the tree was revealing to me. When the tree was done, I reached out and touched my name. It was carved deep into the bark. Even William's name wasn't as deep as mine. I looked up at the tree.

"Why me?" I asked it.

"Because the tree thinks you are worthy," a musical voice said.

I spun around. It was Levora, Queen of the Fairies. She was a stunning creature. Her long hair was as green as this land. Her eyes were pink like sapphires. Her peacock-like wings spread across her back like a fan, painted with vivid colors. I quickly bowed to her.

"You Majesty," I said.

Her musical voice rang out when she answered.

"You may rise, Ethan."

I rose to my feet, but kept my head bowed. It wasn't very often that Levora took this form. She was usually the most colorful sparkle around the waterfall. What had I done to earn this privilege?

"Forgive me, Your Highness. I did not mean to intrude. I was only curious of the three."

"All is well, young prince."

Her voice had such a musical tone to it. The notes wrapped themselves around me and made me feel at ease. Her fragrance was like a garden, one filled with all the flowers of the world. I was honored to be in her presence.

"I see the Tree of Life has revealed the future to you," she said, looking toward my name. "Not many have lived long enough to have that honor."

"Why me?" I asked. "I've done nothing to deserve this."

When she smiled, a bright stream of light was cast all around me. She moved closer, looking at my name.

"The Tree of Life has made its choice. There is no changing what is written. All kings before you have felt as you do now."

She turned and looked into my eyes. She slowly put her hand out.

"May I?" she said, holding it out.

I placed my hand in hers. She wrapped her fingers around it and closed her eyes.

"Love cannot be forced," she said, in her musical voice. "What does not grow, will die without nourishment."

"What do you mean?"

She slowly let go of my hand. She looked up at the fairies, then at my name. The fairies began flying down and all around us. Levora spread her wings as the fairies awaited her command. She looked at the spot where the names were.

"Show him," she whispered.

The tree began to release new beads of water. I noticed the new beads had images moving inside them. The fairies began collecting the beads, then flew just over my head. Before I could ask why they were doing that, the fairies released the beads all over me. I had the sensation of falling as I felt compelled to close my eyes. I felt I was drifting into a dream. Images soon started forming and going through my head. I saw a throne made of gold, with a bearded man sitting on it. I first thought it was William, but this man's eyes were blue. He looked so tired and restless. Had he just fought a battle?

The images began to change, showing me different kings on that throne. I soon realized the tree was showing me past kings of Magia. I saw how much each king had suffered during his reign. The tree showed me all the misery and sorrow in their lives. I saw the evil that each king had battled. Their war against evil had not been easy. Their loss of loved ones had been many. Each time, the king never lost faith in himself. I could see it made him stronger, more confident and determined.

I began to see different realms of the past. One was the human world. It was clear this time frame was hundreds of years ago. I saw chariots and horses, covered in armor. There were many battles going on. Beasts I'd never seen, were killing and eating the humans. Then it changed, I was taken even further into the past. It was a different realm, with people chained by the neck. They were slaves to the demons that ruled. I saw the king, mounted atop a dragon. He sent his magic toward the demons, sending them all back to hell.

The images changed again. I was taken to a dark, evil place. The king was there, his arms spread and bound. He was covered in blood with wounds all over his body. Seven demons danced around him as if to celebrate his capture. An image of two tall, black iron gates began to appear. The gates had tall flames of fire burning all around them. The demons began to move the king closer to the gates.

"Open them," they said, in unison.

The king slowly raised his head. I was shocked to see it was William. He was much younger, but I knew it was him.

"Never!" he shouted.

A dark cloud began to surround William. When the cloud drifted away, a beautiful woman was left standing. She was much more than beautiful; she was magnificently breathtaking. Her red eyes searched for William's. She pressed herself against him as he looked away from her.

"No," he said, shaking his head.

"Look into my eyes," she whispered in is ear.

I could almost see the battle going on in William's head. The woman knew he was becoming weak and pressed herself on him even more.

"Open the gates," she said, trying to get him to look at her. "Open them so that nothing will ever separate us, my Lord."

William finally gave up and looked into her red eyes. His smile grew wider as the woman began to untie him. She knew she had won. William was about to open the gates of hell for her master. When the woman leaned in to kiss him, a wall of fire came up and roared all around them. I never saw the kiss; the fire was burning too high. When it finally died down, William and the woman, were gone. The demons were sent into a panic when they didn't see the woman. They cried out and called to their mistress, but she never came.

The surroundings changed again. I kept my eyes closed as images of the past flowed through my head. I made a fist as I witnessed each battle being fought by a king. Each king ended his battle in that dark, evil place. Each time, the beautiful woman was there. She promised them the world; made them feel they couldn't live without her. I was starting to understand the point of that love spell.

    I began to feel as if I was being pulled forward. I soon realized I was about to be shown the future. It was another king, and he was battling several demons around him. The confidence in his eyes was unmistakable. He was brave and fierce; he battled the demons as if they were ants. The black gates were steps from where they fought. A dark beast, I couldn't make out, was waiting for the gates to open. A dark cloud slowly drifted into the melee. When the cloud disappeared, the beautiful woman was back. The king stopped fighting the moment he noticed she was there. He dropped his sword, took the woman in his arms, and….

    I was awoken by a rush of air. It knocked me to my knees as I tried to catch my breath. I was drenched in water. My heart was racing from what I witnessed. I recognized that king. Although I was a bit older, I knew it was me.

    I reached out my hand, placing it on the wall of kings. I ran my fingers along my name as tears streamed down my face. I understood everything, *witnessed* everything. My life made sense now. I accepted who I was, and who I would be. I rose to my feet as a new kind of energy rushed through me. I felt strong. No, that wasn't it. I felt *invincible*. The path my life would take began to shuffle through my head.

Every step, every moment I lived, I knew where I would be. Everything I once thought were riddles, made perfect sense to me now. The way William spoke, the words he said, all had important meaning. I understood what Levora said about love. It couldn't be forced; therefore, my mind couldn't be controlled. It was a spell, and *real* love could never be erased.

William never fell for the darkness spell because he already loved my grandmother. It was too late to make him love another. His mind was strong enough to know the difference. I was finding that strength, and it was making me more confident than I ever imagined. My doubts about my love for Viola vanished in an instant. I found a new level of trusting myself and my choices. I thought back to William's words. He always said to find the wizard inside me. Guess what, William? I found him. I looked up at the tree, knowing what it wanted from me.

"I'm ready," I said, confidently.

I heard Levora spread her wings. She reached for a large bead of water, then held it out to me. When she dropped it in my palm, I realized it was a ring. I didn't need an explanation. I knew what the ring was for. I thanked her and placed it in my pocket.

"Your Highness," she said, bowing.

"Not yet," I laughed. "I don't believe that position is available right now."

It was like getting a new set of eyes as I looked at her. I instantly knew she had been in love with William for hundreds of years. I saw the moment she learned that William had fallen in love with a witch and how her heart was broken and shattered.

"Did you find your answers," she asked.

"I didn't realize I had questions," I teased.

I looked toward the exit of the tree. I was ready to face the world. I smiled at Levora and held out my elbow.

"Shall we?" I asked, offering it up.

She took hold of it, and I escorted her out.

"Hello, William," I said, not bothering to look his way.

I could sense him even before he got here. I knew where he would be standing. I knew the clothes he would be wearing. I also knew he would be emotional.

Levora's wings spread out like a peacock. She quickly looked around for him.

"William is here?"

"Behind that tree," I said, motioning with my head.

When William came out from behind the tree, I saw tears in his eyes. He nodded at Levora then looked at me.

"I always knew it would choose you," he said. "There wasn't a doubt in my mind."

I nodded knowingly.

"Can't say the same for me, can we?"

He raised his brows.

"I don't know, can we?"

I looked at the Tree of Life. I smiled and looked back at William.

"We cannot, William."

A huge smile spread across his face.

"Your Majesty," he said, bowing.

"Not yet, William. That position is still occupied."

He laughed. "Not for long."

"Vacation?"

"Perhaps."

"I hear Fiji is nice this time of year."

"Oh? I was thinking perhaps, Egypt?"

"It's not too dry for you?"

"Perhaps, a bit sandy."

We both laughed as Levora looked at us with a confused look on her face. William took two giant steps, his tears spilling over, and threw his arms around me. I didn't want to ruin the moment by bringing up our fight. I let it go and returned the embrace.

"Forgive me, William."

"That is not necessary," he said, squeezing me tight. "You are Kintsugi, Ethan."

"You've been talking to Attor," I replied.

"Did that *bird* tell you that *he* thought of that?" he chuckled, pulling away from me.

"Took full credit, if I remember correctly."

"I'll make him lay an egg for that one."

We both laughed again.

I thanked Levora and gave her a moment with William. I saw the side eye he gave me for doing that.

"When will you be home again, Your Highness?"

"Soon, Levora. We will *all* be home, soon."

I pulled out my wand, commanded it to grow, and mounted my staff. I was whistling as I waited for William. When he returned, he was still giving me the 'eye'.

"Mind if we stop by the village?" I asked.

"Just so you know, I knew you were going to ask that," he said, mounting his own staff.

"Well, aren't you a know-it-all," I said, taking to the sky.

He quickly caught up to me.

"Is this going to be how our conversations will be going?" he asked.

I looked over at him.

"You know she still loves you, right?"

He looked straight ahead.

"Apparently, it is."

He flew ahead of me as I laughed.

"You're Kintsugi, William!"

I felt my spirit was revitalized as I flew over the land I loved so much. Although I would miss the human world, it could never compare to how this magical place made me feel. My purpose was clear to me now. I would work very hard to show the tree and Magia that I would be the best king possible.

"Woo-hoo!" I shouted, as I spread my arms as far apart as I could.

Chapter Seventeen: Torn Dress

William was already in the village when I arrived. I wanted to offer my help before I went back to Salem. After we said hello to everyone, William began to make an aisle. He didn't use his magic. He gathered stones and placed them along the path. I saw Cory was still building the arbor, so I quickly went to help. It didn't take us long to finish it.

Cory began drilling holes for the flowers. I wanted to use my magic, but I had to respect Fish's wishes.

"Where did you get a drill?" I asked.

Cory rolled his eyes.

"Walter, who else. Fish has that orb working overtime. There were some things we couldn't do without. Took Walter a few times to finally understand what a drill was."

I laughed at the thought.

"What else still needs to be done?" I asked.

"Honeymoon suite," Cory said, winking at me.

"I think I can help with that," I said, reaching for my staff. "I know a real nice place by a waterfall."

"Your house?" Cory asked.

"No, not that waterfall. It's a place I used to go to as a kid. I think the newlyweds will like it there."

I disappeared for a few hours, and when I returned, the arbor was full of flowers. William had placed different colored gems along the aisle. By now, all of Magia was lending a hand. The wizards were busy welding a special gift for Steven and Vera. Women from the nearby village, were sewing a beautiful wedding dress. Not one wizard was using their magic. I was glad I was able to come and help.

"Ethan, come here," I heard someone whisper.

I looked around but couldn't see who it was.

"Pssst, Ethan, over here."

"Fish? Where are you?"

"I'm hiding behind the cottage."

"Why are you hiding?" I asked, making my way there.

Fish was looking in all directions, making sure no one spotted us. He looked nervous and scared.

"Get back here, hurry," he said, waving at me.

"What's going on?" I wondered.

"Did anyone follow you?" he asked, peaking around the corner.

"No, but I think the whole village heard you calling me over."

He kept looking around the corner of the cottage. What was wrong with him?

"Fish, what's the problem?"

He put the tips of his fingers to his mouth. He

looked like a child that was caught doing something wrong.

"I think I killed Walter," he blurted out.

I had to admit that it really made me chuckle. "What?"

"I killed him, Ethan. I don't know what to do."

"What makes you think you killed him?" I laughed.

By now, I knew the orbs were fairies. There was no way he had *killed* Walter.

"I think I gave him too many orders," he said, biting his nails. "Maybe I overworked him or something? He's gone."

"Fish, I'm sure there is a perfectly good explanation for this. Didn't you say you wanted to put in the work for the wedding yourself?"

"Yeah, but what's that got to do with it?"

"Well, maybe Walter heard you? That would mean he's simply obeying your wishes."

"You think?"

I couldn't help but laugh. Fish had no way of knowing this, but the fairies didn't need to hear his request. They could read minds and knew what he needed before he even said it.

"I'm sure Walter will be back very soon," I assured him.

"There is one more question I need to ask," he said, looking toward the others.

I already knew what he was going to say.

"Ask away."

"Well, I noticed that every time I ask Walter for something to eat, he prepares mostly vegetables. I asked him for a pepperoni pizza the other day, and he made me a pizza covered in peppers. Do they eat meat, here in Magia?"

He was killing me. My laughter echoed all over the village.

"Shh, someone will hear you," Fish said, waving at me.

"Fish, the only reason Walter made you a pizza covered in peppers is because he must not know what pepperoni is. Don't you think?"

"He doesn't know what pepperoni is?"

"I didn't know," I reminded. "I had no idea what most food was when I first arrived in Salem. Even now, when William cooks, I still find some food foreign to me."

"You *were* clueless, weren't you?"

"I was. I still don't know what everyone means when they say they are going to order Chinese. How about, Italian? If you asked me to make you Italian food, I would have no idea where to start."

"Wow that makes sense, Ethan."

"Glad I could help," I laughed.

I turned to leave.

"Ethan, wait," Fish said, calling me back.

"Yes?"

"Do they?"

"Do they what?"

"You know, eat meat here? There's a special meal I want prepared for the wedding. How do I tell Walter what to make if he doesn't know what it is?"

"Walter will be doing the cooking then?"

He gave me a look.

"Do you honestly want *Delia* to cook?"

"I see your point."

I gave his question some thought.

"I'll tell you what, Fish. Why don't you give me the menu, and I'll make sure that Walter understands it. I'll tell William as well. Does that sound like a plan?"

Fish was looking at me with a strange face.

"Yeah, that sounds fine," he said, tilting his head. "You know what, Ethan? Is it me, or do you sound smarter?"

I burst out laughing.

"No really. You kinda sound like a young… well… William."

I shook my head. This kid was very funny.

"I'll take that as a compliment," I said, walking away.

I decided to sit near my mother's lake. I couldn't believe what a good job James and William had done. It was an exact replica of my mother's lake from Salem. I moved a dead branch out of the way as I neared the lake. I leaned back on a tree and took a deep breath. I had so many thoughts running through my head. Some were of Cory, others of Fish and Delia. Then, I started thinking of William.

"Hello, William," I said, gazing at the lake. "I was just admiring your handy work."

"How did you know it was me?" he asked.

I looked up, my brows raised.

"Really?"

He laughed a bit.

"It may take you a few years to become accustomed to all the thoughts."

"Do they ever stop?"

"Not for one moment."

He took a seat next to me.

"There is one thing you must understand."

"What's that?" I asked.

"You must never change what you see coming."

"I haven't changed a thing, William."

He looked at me from the corner of his eye.

"When you were walking over here, you moved a branch out of the way. Why?"

"Delia was going to trip over it. It would have torn her dress, thus, blaming Fish and causing an argument."

"She is still going to trip," he informed me. "By moving that branch, you only changed *where* she would fall, but not the fall itself. She and Fish will still argue over her torn dress."

"I never thought of that, William. Tell me; what would you have done differently?" I asked curiously.

"I would have suggested to Fish that he surprise her with a new dress, *before* she fell."

Just then, "Fish!" we heard Delia yell.

William was smiling as Fish ran out of the cottage to see why Delia had shouted his name.

"Are you okay?" he asked her.

Delia was sitting in a puddle of mud, her dress torn and dirty.

"Did you leave that drill out here?" she yelled at him. "I almost broke my neck."

"No, Cory was using it."

"Wasn't it *you* who asked Walter for it?" Delia shot back. "Look at my dress, it's ruined. It took two days to make this dress."

Fish helped Delia to her feet, then snapped his fingers.

"Hold on, Dells. I'll be right back."

Fish ran back into the cottage. I looked at William with suspicious eyes.

"Wait for it," he said, with a big grin on his face.

Fish came back out with a box in his hand. It had a red ribbon, wrapped all around it.

"I wanted to surprise you with this tomorrow," he said, handing her the box.

Delia wiped her hands on the torn dress. She took the box from Fish and pulled away the ribbon. I saw the look of glee on her face when she pulled out the new dress.

"I hope it fits," Fish quickly said.

"Oh, Fish," Delia said, wrapping her arms around him.

I looked at William.

"When did you give Fish the box with the dress in it?

"Oh, let's see. I believe it was two weeks ago."

I smiled. "Touché, William."

"You see, Ethan, there was no need to move that branch. It was only going to be something as simple as a fall. It doesn't matter that it would cause a small quarrel between them. They would have made up that same day. You must never waste your efforts or energy on insignificant things like that. You already knew she wouldn't be hurt. Why change it?"

"I think I'm starting to understand, William."

"Leaving things alone will become second nature to you. Your wizard energy will warn you if your help is needed. You will have to learn when to help, and when to stand back. When I knew Thea was suffering, it killed me to stand back and watch. Those will be the most troublesome times for you."

"I'll have to remember that," I said, looking toward Delia.

I told William about Fish's menu. He said he would make sure the fairies got it right.

"Do you have any questions for *me*?" William said.

"How did you know?"

He rolled his eyes.

"Those kinds of jokes will quickly get old, Ethan."

"Okay, my apologies. I do have a few. Why do I feel an urge to cook? I almost told Fish that I would cook the entire meal for the wedding."

"Aww, the cooking. Well, I find that it slows the thoughts down a bit. It allows me to sort through them carefully. I tried building things at one point, but I'm afraid I wasn't a very good carpenter."

"I see," I said, thinking of what I could cook.

"What is your next question?"

"It's about Viola. Did I mess things up with her? I'm not getting any reading about her. It's starting to worry me."

"I'm afraid you'll have to find your answers when we get back to Salem."

I looked at William as he gazed at the lake. I could sense the magnitude of love he felt for my mother. Although he criticized her, his love for her was endless. Throughout his life, most of his energy was spent trying to make her life easier. I saw the many times he had to rescue her as a child. My mother had not been easy to live with. She got herself into a lot of *pickles,* as she would put it. William was a good father to her. I knew he watched over me because of my mother. He didn't want her suffering the loss of a son.

"Are you done analyzing me yet?" William asked.

"Not yet," I answered.

William was a decent and fair king. He wore his wisdom like a badge of honor; wisdom that grew with every century he lived. I could only hope to be as wise as he one day.

"Okay, I'm done."

"William!" Fish called.

We both turned. Fish was running toward us. I wanted to laugh when I saw his face was covered in Delia's lipstick. He looked happy as he almost skipped his way to us.

"William, thank you for the dress," he said, out of breath. "I mean, I was going to buy her something, but the dress was a good idea."

"It was my pleasure, Fish."

He thanked William again and ran back to

Delia. Cory soon joined them as they began to pick more flowers.

"Have they told my mother yet?" I asked.

William sighed.

"They are waiting for the right time."

"Has she told *them*?"

"She hasn't even told *me*," he answered.

We watched my mother's loved ones as they put the final touches on the arbor. Viola and Steven came out to see it all done. She was in tears as Steven put his arm around her.

"It looks perfect," Steven said, kissing Vera on the head.

"It will look even better tomorrow," William murmured.

We both got to our feet and joined the happy couple. We told them how much we were looking forward to the wedding. We finally said goodbye and prepared ourselves to leave.

"One more thing," Fish said.

"Yes?" William answered.

"Will Walter know what a tuxedo is?"

William smiled.

"I will make sure of it, Fish."

"Thank you, William."

William shook his head as Fish walked away.

"Where did he get the name, Walter from?"

I laughed. I seem to be doing a lot of that lately.

"The fairy is lucky he didn't name her, Chuck."

We both removed our rings, and we were gone.

Chapter Eighteen: Thoughts

It was very late by the time we got back to Salem. Everyone was sleeping. William and I decided to have a quick cup of coffee before heading to bed. It was strange to come back here and feel so different. I had hundreds of thoughts, flowing into my head. I knew Viola and her guardians were here. They were sleeping in the guest rooms. I knew the guardians and my mother had developed a plan to help me notice Viola more. They had spent the day giving Viola what Delia would call a makeover.

I knew Netiri was also here. He wanted to speak to William about me. He was very worried about my state of mind lately. He planned to warn William how forgetful I was becoming. I also knew we would be getting visitors in the morning. Thought after thought, drifted right into my head. Was I going to be able to sleep tonight?

"Maybe coffee isn't such a good idea," I said, realizing it may keep me up.

William was already brewing a pot.

"I find that coffee relaxes me," he said, reaching for two cups. "Tea also helps."

"When did it happen to you?" I asked. "How old were you when you realized you would be king?"

"Why do you ask?"

"I'm just wondering how long it took you to manage all these thoughts. It feels like someone is constantly whispering in my ear."

"You'll grow accustomed to it. A time will come when you won't even notice it."

I watched as William poured the coffee into the cups. I couldn't help but think of the image of him in hell. What happened with that woman? He obviously won, but how?

"I can't tell you that," William said, handing me a cup. "I will say this, it wasn't easy."

I took the cup from him.

"Is that why you never saved Steven yourself? Why did you have to wait for me to do it?"

A sad look washed over him.

"I knew how much that poor boy was suffering. I was tormented knowing I couldn't save him. When I was taken there, I had my Emma. She hadn't been killed yet. My heart was strong because I loved her. That love was unbreakable. If I was taken now, the results would not be the same."

"Why was I able to save him?"

He smiled.

"Your heart is strong because of your innocence. You have not been tainted with heartbreak. Evil thrives on any bad experiences in your life. It will take any weakness and use it against you. When Irene pulled you into her hell, that place had nothing to show you. It had no choice but to torment you with Irene's memories, not yours. If I was pulled there now, hell would have plenty to show me. I knew I could never take seeing my Emma dying. It is the one thing that would have broken me."

"I think I understand."

"Love is powerful, Ethan. It cannot be forced. There is no love spell that can force you to love. *Real* love, that's what will make you strong. You must learn the difference."

"That reminds me," I said, putting my cup down. "A pit? You used a *pit* to make me believe I had swallowed evil?"

He laughed.

"It was the first thing that entered my mind. Don't forget; I also blamed those witches for your bad mood. I believe I said they had put spells on you to make you angry."

"Well, I'm hoping there will no longer be a need to trick me," I said, taking a sip.

"Why is that? Do you feel you have all the answers now?"

"Don't I?"

"I see," he said, reaching for his coffee. "Let me inform you of something, Ethan. Knowledge does *not* come cheap. You haven't even come close to paying the price."

"I apologize, William. I didn't mean to come off as a *know-it-all*."

Images of Netiri began to form in my head.

"Netiri is coming," I said, putting my cup down.

"Stop saying things like that out loud, Ethan," William warned. "You may say something important one day and not realize it."

I heard when Netiri pushed the door open.

"I didn't know you were back," he said, taking a seat next to me. "How you doing, kid?"

The last time I saw Netiri we were on our way to make ourselves some sandwiches.

"Much better now," I said, looking into his eyes.

I began to see his past. I saw the *real* reason he never found a woman. It wasn't because he was awkward around them, it was much more than that.

"Viola and her guardians moved in yesterday," he informed us. "Thea said they would be staying here for a while."

"We'll have to make them feel welcomed," William answered.

"Oh, before I forget," Netiri said. "Sean came by. They're back from vacation and he wants to get the deli ready to re-open. He said he wants to give it a good cleaning."

"I'll go see him tomorrow," I replied.

We talked for a while then headed up to bed. I spent most of that night trying to keep the thoughts away. Why did I need to know that Netiri would be wearing a blue shirt tomorrow? Some of the thoughts were just pointless. By morning, all I wanted to do was slow down my thoughts. It was too much information all at once. I remembered what William said about cooking. I decided to give it a shot.

When I got out of bed, I found a note from William on the nightstand that read, *This will help.* Under the note was a book. I picked it up and smiled when I saw the title: *The Art of Cooking*.

I put the book down and jumped in the shower. The water felt good as it hit my face. My original plan was to sleep in today, but there were far too many thoughts keeping me up. I was really hoping that cooking would slow them down, like William said. I felt tired and drained. I must have only gotten about two hours sleep. I wasn't sure if I liked this part of being a wizard king. Maybe once I got used to controlling the thoughts, things would get better.

As I dried myself off, I began to feel the sensation of needles tearing through me. I knew it was time to go see Doctor Crowley. I kept missing my appointments every week. I thought I would be able to handle this nerve pain, but it wasn't getting any better. If anything, it was getting worse. I was still having trouble with material touching the affected areas. It felt as if my skin had been peeled away, and the material was aggravating it. The nerve blocks I was getting were supposed to make that feel better. They worked okay most times, but today, the needle-like feeling wouldn't go away.

After I got dressed, I grabbed the book William left for me and headed downstairs. William was already in the kitchen when I walked in. As usual, he was standing by the stove.

"Any coffee yet?" I asked, placing the book down.

"Are you seeing Doctor Crowley today?" he asked, pouring me a cup.

I nodded and took the cup from him. I noticed he had a lot of ingredients on the counter. William followed my eyes and realized what I was looking at.

"I thought perhaps I would help you by prepping a few things. Everything needed for a breakfast is laid out for you."

"I'll get started on it then."

William was in the middle of showing me how the stove worked when my mother, Viola, and her guardians walked in. Netiri was next to enter the kitchen.

"Morning everyone," I said, looking at Viola. "I hope you are all hungry?"

"*You're* cooking?" my mother asked.

Viola put her head down. I think she was disappointed that I didn't say anything about the way she looked. Renee and Cheryl just gave me dirty looks. They took a seat as I walked around the counter.

"I thought I would give it a shot," I said, making my way to Viola.

She looked stunning. Not because my mother had helped her with make-up and things like that, no, she was just simply stunning. Viola was a natural beauty. She didn't need things like make-up to bring out how beautiful she was. It was the quality I loved most about her.

"Good morning, Viola," I said, softly.

She kept her head down.

"Good morning, Ethan."

I was pleased to see that her hair was still a knotted mess. Although it was pinned up, I could still see the love. She wore tight jeans and a yellow sweater. Her perfume was subtle and pleasing. I began to get reading about her. I didn't like that she thought so little of herself. Didn't she know? Any man would be lucky to have her.

"Will you not look at me?" I said, placing my fingers on her chin.

I slowly lifted her chin up. I could see that she wanted to cry. I never meant to make her feel this way.

"I almost didn't recognize you," I lied. "It took me a moment to realize it was you. You look beautiful."

Her honey-brown eyes made my heart race. She was my person, my one true love. I no longer had doubts about marrying her. She was the one, my strength and my life.

"Thank you," she said, looking down again.

"Told you it would work," I heard my mother say.

I kissed Viola's hand and led her to the table. I pulled out her chair before returning to the stove.

"I'm cooking everyone breakfast," I said, reaching for a pan.

William began sending me instructions in my head. There was no need to answer him. I simply nodded and did as he said. William grabbed the cooked bacon and placed it on a platter.

"The sausage is almost done," he said, motioning with is head.

I nodded and reached for another platter.

"*What are the pancakes going on?*" I asked.

"*Bottom shelf, there's a green platter.*"

I nodded and pulled out the platter.

"*Syrup is in the cabinet above,*" William said.

I nodded and reached over the stove. I gave him the syrup as I checked on the eggs.

"*Don't overcook them,*" he warned. "*It's nice to have yolk when eating eggs Benedict.*"

I nodded and began to take the eggs out of the water. I put ham on an English muffin, placed the poached egg, and topped it with a yellow sauce William made.

"*Does this look right?*" I asked, holding it up.

William nodded and reached for another platter. "*The hash browns are ready,*" he said.

I nodded and shut the stove off. When I looked toward the others, everyone was staring at us. Netiri had such a confused look on his face.

"When did you learn how to cook?" he asked.

"That's it," my mother said, pulling her chair out. "What's going on? Why does Ethan keep nodding? Since when can he cook?"

"*Tell her you wanted to surprise Viola,*" William quickly said.

"I wanted to surprise Viola," I answered.

"*Tell her you feel bad for the way you've been acting.*"

"I felt bad for the way I've been acting."

"*Tell her…*"

"Stop!" I yelled. "William, I can't do this right now."

"Do what?" my mother asked.

I headed out the back door and pulled out my wand. I just needed a moment alone. This was too much for me. The pain, the thoughts, I couldn't stop any of it. I commanded my wand to grow and mounted my staff. I took to the sky in hopes that the air would clear my head. The thoughts I kept having were becoming like voices in my head. They were getting louder and louder. How did William do this?

It felt impossible to give my brain any kind of rest. Even now, I was getting thoughts of the people I was flying over. I couldn't see them or hear them, nor had I ever met them. But yet, the universe felt compelled to tell me their life story. What did I care if the postman was having an affair with one of his stops? I didn't care if the grocery store was about to lose power. What was the point of all of these thoughts?

I flew faster, hoping I would fly faster than the thoughts could reach me. It didn't work. I began to get an image of a woman; she was carrying witch hats. I drew breath.

"Melanie," I said, to myself.

I began to follow my instincts. There was only one place I knew she'd be heading to—Willow Park. Could it be that she had made contact with Irene? I knew the Black Witch would never let her out of her sight. Irene was giving her too much trouble. She would never take a chance on Irene pulling herself out of the darkness. I saw the progress Irene was making. Knowing her daughter was still alive had given her hope.

I beat Melanie to Willow Park and waited behind a tree. The park was empty, since Salem was quiet this time of year, so Netiri and I did a lot of flying, unworried if human eyes would see us. Besides, we usually stuck to flying high in the clouds.

Twenty minutes had gone by and still no Melanie. Where had she gone? She wasn't very far from here when I flew over her. I looked at the spot where Melanie sat the last time she called her sister. Did I even need Melanie? I came out from behind the tree and looked down at the spot.

"Abrir," I whispered.

It was the one-word Irene had chanted just before she made the ground open. I held my breath as I waited to see if it would work. When I heard the ground begin to crack, I smiled. I was expecting to smell sulfur the moment I jumped in. Instead, it only smelled like a rotting plant. Delia had killed several plants before, so I knew that scent well.

I looked around the dark, damp place. It didn't even look like it usually did. There was no orange sun, no feeling of despair and sadness. It was simply dark and damp. I followed a small creek until I reached a dilapidated cabin. I knew this cabin, it's where I found Steven in that cage. I made my way in and looked around. The place was covered in cobwebs. The dust must have been an inch thick. There was a stairway that led to the second floor. I could sense that no one was up there. I checked the fireplace to see if it was warm, but it hadn't been lit for a while. I knew this was where Irene lived, but where had she gone?

I was about to leave when I spotted a brown piece of paper on the floor. It was laid out as if someone wanted it to be found. I picked it up and tried to make sense of what was on it. There were symbols I'd never seen before, marking different parts of the paper. I looked closer, I noticed a small sun was drawn on a corner of the paper. I looked at the symbols again, what did they mean? I turned the paper over and drew breath. One word gave away what I was holding. It read...*Salem.*

I instantly knew I was holding a map. Irene was trying to tell me where the Black Witch was planning on pulling me down. One of the marks was at the park where I had just been. I recognized the second mark, and it was the mansion. The fort in New Bedford was also there. One mark stood out to me. I couldn't be sure, but I think it was Doctor Crowley's office. Was he helping her?

As I examined the map, I saw wavy lines I assumed meant water. That one didn't make sense to me. Then I saw three small symbols, down at the bottom of the map. I wasn't sure what they meant, but they looked strange. Then I noticed the edges of the map. It appeared that someone had torn it out of something. Perhaps a book?

I placed the map in my pocket, checked around one last time, and made my exit. I jumped back out and chanted, *abrir*, to close the ground. Now that I knew I could open and close it, checking those other spots would be easy. I was about to leave when I spotted Melanie. She was walking toward the closed snack shops, with her hands full of witch hats. I stayed out of sight as she made her way to a ramp on the water. She put the witch hats down and began to look around. I moved closer as she picked up some of the hats and made her way to another ramp. What was she doing? When she left some of the hats near a small tugboat, I decided to come out and talk to her.

"Has Irene started swimming?" I asked.

Melanie spun around. She didn't look very happy to see me. I didn't miss it when she began to glance around for her sister.

"She's not here," I said, moving closer to her. "I've already looked."

"Why? So, you can kill her? I saw what you've done to her. What kind of magic did you use on her?"

Melanie had no way of knowing about what the black book of spells had done to Irene.

"You are mistaken, Melanie. I have done nothing to cause the way she looks now. But it's good to know that you *have* seen her."

She bit her lip, realizing what she had given away. I had to assure her that Irene was making progress. If she knew anything that could help me, she needed to fess up.

"Melanie, have you been meeting with her?"

"That's none of your business."

"When did you see her?"

She didn't answer.

"I think she wants you to know that you haven't lost her," I said, moving closer. "She's trying to connect with both of us. I want to help her, Melanie."

It didn't seem like I was getting through to her.

I had to show her that I was sincere. There was one thing Melanie didn't know about, and I was about to show her.

Before Melanie could look back at me, I placed both my hands over her head. I showed her what happened with the Black Witch and how Irene had helped me. The most important thing I showed her was—Viola.

Chapter Nineteen: Viola

Melanie's eyes were glazed over as my magic filled her head with my memories. I was careful not to show her too much. I didn't want her to see how much her sister was suffering.

"Impossible," Melanie muttered, as I pulled my hands away.

"She's alive and well," I assured her. "Her name is Viola."

"But how is that possible? She killed her children, and they were boys."

"No. One was a girl, and I can't tell you how that came to be."

"Does Irene know?"

"Yes. William told her."

"This is impossible," she said, breaking down in tears.

"Melanie, you saw how Irene helped me. She is trying to fight her way out of the darkness. I want to help her. I truly believe I can get your sister back."

I could see she was thinking it over.

"I don't wish to harm her, Melanie. I want to save her."

Her hands were shaking as she wiped her tears away. I didn't know if it was because of her sister, or the fact that she was in emotional distress.

"When Irene first made that blood promise," she began. "She would leave me notes to meet her. I had already noticed the changes in her. She was becoming angrier by the day. But the one thing that never changed was the notes. That's when I thought of making those witch hats with 'absorption' spells to help her keep the evil thoughts away. Two days ago, I began to get the notes again. It was *her*, the sister that used to reach out to me."

"She's fighting back, Melanie. I witnessed it. Let me help her."

"I'll agree only if you let me come with you."

"I can't do that."

"Fine, I won't tell you where I've been meeting her."

"I understand."

What Melanie didn't know was when I placed my hands over her head, I got all the information I needed.

"I'm serious, Ethan. I won't tell you."

"I heard you. Like I said, I understand."

She wiped away her tears.

"Okay, I'll think about it. I can meet with you tomorrow, if that's possible?"

"Of course."

"What about Viola? Does she know any of this?"

"I believe so. I'm not certain of the extent of her knowledge on it, but she knows Irene is her mother."

"Does she know about her brother, and what Irene did to *him*?"

I didn't know the answer to that question. I was wondering the same thing. I would make it a point to ask William about it.

"I can't answer that, Melanie."

She put her head down, tears streaming down her face. I wanted to comfort her, tell her that everything would be okay. Truth was, there was a very bad feeling growing inside of me.

"I have to go," I said, turning on my heels.

"You'll come see me?" she asked.

I nodded yes and pulled out my wand. I looked around for human eyes as my wand grew into the staff.

"You're going to be seen one day," she warned.

I smiled.

"It won't be today."

I took to the sky and headed back home. I felt bad for leaving the way I did. I just hoped that William understood that all the thoughts were overwhelming me a little. I felt there had to be some trick to controlling what entered my head. It was hard to believe that William was able to live this way. He always looked so calm and collected. How did he do it? He did say that I would become accustomed to it, but right now that seemed impossible. I knew I had to try my best to show him I could handle this. The Tree of Life makes no mistakes, I had to remember that.

I landed in the backyard and took a deep breath. I could already sense they had been talking about me. I could sense Rapoza and his men. Brad wasn't with them. It was only Rapoza, Lima and Moe. I shrunk my staff and placed it in my pocket. When I opened the sliding doors to the kitchen, the room went silent.

Any food left?" I asked, hoping to break the silence.

Rapoza and his men were having coffee with William at the table. My mother, Cheryl and Renee were cleaning the kitchen. Viola wasn't there. Netiri was shaking his head at me. William gave me a look, got up, and began to make some coffee. I said hello to the warlocks and joined William in the kitchen. Renee gave me daggers with her glares as she wiped the counter.

"I apologize for leaving so abruptly," I said, reaching for a cup. "I just wanted to clear my head a little."

William only raised one brow.

"You are apologizing to the wrong person," he snapped at me.

"Excuse me," Renee said, almost throwing me into the cabinets.

She put away a platter and almost broke my shoulder when she walked by me again. Cheryl gave her a huge smile and handed her another platter.

"Put this one away, harder," she said, glaring at me.

"No problem." Renee said, grabbing the platter from her.

This time, I moved out of the way before she could push me. Why were they so mad at me? I couldn't help but feel the tension in the room. What happened after I left? Was this about Viola?

"*You know what to do,*" William said, in my head.

"*Where is she?*"

"*In her room, crying,*" he snapped.

"*Why?*"

"*If you have to ask, then you have not been paying attention.*"

My mother opened a cabinet next to me, almost hitting me with the door.

"You're just like your father," she mumbled.

Okay, I was obviously the problem. I excused myself and left the kitchen. I ran up the stairs and made my way to Viola's room. I wasn't sure what to say as I knocked on the door.

"Go away," she cried.

"Viola, it's me, Ethan."

I waited a few moments before I opened the door. I walked in and heard running water. The bathroom door was open, so I took a peak. Viola was over the sink and washing her face. I looked around the room and saw the dress she had worn this morning. It was lying on the floor and looked like someone had ripped it to shreds. On the bed were containers of make-up, all broken and scattered about. I instantly felt horrible. I knew I hadn't been the best boyfriend lately, constantly forgetting all about meeting with her. It wasn't her; I was just being very forgetful these days.

"How may I help you?" Viola asked, as she came out of the bathroom.

Her tone was cold. I could tell by her red eyes that she'd been crying. She was holding a towel that she used to keep wiping her face.

"Can we talk?" I asked.

"Why?"

"I need to explain some things."

"You don't have to, Ethan. I understand."

She wouldn't look at me. She only kept wiping the left-over make-up from her face.

"What is it that you understand?" I asked, moving closer.

She put her head down.

"You don't need to explain yourself to me. I'm no one. You've made that perfectly clear. You have no problem forgetting that I even exist. I think you should look for someone else to wait for you. Maybe even someone who likes wearing all this make-up?"

I moved even closer, but Viola took two steps back. She put her hand up and shook her head.

"Not this time, Ethan. I deserve more."

"Viola, I just…"

"Do you know why I sat on that bench for so long?" she cut in. "I sat there waiting, because I already loved you."

"Viola, please let me…"

"It's my time to talk," she said, raising her voice. "You had your chance."

"Please, forgive me, Viola."

She pulled out a small box from her pocket. I instantly knew it was a memory box.

"William gave this to me," she said, holding it up. "It's filled with memories of you and me. They were supposed to be the happiest days of our lives. I fell in love with the man in these memories. I waited for him, night and day. It's clear to me now, that man is not you."

Before I could say another word, she threw the box on the floor and crushed it with her foot. She turned away and told me to leave.

"Viola, please."

"Get out, Ethan. I never want to see you again. Go find yourself someone that doesn't care about being neglected."

I couldn't move. This couldn't be happening. How did I manage to mess things up so much? I loved this girl. She was my true love, my life.

"Despite what you may think, Viola. I truly do love you."

She still had her back to me.

"Take your love and get out, Ethan. I can't return that love anymore."

I felt my heart shattering when she said those words. I was numb, heartbroken and full of regret. I kept thinking of the things I could have done for her' of ways I could have shown her how much I loved her. I didn't pay attention to her when they gave her that makeover. I always said Viola didn't need those things.

"I'm sorry," I said, leaving the room.

My first instinct was to fly away from here, but

I was done being a coward. I thought I could fly away from all my troubles. Even today, I left when I couldn't take the voices in my head. Maybe Viola was right; she deserved more. I took one last look at her before closing the door behind me. I waited in the hallway, expecting to get a reading from her. I think I had hopes that she would change her mind. That she would open the door and tell me she was only angry. That didn't happen. I only heard when she broke down in tears.

    I headed back downstairs. I knew there'd be angry faces that awaited me. Once again, the room went silent when I walked in. I was surprised to see my father there. I didn't see him this morning when I was making breakfast. My mother gave him the same dirty looks she had given me. I looked and Renee and Cheryl, the daggers were still coming my way.

    "I hate men," I heard Cheryl say.

    "Especially him," Renee added.

    Netiri leaned over and whispered something in Rapoza's ear. He looked my way and began to laugh. Are they friends now?

    "You didn't eat," my mother jeered, tapping Renee with her elbow. "Maybe *Renee* can cook you something?"

    I wasn't sure if I wanted to be poisoned right now. I said no and took a seat at the table. I held my side as that feeling of needles began to get worse. It was climbing up my back and rib area. I really needed to go see Doctor Crowley.

    "She dumped you?" Netiri asked.

    "We've all been there," Rapoza said to me.

"I have two doghouses at my house," Moe laughed.

"I've been in mine all week," my father added.

Doghouses? What did that have anything to do with this?

"When you're in the *doghouse*," Netiri explained. "It means your girl is mad at you."

"I wasn't asking," I replied.

William cleared his throat.

"Yes, um, Ron and his men will be staying in the guest house for a few days. I want to make sure we make them feel welcomed."

I already knew why they were here.

"Why don't you go show them where it is?" William continued. "I've made a few changes."

"*Doesn't it look like Magia right now?*" I asked him.

"*Didn't you hear me? I made a few changes.*"

"*Hey kid, did she dump you?*"

"*Shut up, jerk off. Don't mess with me right now.*"

"*I was just asking.*"

"*Both of you, close your mouths,*" William snapped at us. "*This isn't the time. They are staring at us.*"

"*Sorry, kid.*"

When I looked at Rapoza, he was giving us a strange look.

"Are all of you telepathic?" he asked.

"Tele what?" I asked.

The warlocks simply glanced at one another. I thought it was best to change the subject.

"I'll be happy to show you where the guesthouse is," I said, giving Netiri the same daggers I'd been getting.

"Take your father with you," my mother snapped at me. "Two peas in a pod, you are."

"That's my cue to leave," my father said, putting his cup down.

"Are all the women in this house angry?" Rapoza asked.

The men started laughing as we left the kitchen. Once outside, my father gave me a tap on the back. He hit the infected area and sent pain surging through me.

"You, ok?" he asked, when I closed my eyes.

"I'm fine," I lied. "I'm just tired."

"She'll calm down, Ethan. I'm sure you both will work things out."

My father obviously thought I was upset about Viola. Well, I was, but right now I was only upset about the pain. After showing the warlocks the guesthouse, I left to go see Doctor Crowley. I was overdue for a visit. My pain level was at a thousand, at least it felt that way. I couldn't understand why the sensation of needles was back. Keeping a t-shirt on was getting harder and harder. The material against my body felt like sandpaper rubbing against my skin.

Netiri asked if he could come with me. I agreed as long as he didn't ask me any questions about Viola. I didn't want to talk about that right now.

"Are we walking?" he asked, showing me his wand.

"Yes, I don't feel like flying right now."

As we made our way into town, Netiri asked me about the warlocks.

"Do you know why they're here?"

"Yes."

"Is it to help William?"

"To help all of us."

"With what?"

I stopped. I don't know what it was, but I was getting very annoyed right now.

"Can you *please* stop asking me questions?"

"What's wrong, kid?"

"It's these damn voices," I said, grabbing my head. "They won't stop. I think it's making my pain more intense."

"You're hearing voices?"

"It's a long story, Netiri. I'm sorry if I'm coming off as rude. I'm just in a lot of pain."

"Come on, let's get you to Crowley."

I wanted to tell Netiri about the Tree of Life and the visions I had. I wanted him to understand that I wasn't going crazy when I said I was hearing voices. It was making me feel as though I was going mad. Well, it was *driving* me mad, but I wasn't *going* mad.

"Ethan, you, okay? What's wrong? Why are you bending down like that?"

I didn't even realize I was doing that. There was a surge of pain exploding all over my body. I felt as if I was on fire. I usually felt heat when I was in Irene's hell, but this was different. This heat felt like it was burning my bones. I slumped over even more as the heat became more intense.

"Netiri, the fire, put it out!"
"What? There is no fire, kid."
"Netiri!" I yelled, dropping to my knees.

Chapter Twenty: Morphine

I could feel my skin peeling off as the fire burned me alive. Netiri kept saying there was no fire, but I could feel it melting me away. It was a pain like no other. I didn't have the words to describe how intense it was. I began to convulse as I tried to roll on the ground to put the fire out.

"Ethan, there's no fire!"

I heard the steps of people who were coming to help. Soon after, voices began going through my head. I screamed and tried to block them. The voices were only making the fire burn hotter.

"His doctor is right around the corner," I heard Netiri say.

I felt them pick me up and carry me away. The whole time, I screamed out in pain from their touch. It was like they had reached inside my body and lifted me up by my bones. Is that what was left of me? The voices became louder as the fire got hotter. I couldn't take much more of this agonizing pain.

"Kill me, Netiri!"

"*There are humans here, Ethan,*" he said in my head. "*I can't use my magic to help you.*"

"No! Get out of my head!" I shouted.

His thoughts were like red hot daggers, scraping and tearing into my brain.

"He's going into to shock," I heard someone say.

I began to feel a force all around me. Whatever it was, it was strong. The voices became louder, the fire, more intense. By now, I had no voice to cry out with. I only shook as I tried to reach for Netiri. Why wouldn't he kill me?

"What happened?"

It was Doctor Crowley. At last, someone would show mercy on me.

"I don't know. He says he's burning up.

"Quick, put him on that gurney."

I was being moved very fast, but not fast enough to stop the fire.

"I have to call his family," Netiri said, in a panic.

I would have never thought it possible, but the fire began burning even hotter. How was there any of me even left? I should be ashes by now.

"Erika, start an intravenous," Crowley ordered. "Kelly, go get the morphine. I think he's going into neurogenic shock."

"Oh no," she answered.

"Erika, go ask that kid if Ethan fell."

"Right away, doctor."

I couldn't understand why Crowley wouldn't put the fire out. Why was he allowing me to burn alive?

"Dammit, his blood pressure is dropping."

"He says they were just walking, doctor."

"That doesn't make sense."

I began to feel Crowley's hands on my chest. For some reason, he was pushing down on it with force. Then I felt someone pry my mouth open. Soon after, they were blowing air into my mouth.

"Give him extra morphine," I heard Crowley say. "He's a wizard and I don't know if our medicine will help him."

"*Ethan*," a raspy voice said in my head.

I knew that voice. It was the Black Witch.

"Did you hear something?" I heard Crowley ask.

"Something is wrong with the door. I can't open it," I heard Erika say.

"Did you feel that? Did the ground just move?" Kelly asked.

I began to smell sulfur. I knew what was coming next.

"What is that smell?"

I heard the sound of the cracks as they opened the ground. The smell of sulfur became stronger. That feeling of despair and sadness washed over me.

"The ground, it's opening up!"

"It's a sinkhole. Quick, move the gurney."

I couldn't make out whose voice belonged to whom. They all blended together as something strange was going through me. I couldn't be sure, but I think it was something in my veins. The feeling of burning began subsiding. Finally, they put out the fire. My body felt relaxed and calm. Then, that raspy voice called to me again.

"Ethan."

Had I died and gone to heaven? My body certainly thought so. I opened my eyes as a wonderful feeling washed over me. I couldn't help but smile, smile at how wonderful I felt. I thought I heard muffled screams coming from the nurses. When I sat up to tell Crowley I was fine, I saw some kind of tube in my arm. I looked around the room, the nurses and Crowley were there. I could see their lips moving, but couldn't hear what they were saying. Why did they have a look of shock on their faces? They were all looking down at the ground with terror in their eyes.

When I looked at the ground, I saw several skeleton hands reaching up for me. That wasn't so bad. Why were they scared? My mood was so pleasant and calm as I jumped off the gurney.

"Ethan, move this way!" Crowley shouted at me.

He was reaching over the cracks and trying to pull me over to him. I couldn't understand why they looked so scared. It was just hands. Yeah, they were skeleton hands, but nothing to worry about. I saw those all the time.

"I'll get rid of them," I said, tapping myself on the chest.

"Ethan, it's the morphine. You're not thinking straight," Crowley yelled.

I pulled on the tubes that were on my arm, noticing there was a needle on the end. I pulled it out and tossed it aside.

"I knew there were needles inside of me," I said, almost joyful.

I looked at Crowley.

"I found the needles."

Crowley tried to grab me, but every time he moved away from the wall, a cloud of smoke would block his way. Something didn't want him getting near me.

"Well, that was rude," I said, looking down. "He's, my doctor!" I yelled into the cracks.

"Ethan, get away from there!" Kelly shouted.

I tapped myself on the chest again.

"I got this, Kelly," I said, winking at her.

Erika, the other nurse, was pounding on the door. She kept pulling on the knob, then would pound on the door again.

"I'll get that for you," I said, taking two steps forward.

When I got near the cracks, the skeleton hands grabbed my ankles. The cracks began to get wider and wider. The gurney fell through along with some equipment. I began to get pulled under. Half my body was in the hole as I hung onto the edge.

"I'll go talk to them," I said to Crowley. "They shouldn't do this to your office."

Crowley jumped forward and grabbed my arms. He tried to pull me out as a puff of sulfur was blown in his face. I looked into Crowley's eyes as he began to sob. Why was he crying? Then Kelly and Erika also began to sob. I knew those sobs of misery anywhere. Hell was making them feel sad.

"That place does that to you," I said, as if it were normal. It's real sad down there."

Another puff of sulfur blasted through the floor. Crowley began getting pulled down with me as the nurses screamed out in terror. I heard what sounded like an explosion. The door Erica had been pounding on went flying across the room like a rocket.

"Grab Crowley's legs!" someone shouted.

Crowley was losing his grip on me. The more he tried to pull me up, the more the skeleton hands pulled me down. With one last pull, Crowley was pulled into hell with me. The cracks immediately began to seal themselves shut.

"Quickly, before the ground seals itself."

Whoever that was, they didn't make it in. A fire began to roar when the cracks were gone. Crowley grabbed at his chest as he fell to his knees. He was choking on his sobs as he looked around. I can't describe the terror in his eyes, but it was awful. He grabbed onto my leg and begged me to help him.

"Get me out of here," he cried.

"I know, it's sad down here, isn't it?"

I was about to help him to his feet when a thunder-like fire began to roar behind us. I saw a dark cloud come out of the fire and move toward us. Then I saw it, two black iron gates began rattling. There was a beast, large and dragon-like, dancing behind the gates. The beast wanted out. It would grab the gates, shake them, and continue its dance-like ritual. The dark beast sent a wave of fire toward us. Crowley instantly began writhing on the ground.

"It burns!" he cried.

"I know. Do you want me to get you out here?" I asked, pointing out. "I know the magic word."

I began to hear something that resembled, marching. Yes, it was marching. What was marching their way here? I thought it best to get Crowley out of here. I had no idea what that marching meant. I looked up and chanted, *Abrir*.

I seemed to *really* piss off hell when I did that. The gates disappeared behind huge flames of fire. The dark cloud began to engulf me as I tried to help Crowley to his feet.

"*Ethan*," the raspy voice called.

I dropped Crowley when a sensation of utter love filled my heart. The dark cloud began to fade, revealing a pair of red eyes. A stunning woman, with porcelain skin was looking back at me. My heart began pounding, like it wanted to beat with hers. The woman would fade in and out. Sometimes I could see her beauty, and other times I would see a skeleton with maggots crawling all over it.

"I remember you," I whispered. "Why do you keep changing? Don't be the ugly one anymore."

I ignored Crowley's cries for help as she got closer to me. I looked down at her lips; I wanted to touch them. She was a stunning beauty who had stolen my heart. When the image blurred again, the maggot-covered skeleton was back. It wanted to kiss me as it got closer to my lips.

"Eww," I said, leaning back. "Bring back that other woman."

Before our lips could meet, a sword with blazing light coming from it, got between us. I began to hear the thumping of people jumping in. Soon after, the sounds of wild animals surrounded us. The beasts squealed as if they were wounded. The beautiful woman began fade away into a dark cloud.

"Hey, where are you going?" I asked.

I was suddenly slapped hard across the face.

"Snap out of it!" someone shouted.

"That wasn't nice," I said, grabbing my cheek.

I had the sensation of being carried away. It was then that I saw Sean and the warlocks, all carrying shiny swords. The blades of the swords were emanating light all around us. They swung the swords at my feet. It took me a moment to realize that something was trying to carry me away.

"What are these things?" I asked, looking down. "Are they taking me for walk?"

Sean looked at me, tilted his head, and then continued fighting. He kicked something away and swung his sword. I was able to see a creature with red eyes before Sean's sword pushed it toward Rapoza. Six other creatures came at him. They had rotted, burnt skin still hanging from their bones. Their hands were long and narrow, with black, cracked fingernails that resembled daggers.

"Those things are ugly," I said.

Sean and the warlocks glanced at each other, not knowing what to make of my demeanor. When one of the creatures grabbed onto my neck, Sean almost decapitated me trying to get him off.

"Good aiming, Sean," I praised him.

He gave me a look I couldn't understand. I would say he looked confused. The demons started hissing at the warlocks and Sean. Rapoza swung his sword at one. The beast began evaporating, leaving behind a cloud of sulfur.

"That stuff really smells," I warned them. "Smells like a dragon took a poop, doesn't it?"

I don't know why they kept stopping when I said something. They would look at me, shrug their shoulders at each other, and keep fighting. I looked down at Doctor Crowley, he wasn't doing very well. I bent down to help him.

"Hey, Crowley wants to get out of here," I said, trying to pick him up again. "I think he's scared. He doesn't look like he's having fun."

Out of nowhere, the fire died down, the beast turned into dark clouds, and the smell of sulfur faded away. Where there had just been a battle, was now only a dark, damp place.

"Hey, where did the gates go?" I asked, looking toward where they had been.

I looked at the others.

"That guy was big. Did you see him?"

Sean shook his head, handed Rapoza his sword, and threw me over his shoulder. It was like he was picking up a feather.

"You are strong," I said, patting him on his butt.

"Let's get the hell out of here, before those things come back," Lima said.

"Lima! *Protector of the North*!" I yelled. "You are *King of the Corner*!"

"What the hell is wrong with him?" Rapoza asked. "Is he drunk?"

"The hell if I know," Sean answered.

"How the hell do we get out of here?" Lima asked.

I was still hanging off Sean's shoulder.

"Hey, use my wand. It's magical and will fly you out of here. Go ahead, it's in my pocket."

Lima pulled my wand from my pocket. I laughed when he shook it and it didn't do anything.

"Wand, you better listen to them. Get us out of here, okay?"

As my wand responded to my voice, it grew in Lima's hand. I told the wand to hover then looked at Lima.

"Don't forget Doctor Crowley. He's been crying the whole time. I don't think he liked it down here."

Lima shook his head at me, then leaned down to help Crowley up. He was white as a ghost as he leaned his head against Lima.

"Let's get you out of here, Henry," Lima said, trying to hold him up.

"Who is Henry?" I asked, over Sean's shoulder.

Lima draped Crowley over my staff then jumped on. "Up, up and away," I cheered, in a drunken-like voice.

When my staff flew out of hell with Lima and Crowley, it didn't take long for it to come back for us.

"Someone call for a ride?" I laughed.

Rapoza looked at Sean.

"I don't know how I can laugh at a time like this, but I really think he's drunk."

"Get us out of here, staff," I called out. "Hey, I should name you. I always call you, *staff*."

Moments later, we were flying out of hell. The first person I saw was William. He had a look of concern on his face.

"Is he dead?" he asked Sean. "Did he kill any of you?"

Sean dropped me on the ground.

"I think he's drunk, William," Sean answered.

"Drunk? I don't understand?"

"You were wrong about fighting him," Rapoza reported. "He wasn't the one we battled with."

"William!" I said, trying to get to my feet. "It was hot down there. Henry was crying, a lot. There were dead wolves running around and attacking us. I think I saw a dragon that's made of fire. Someone locked him behind some black gates. I think he was mad."

William wouldn't look away from me. He had the same confused look on his face as everyone else.

"Guess you had to be there," I said, when he wouldn't answer me.

William looked at Sean and the warlocks.

"There was no fight?"

"Not with him," Rapoza answered.

"No begging to stay? No trying to open the gates?"

"I'm telling you; he was just as he is now."

"I don't understand?" William said, looking back at me. "There should have been a battle with him. The beast was calling out his name."

"We didn't see a beast," Rapoza answered. "The only thing we witnessed were the soldiers you warned us about. The spell you placed on the swords worked, just as you said it would. Ethan never tried to open any gates; never tried to kill us as we expected."

"Hey, where is Henry?" I asked, looking around. "Did he stop crying?"

I spotted Kelly, Erika and Crowley lying on the floor. William had put them all to sleep.

"That looks like a good idea," I said, as I sat on the floor. "I think I'll take a nap with them."

William instructed the others to pick me back up. He crossed the room and took a whiff of my breath.

"Are you trying to kiss me?" I asked.

William looked into my eyes, baffled by my demeanor. He looked back at Crowley and the nurses. Sean and Rapoza were still holding me up as William placed his hands over Crowley's head.

"Don't mess up his hair," I said. "He has nice hair, doesn't he?"

Rapoza and Sean were laughing as William closed his eyes. He held his hands on Crowley's head for a few moments, then slowly looked at me.

"It's morphine," he explained. "A very high dose."

"That explains it," Sean laughed.

"Hey, how was your vacation?" I asked him. "Did you go somewhere far?"

"Wow, maybe I should try a little morphine," Moe laughed. "Seems to work better than alcohol."

William was the only one *not* laughing. He kept looking into my eyes with a serious look on his face. I wanted to tell him that I needed a nap. I had an uncontrollable need to close my eyes.

"Take him home," William instructed. "I'll be along shortly. I need to clean things up here."

"Is Henry coming with us?" I asked, as Sean threw me over his shoulder again.

Rapoza kept laughing and shaking his head.

"Hey, you're my favorite," I said to him, as Sean opened the door. "You kicked my ass, remember?"

As Sean and the others walked out, I saw William with a small bottle in his hands.

"Morphine?" he said, mostly to himself.

Chapter Twenty-One: Explanation

When Rapoza drove into the driveway of the mansion, they were all still laughing. I wasn't sure what they all found so funny. I saw Netiri and my parents outside. They were pacing back and forth. They all ran to the car when it came to a stop. Sean opened my door, pulled me out, and threw me over his shoulder again.

"How is he?" my mother quickly asked.

Rapoza started laughing. In fact, they all did.

"What's so funny?" my father asked.

"Lucy, I'm home," I said, waving hello to my parents. "Fish taught me that one. By the way, who is Lucy?"

My parents looked at Sean.

"William said it was the morphine," he explained.

"Morphine? Was he hurt?" my mother asked, looking me over. "Why wouldn't he use a spell

"William can explain when he gets here," Sean said, making his way inside with me.

"Isn't he strong?" I said, patting Sean on his butt again. "He's got muscles everywhere."

Once inside, I saw Viola and her guardians at the top of the stairs. Viola had a very worried look on her face as Sean began ascending the stairs.

"Is he okay?" Renee asked.

"He's more than okay," Sean answered. "What room am I putting him in?"

My mother was right behind us.

"Put him in William's room," my mother said, walking around us.

As Sean passed Viola and her guardians, I was able to touch a strand of Viola's hair. She began crying when we locked eyes.

"Hey, you dumped me," I said, as Sean walked away.

I don't remember much after that. I knew Sean placed me on a bed, told my mother I would be out for a few hours, then said he would be in the guesthouse. My dreams were so odd that day. I dreamt of a powerful force in the form of a dragon. The dragon was set ablaze as it tried to destroy the gates that held it. The Black Witch was there, only, she wasn't the beautiful woman I'd seen. Her skeleton-like appearance was dreadful. Maggots crawled all over her as she looked at her master.

She held a black book of spells in her hands. It was a book I'd seen in my dreams. The cover had skull faces of souls that had lost their battle with evil. They moved and cried out for mercy from their master. I heard an odd ticking coming from the book the Black Witch held. It reminded me of the sound a clock would make as it ticked away each second. There were wolf-like creatures, bowing at the dragon's feet. A wave of fire, high as a mountain, began to form behind the dragon. As the wave of fire grew larger, I saw an army of beasts within it. They were the same kind of beasts the Tree of Life had shown me. They carried weapons I'd never seen before. They were chained by the necks, awaiting their master's command.

"We are running out of time," the Black Witch said to her master.

When she opened the black book of spells, that ticking sound grew louder. That seemed to upset the dragon. It hit the gates with its tail, trying to knock it down. The dream suddenly changed. I was back in hell. The Black Witch had transformed herself into that beautiful woman. She was smiling at someone who was holding a sword. I could only see his hands, but I could see that his hands and sword were covered in blood.

When the beautiful woman reached out to touch him, I saw it was me. Near my feet were bodies, bloodied and scattered about. Those bodies were not beasts, they were my dead friends. Rapoza and his men were there, so was Sean. When the Black Witch kicked something out of her path, I saw that it was Netiri's head rolling away. I had no reaction to their deaths. I only looked at the Black Witch with love in my eyes. I seemed to be happy that I had pleased her so much.

"Well done," she said, looking at the massacre on the ground. "He will reward you for this."

"My Queen," I said, pulling her into my arms.

The sound of someone weeping ruined our moment. I smiled at my queen as I turned away from her. I raised my bloody sword, then made my way toward the weeping. I saw two women on the ground, holding each other tight. I raised my sword above my head, preparing myself to kill them.

"Ethan, come back to me."

"No!" I shouted, as I awoke from my nightmare.

I was drenched in sweat; I couldn't catch my breath. I looked around the room, unsure of where I was. My heart was beating so fast. I put my hands over my head, trying to forget that horrible dream.

"I'm sorry I had to do that," a voice said.

I spun my head around. William was sitting in a corner of the room, a cup of tea in his hand.

"Why did you make me dream about that?" I said, trying to catch my breath.

"That wasn't a dream, Ethan."

Before I could question him, he got up and moved his chair next to me. He reached for a cup of tea that sat on a table next to me. He tapped it to warm it back up and handed it to me.

"Here, this will help."

I took the cup from him, afraid of what he was about to tell me. I knew who one of those women that I was about to kill. It was Viola.

"If that wasn't a dream," I said. "Nothing is going to help."

"What you experienced was my vision, Ethan. The only reason I was able to show it to you is because my vision has taken another course. Something happened yesterday, or should I say, what *didn't* happen yesterday, changed everything. Therefore, there's no need to keep it from you now. For once, I can be completely honest with you."

"I don't understand?"

"There should have been a battle yesterday, but that battle should have been against *you*. Instead, it was against the beasts that thrive there."

"Yesterday?"

"You've been sleeping since then," he explained.

I began to think back. I remember Netiri and I were walking to Doctor's Crowley's office. I remembered the immense heat that overpowered me. I felt I was burning alive.

"That heat you felt was the beast," William said, taking a sip of his tea. "It's a heat *not* of this world. I have felt that heat before. When the beast is near or at the gates, he lets it be known. Only wizards like us can feel and tolerate that heat. That's why I've been trying to build your tolerance to pain."

"The tree," I said, remembering what it had shown me. "I saw you there, in hell. You were much younger, but I knew it was you."

"Every king before me has fought that battle. We are magical beings, created by the gods to protect all the realms. Only beings like us are capable of opening the gates of hell. The gods also knew that only beings like us, are capable of keeping them closed. The Tree of Life was created to choose those kings. The tree has the capability of knowing our hearts and our intentions. It chooses only kings that are strong-willed and brave. We have been keeping the gates of hell closed for thousands of years."

"Am I going to be the one who opens them? Because that's what it sounds like."

"I must admit, I was uncertain for a moment. I was prepared to switch places with you if my doubts continued. You see, I never had to fight the magic of that black book of spells. In the many years I've breathed in air, this is the first time the Black Witch has gotten her hands on it. That's why I began to have doubts. I relied on my faith in you to keep pushing forward. The last thing I ever wanted to do was kill my own grandson."

"You didn't answer my question, William. Am I going to be the one who opens them?"

He looked deep into my eyes before answering. I was afraid of what that answer was going to be.

"The Tree of Life makes no mistakes," he answered. "When I had my vision, I didn't know you would be king. The Tree of Life had yet to write your name. When you were born and I first held you, I saw the path to being king had started. I paid visits to the Tree of Life, waiting to see your name on its bark. There were times I had doubts about what I had sensed about you. That day, when you came out of the Tree of Life, I knew I was looking at the next king."

"That doesn't make sense, William. You've been telling me my whole life that I would be king."

"That's because I sensed it. I have faith in my predictions. They have never failed me."

"You still didn't answer my question. You keep deflecting."

"I can't answer that, Ethan. My vision has changed. Only *you* know the answer to that question. What happened in Doctor's Crowley's office should not have happened that way. A new course has started. I have no idea what the outcome will be."

"Will you tell me the original course of it? Show me the rest of it," I asked hopeful.

He gave it some thought.

"I will tell you this; there should have been a battle between you and the warlocks. Your need to protect the Black Witch would have overpowered you."

"I killed them, William. I killed them all. I saw it in my nightmare."

"That part of my vision has changed. It began changing when you found your way out of hell that first time. You were stronger than I ever imagined. I expected to kill you that day. I never imagined you would come out of there, well, still you."

I drank the rest of the tea and looked out the window. I couldn't shake the memory of Netiri's decapitated head. I saw the evil look in my eyes as I was about to execute Viola.

"Would you like some more tea?" William asked.

"Yes, please," I said, handing him my cup.

He tapped the pot to re-warm the tea, filled my cup, and handed it back to me.

"Ethan, do you remember what I said to you when you first arrived in Salem?"

"Are you talking about the instructions you gave me?"

"Yes. What did I say to you?"

"You told me that I would find evil here. You tried to help me understand that it may become part of me. You told me to embrace it and not allow it to control me. You feared that evil would someday change me.

"I wanted you to know the difference," he answered. "It was vital to me that you understood how evil worked. I didn't want you losing yourself to the darkness. I almost lost hope when you hunted down those witches. The way you chose to kill them gave me concern."

I looked down at my cup.

"I remember being filled with rage. For some reason, their deaths weren't painful enough. I still smile when I think back to that. I know it sounds horrible, but I can't help it."

"You are not to blame for that, Ethan. Since birth, evil knew that it needed to seek you out. Why do you think we kept you in Magia for so long?"

"What are you talking about? It was my parents that didn't want me to leave."

"It was mostly your mother. Her vision made her fear your departure. By the time she had that vision, I had already put things in place. I've known she would give birth to you for hundreds of years."

"Wait, why did you say that evil knew it had to seek me out?"

"As I said before; I always sensed you would be king. Evil always seeks out the new king. My theory is, evil can sense when that king is born. It targets them, causing despair in their lives. It throws everything it can at the king, hoping that hard times will change him and make him evil. My battle with evil began the moment I went into the human world. You lived a sheltered life in Magia. Your troubles began when you arrived in Salem. I am convinced that evil felt your presence. It began its work on you; looking for people to help it."

"The witches," I said, looking away.

"Those witches you killed were willing participants. They cared only about the reward the Black Witch had promised them. As for Irene, evil gave her the idea of making a blood promise. She broke that promise, but lost her soul to the darkness as punishment. Now she does their bidding. She's not strong enough to pull herself out. Evil also used warlocks to do its dirty deeds. When evil went after your mother, it believed that *she* would someday be Queen of Magia. Evil made the warlocks hate and envy her. When she broke her blood promise and never surrendered herself to the darkness, it only made the darkness want her more."

"It still wants her?" I asked.

He filled his cup, always tapping the pot before pouring.

"Perhaps the darkness doesn't want her, but the woman does."

"Irene?"

"No. It's the woman with the red eyes. She's been down there for thousands of years. It's the same woman that lures kings by transforming herself into a beautiful woman. She feels if she can find the king who will finally open the gates, Satan will set her free. She lost her soul to the darkness when she made a blood promise. She doesn't see a way out, not until she witnessed what your mother did. Thea pulled herself out and never allowed the blood promise to change her."

"I didn't make a blood promise, William. Why am I changing?"

"It would be much easier if I showed you. Are you ready to see the truth?"

"I am."

"Come with me," he said, rising to his feet.

Chapter Twenty-Two: Hardest Worker

He put his cup down, walked over to a wall near the bed, and looked over his shoulder at me.

"Come stand next to me, Ethan."

I did as he said and looked at the wall.

"What am I supposed to be seeing?"

"The room I put behind this wall was in the guest house for a brief time. I had to move it back when Sean started training back there."

"He was never on vacation, was he?"

"No. He was training, with *me*."

"To fight me?"

"Yes."

"And the warlocks? What are they training for?""

"To kill you if you got near the gates."

"What kind of spell did you put on their swords? I remember the light coming from them."

"That was for the demons. It may not kill them, but it would have given the warlocks time to kill *you*.

Now, let's continue, shall we?"

I looked at the wall. I remember William made the guesthouse look like Magia. William used it to stay strong and remember where he came from. At least, that's what he said.

"No more lies," William said, waving his hand.

His magic spread throughout the wall. It soon formed a door with a bright light coming from it. William pushed it open.

"After you," he said, stepping to one side.

My mouth was dropped when I walked in. There were thousands, no, millions of memory clouds floating all around the room. The room wasn't very big but felt enormous none the less. Magia's flowers were here, spreading their sparkles of light into the air. I heard the sound of a waterfall, but knew it wasn't really there. William waved his hand and sealed the door behind us.

"What is going on with all these memory clouds?" I asked, looking all around the room.

Each one was filled with moving images of people I didn't know. I looked closer and noticed some of their clothing was strange. Some were clearly from a different time in life.

"These memory clouds go back about five hundred years," William said. "Some are from the present, some from the future. They each mark an important event that brought us to where we are today. Each person in these memories either helped, or fought against evil."

He looked through the memory clouds until he found the one he was looking for. He tapped it with his finger and it floated closer to us. I looked inside of it. There was a small boy crying in the street. The cars that drove by him were strange. They looked nothing like the cars you'd see today. Passersby just ignored the boy and didn't stop to help him.

"That is Simon," William explained. "This was right before I found him and took him to Magia. His human father had been molesting him. I thought I could help him by taking him home. I never imagined that evil had already touched his heart. He grew up despising humans. That's why he turned the warlocks against them. He wanted everyone to hate humans as much as he did. It's the one thing he hated most about himself; he was half-human."

He flicked it out of the way and tapped another one. It too, floated closer to us. I saw a thin man with a pointy nose. He was hiding behind a tree, watching a much younger William. There was another wizard there, William was telling him that he was leaving to venture into the human world.

"That is Wendell," William continued. "He wanted desperately to be king. He used Simon to plot against me and take my powers. I had no idea that Wendell had taken Simon under his wing. He betrayed me and all the wizards in Magia."

Again, he flicked it away and tapped another one. When it got closer to us, I recognized my mother in an instant.

"What are they doing to her?" I asked.

"Those are warlocks, and they are dragging her through the forest. Simon wants to cut you out of her womb. This is the vision your mother had before placing you inside that crystal. Evil had already instructed Simon to kill you, he just didn't know it."

Another flick, another tap.

"What is this one of?" I asked.

He looked away.

"That is my Emma. Someone had poisoned her. She suffered before her death. This is the way I found her."

I looked back into the bubble. I could see William sobbing like a child as he held her. My mother was there. She was about nine years old. She stood behind a tree, watching her father weep over her dead mother. I saw when a witch named, Sharron finally took my mother away.

Another flick.

When the memory got closer, I saw Netiri. He was ripping a woman's dress away. I knew he was about to rape her. The other warlocks were waiting their turn at her. Before Netiri could finish the deed, a group of men saw them and chased them away. He never raped the girl. He left her naked and crying on the ground. The men who found her spread rumors, saying that all the men had taken a turn at her. I saw when the girl hung herself because of that.

"Is that the real reason Netiri has never been with a woman?" I asked.

"Yes," William answered. "When he found out the girl had taken her own life, he became riddled with guilt. I think he's been punishing himself by never seeking out a woman again."

"I knew," I said, looking into the memory. "I just didn't know she had killed herself."

William flicked it away.

"Why are you showing me all of this?" I asked.

"I needed you to understand that evil *never* takes a break. Satan is the hardest worker there is. He uses all the deadly sins against us. Envy, gluttony, sloth, lust, pride, wrath and greed. I've seen others, but those are the most common. You see them everywhere, in one form or another."

He looked at the memory clouds.

"Satan touched all these people with those sins. Not one of them knew it or felt it. He lives in every realm but ours, searching out helpers. They never see it coming, never realize he's watching. The more souls he collects, the more powerful he becomes. It's a battle between good and evil. Some change their ways, others get lost. Satan may not walk the earth, but his sins certainly do."

He looked at the memory clouds again.

"I myself, have fallen victim to several of those sins. I've had to lie in order to keep my secrets safe. I put on some incredibly good performances here in Salem. I had to act surprised, shocked, and even scared sometimes. All to keep the truth buried."

"What truth is that?"

He looked at me.

"Haven't you been paying attention? The truth to all of this," he said, motioning toward the memory clouds. "It's our purpose, the reason we were created. We are not meant to benefit from our powers. They were given to us as a gift, one that is used to fight evil. Our job is to search out these happenings, and spot when Satan is getting the upper hand. Our powers are tools, Ethan. We use them wisely. We don't change things, don't interfere, and we keep the gates closed. That's it. We have no other purpose. Any form of happiness we find in our lives, it is only an added bonus. I need you to understand these things because evil will always try to change you. And for the first time, hell had a book of spells to help it."

I looked at the memory clouds. I could see the many sacrifices William made in order to make me and my mother strong. He stepped in when needed, fought when he had no choice. He spent his life putting puzzles together in order to find the truth. His whole life was dedicated to fighting evil. I saw the many times he had to look away because he couldn't change things. He knew the work that evil was doing, but his only job was the keep the gates closed.

"Keepers of the Gates," I whispered.

He began to show me one memory after another. I saw my father's suffering when my mother sent him away. She didn't know it, but evil needed her to do that in order to make her weak. But William was right, love really was a powerful force. That was the only thing that kept my mother fighting, her love for my father, and her love for me. It really was never-ending. One of the memories I couldn't understand. Two men, holding golden swords, were in it.

"What's this of?" I asked.

"That is Sammy and Javier. They are no longer

here. No one remembers them because their purpose is over."

It all began to make sense to me. Each soul, each life, had a purpose in this world. We all made our choices when crossing those roads. There was the easy road, or the road less traveled. We started our lives like a blank page of a book. Our choices wrote the pages, and our decisions wrote the end.

Willian tapped another memory.

"This one is important," he said, tapping the memory closer to us. "It's the future, so I can't show you much of it."

I looked closely at the memory. I gasped when I saw myself inside of it. I was much older than I was now. It looked to be fifty years into the future. I was waiting behind a tree, looking around it and waiting for something. Then I saw it, a boy, around seventeen years old, came out of the Tree of Life. I cried tears as the boy looked at me. There was torment in his eyes. The boy dropped to his knees and begged for forgiveness. I came out from behind the tree and looked over the boy's shoulder. I saw a woman, she was lying dead inside the tree. Before the memory could show me more, William flicked it away.

I quickly spun around.

"Bring it back!" I shouted.

"I will not."

"You said, no more lies!"

"You know I can't show you, Ethan."

"Was that my grandson?"

"Yes."

"Who did he kill?"

"He hasn't killed that person, remember? It's the future. Many things can happen to change it. *You*, can change it. Just as things changed in Doctor Crowley's office, you can change the outcome of that day."

He held out his hand. His fingers were wrapped around something.

"What is that?" I asked.

He slowly spread his fingers. He was holding a small glass bottle. It had one word on it…morphine.

"To have what you've never had, you must be willing to do what you've never done," he said, looking down at it.

"Morphine?"

He smiled.

"Doctor Crowley gave you a large dose of this right before you were pulled under. I was shocked to see your good mood when they brought you out. I was even more surprised to see there were no casualties. Something as simple as this," he said, showing me the bottle. "Changed the future. Not a word was said, not a secret told. No rules were broken, and yet, it changed everything."

"Is that bad?"

He laughed.

"No, but it opened my eyes. Every king before you has battled in that dark place. You are the only one in history that has come out smiling. The dead should have been many, Ethan. All killed by your hand. That didn't happen, did it? If this helped change that, imagine what else it will change."

I wasn't sure where he was going with this.

Did he want me to live my life on morphine?

"No," he said, shaking his head. "I simply want you to understand that the future is not written in stone. This little bottle helped me understand that. I have always said that things will *still* happen, even if you change them. I was wrong. You unknowingly changed the future. Nothing was done by your hand or mine. And yet, it changed everything."

I think William noticed I was trying to make sense of what he was saying. He put the bottle down and placed his hands over my head.

"I will spell it out for you," he said, closing his eyes.

Chapter Twenty-Three: I Do

I was looking out my window as I watched Sean and the warlocks, going into the guesthouse. A day had passed since William placed his hands on my head. I knew what was coming, and it would be up to me to change it. The trick was, I couldn't lift a finger to do it. I sat up all night, thinking of ways I could get away with it. I thought of the things the Tree of Life had shown me. I felt empathy for every past king of Magia.

Now I understood that evil tried to change every king before me. It worked slowly, never allowing its victim to realize what was going on. I thought of the many people I encountered here in Salem. Some were kind, others impatient or mean. I thought of the deadly sins William spoke of. I could see them everywhere now. The bank robbers, murderers, rapists, the list went on and on. All these things happened to give Satan another victim, and another page for his book of lost souls.

"Ethan, are you up?"

It was my mother.

"Come in."

"You didn't come down for breakfast," she said, closing the door behind her.

"I wasn't hungry," I said, looking out the window again.

She stood next to me.

"What are you looking at?" she asked.

I remembered the memory clouds I'd seen of her. I looked at her as my admiration for her grew. I don't know why the Tree of Life never chose her to be queen. She was certainly worthy of it. I knew no one braver, no one more capable of fighting evil. She thought nothing of her suffering if it meant lessening mine. She was a good mother, a good wife. It was time for life to stop giving her anguish. I wanted her and my father to be happy. I didn't want their lives to revolve around protecting me. It was time to let her go. She had to prepare herself for my sister. It was time to place her back where she belonged.

"When are you telling them?" I asked.

She was still looking out the window.

"I'm sorry, what?"

"When are you telling Fish, Cory and Delia that you and my father are moving back to Salem?"

She seemed surprised that I knew. She looked back out the window and smiled.

"Isn't it beautiful here? I always loved Salem this time of year. It's the only place that has ever felt like home to me. I like to call it *my palace*. My heart aches every time I think of this magical town."

"You told me so many stories about this place. I always knew how much you missed it. Maybe you and my father belong here."

Her liquid brown eyes began spilling over.

"I left my heart here when we moved to Magia. I always wanted you to experience Salem the way I did. I always pictured you begging for candy, opening gifts at Christmas, and decorating a tree. I wish I had the beautiful memories of you doing those things."

"You still can," I said, facing her. "It's not too late. You're going to be a mother, remember? You can have all those things. Magia will always be there. You belong here, Mother."

She put her arms around me and leaned her head on my chest. I knew what she was waiting for.

"I'll still be here, Mother. I'll be around for as long as you need me."

She looked up at me.

"I love you, Ethan. There isn't anything I wouldn't do for you."

In that moment, I knew why the Tree of Life hadn't chosen her to be queen. A mother's love is too powerful. She would do anything for her child. There's a reason William kept things from my mother. She would have changed the future so many times, all to save me.

"I know," I said, kissing the top of her head.

"So, are you feeling better?" she asked.

I pulled away from her.

"Well, the last few weeks have been good. I haven't killed anyone, skinned anyone alive, or hunted anyone for revenge. I would say that is progress, wouldn't you?"

She laughed.

"What about Viola? Is it truly over between you both?"

I just looked out the window and didn't answer. I think my mother realized that I didn't want to talk about it.

"We're leaving for Magia soon," she said. "The wedding is today. Fish and Delia are really looking forward to seeing you there."

"I'll be there, Mother."

I was still looking out the window when she walked out. Sean, Netiri, and the warlocks were coming out of the guesthouse. They spread out in the yard, all holding swords in their hands. I knew what they were doing, and I had to help them. I hurried down the stairs and right out the back door to the kitchen.

"May I join you?" I asked them.

They all looked at one another, unsure of what to answer. I pulled out my wand, placed it on the ground, and walked over to them.

"Listen, we already know that my sword can't kill you. I will probably be fighting you with my bare hands. I assume I will want to steal one of *your* swords in order to kill you with it. I can show you how I fight, so it never gets to that point."

More glances back and forth. I looked into Netiri's eyes, thinking of William's vision.

"I never want to hurt any of you," I said, looking at them all. "If it gets to the point where I lose control, I'll welcome your swords across my neck."

"I never want to hurt any of you," I said

"Okay," Sean said, stepping forward. "But no magic. No waving your hand, no thinking of spells, no nothing, understood?"

"Understood."

I looked at Rapoza.

"I'll probably come after you, first. You have the biggest sword, therefore, making me want it. Let me show you all my weaknesses so you know where to strike."

"You have weaknesses?" Moe asked.

"Many of them," I confessed. "I'm a wizard, so I've relied on my powers to do most of the work. Remember how you kicked my ass in Fall River?"

Lima smiled.

"We did kick your ass, didn't we?"

"And it hurt," I said, grabbing my chin. "I can still feel that boot in my face."

"Okay, show us those weaknesses," Rapoza said.

We must have practiced for hours before William came out and reminded me about the wedding. I had completely lost track of time. I hurried into the house and up the stairs. I showered, put on my best robe, and headed back down. I was surprised to see the warlocks and Sean waiting with William. I didn't realize they would be coming with us. Why wasn't William worried about them becoming enchanted with Magia? I didn't question it and smiled at the men.

"Your father and mother have already left," William said. "We are just waiting on Netiri."

They were all dressed in tuxedos. I've never seen Sean look so handsome. I was used to seeing hm in work clothes.

"Don't you look spiffy," I said, touching his jacket. "You look like a million bucks."

"How does my ass look?" he said, turning around. "I know how much you like touching it."

The warlocks laughed. Lima spun around so I could check him out.

"How do I look?" he asked. "Do I look like the Protector of the North?"

I smiled.

"Indeed, you do. As do all of you."

William was wearing a robe I'd never seen before. It was black in color, with a gold oak tree all along the back. The branches of the tree were draping to the ground. It was no secret what tree he had put on it.

"I'm ready," I heard from the stairs.

We all turned; it was Netiri. For the first time, he was wearing a wizard robe. It was a beautiful blue with fire breathing dragons all over it.

"How do I look?" Netiri asked, as he made his way down. "Do I look funny?"

"You look like a virgin," I said, placing my hand on his shoulder. "But a very handsome one."

"Thanks, kid. You look nice as well."

"We should be going," William said.

You could feel the energy in the air when we arrived in Magia. The flowers sparkled like I'd never seen them sparkle before. Stars, big as moons, were hanging above the land. The sun's rays also seemed brighter than ever. You could hear the ivy whistling a beautiful tone. I could smell the cherry blossoms from here.

"Wow," Rapoza said, gazing around. "I never thought this place could get any more beautiful. I didn't see stars the first time we came here."

"I was going to say the same thing," Sean added.

It was obvious that William had brought Sean here before. He didn't seem shocked or surprised about the vortex, either. We began making our way toward the village. We were talking about the bright rays from the sun when William came to a sudden stop.

"What in the world?" William gasped.

The dragons were lined up, forming a path right into the village. At the end of the path was Attor. He wore a huge, and I mean huge, bow around his neck. He leaned his head down as we approached.

"Bride, or groom?" he asked.

"W...what?" I laughed.

"I was told that's the way humans do this," he said, looking toward Fish.

Fish was at the end of the village, talking to Walter. I had to hold in my laughter. William's eyes were still locked on Attor.

"Bride, or groom?" he asked again.

"Both," I answered.

Attor looked toward Fish again.

"I'll be right back," he said, taking to the sky.

He flew over to Fish, leaned down to ask him 'who knows what'. Fish looked profoundly serious when he gave him his answer. Attor swiftly flew back to us and leaned down.

"You will have to place half of yourself on one side, and half on the other."

The warlocks and Sean burst out in laughter. I quickly reminded them about Attor being a *fire-breathing* dragon. They didn't laugh much after that. William stepped forward, looking up at Attor. His voice started off nice, but it didn't end that way.

"Attor, come here, please," he said, motioning with his finger.

Attor leaned down.

"No, closer," William motioned, with his head

"Yes, My Liege?"

"Attor, I know I asked you to be very accommodating to our guests. In fact, I asked that as a personal favor to *me*."

"I have done just that, Your Majesty."

William glanced at the bow.

"I relieve you of your obligations. You may resume your normal duties. And take off that ridiculous bow!" he shouted.

"Yes, My Liege."

Everyone's shoulders were bouncing up and down. I was having a challenging time keeping my laughter in. Attor raised his talons, pulled away the bow, and blew fire at it.

"I'm going to kill Fish," William said, storming off.

I was still laughing when we got to Fish.

"Fish, really? Half our bodies?" I teased.

"Hey, if anyone could do it, it would be a wizard, right?"

I started laughing again as I checked out what he was wearing. To my surprise, he was wearing a wizard robe. The robe was a bright orange, with pumpkins and skeletons all over it.

"When in Rome," he said, spinning around.

"What happened to your tuxedo?" William asked. "I explained to Charles what it was so he could provide it."

"Charles didn't like it, so he made me this."

"*Charles* didn't like it?" William said, looking up at the orb.

The tiny fairy quickly flew away. William shook his head and glared at Fish.

"Fish, leave the dragons alone."

"As the French would say…. Moi?" Fish said, pointing to himself.

William rolled his eyes and said he needed to put the finishing touches on something. We left Fish and took a little walk around the village. It had really been transformed into a beautiful garden. The seating area faced my mother's lake. Each trunk-like seat had red bougainvillea wrapped around it. The arbor Cory built had every inch covered in Magia's flowers. It stood in the middle of the stone-covered aisle.

It seemed all of Magia had shown up for the wedding. The Pismas were here, gossiping as usual. Levora was sitting at a table covered with moss and flowers. The Onfroi were also here but kept their distance. Their bark made Wizards a bit weak. I couldn't wait for the warlocks to see the Venose. They were Magia's version of a lion. Only, our lions walked on two legs. Their manes were long and flowing. When they roared, you had to cover your ears in fear of the sound waves would hurt you.

Wizards of all ages were seated near the stone-covered aisle that the bride would be walking down. I spotted Renee and Cheryl, saying hello to some of the wizards. I didn't see Viola. Had she not come?

Rapoza and his men wouldn't stop looking at Levora. Sean was busy looking at the orbs that were flying around the village. I could smell the aroma of food being prepared. I was curious about what menu Fish ended up deciding on. I made it a point to tell William if he could talk to the fairies about it. It still made me nervous about Fish's choice.

Out of nowhere, the sound of trumpets blared throughout the village. I have to say, it made me jump back a little. I turned and realized it was the guards that were playing the trumpets. I almost lost it when I saw what they were wearing. On their tails were bows, placed every inch or so. They each had on vests, with ruffled collars that almost covered their faces. Just then, William came back and joined us.

"The bride is almost ready," he said, looking around.

"What are you looking for?" I asked.

"I thought I heard trumpets," he replied.

I tapped him on the shoulder, then pointed to the guards. William's face was priceless. He took one look at the guards and yelled... "Fish!"

I was still laughing when I spotted Viola. She was near one of the cottages talking to Cory and his wife. She wore a beautiful yellow dress that hugged every curve of her body. Her hair was pinned up, with yellow and green, emerald flowers. When Cory and his wife began escorting her to her seat, I couldn't help but notice the stares she was getting from some of the young wizards.

"Is that Viola?" Netiri asked.

One wizard got up and offered her his elbow. She nodded and wrapped her arm around his. She never looked at me, never acknowledged I was there. The trumpets began to sound again, signaling everyone to take their seats.

"Come on. Kid," Netiri said, placing his hand on my shoulder.

As we approached our seats, I noticed the young wizard had taken a seat next to Viola. They were talking and laughing as I took a seat behind them. Netiri said we should sit somewhere else, but I ignored him. Rapoza sat next to me, the others sat next to him. They were all looking around with amazement in their eyes. When the Venose walked by to find a seat, the warlocks slowly looked at each other.

"This place is amazing," Lima said, shaking his head.

William took his place at the altar. I had no idea he would be performing the ceremony today. He waited for everyone to take their seats. He looked up at the sky and waved his hand. His magic looked like shooting stars, and it made the sky dim itself. It looked like a cloudy day, but there was not one cloud in sight. He turned and faced the lake, waved his hand, and turned around again. The water from the lake began to rise. I heard the warlocks gasp as the water formed a beautiful waterfall.

There was no mist coming from the falls. Only sparkles of light were coming down its water. William gave the fairies a subtle nod. They began to land on all the rocks that lined the aisle. They spread their wings and made the isle light up with their magic. William waved is hand again, making a beautiful soft, song start playing.

He looked over at the Onfroi, nodded, and gave them a signal. One of the Onfroi began to open its trunk. Steven walked out of the doorway that had appeared. My parents soon joined him and walked him to the altar. My mother gave Steven a kiss on the cheek and took a seat. My father hugged him and did the same. Steven wore a traditional tuxedo that William had gifted hm. His face was one of joy and happiness. He shook hands with William then turned to face the aisle. William waved his hand, making a different song start playing.

"Is that Here Comes the Bride?" Rapoza asked.

We all got to our feet when Fish and Delia walked out of a cottage. They both stood aside as Vera made her way out. Vera had on the most beautiful, white, long veil. Her dress was white as snow, with what looked like snowflakes coming down the dress. She held a bouquet of flowers in her hand. I looked back at Steven; he was in tears.

Fish and Delia began to walk her down the aisle. Fish kept wiping away his tears and kissing Vera's hand. Vera never took her eyes off Steven the whole time. He was beaming with happiness when his bride got to the altar.

"Who gives this woman in holy matrimony?" William asked.

"We do," Delia and Fish said, in unison.

They both kissed Vera, then Fish shook hands with Steven. Fish was still crying when he took a seat. William stopped the music as Steven reached for Vera's hands. They faced each other with such a look of love in their eyes.

"We are gathered here today," William began.

This wasn't the way people got married in Magia, but I knew Fish wanted to give his daughter a traditional service. Although *nothing* about today was traditional, at least the service would be.

Magia's occupants were listening to every word William was saying. They'd never heard a service performed like this before.

"No streams of light?" I heard one Pisma say.

"Do you, Steven Romero, take this woman to be your wife? Do you promise to love and honor her, through good times and bad?"

Steven smiled.

"I do."

"Do you, Vera Fisher, take this man to be your husband? Do you promise to love and honor him, through good times and bad?"

"I do," Vera cried.

"With the honor bestowed upon me, I now pronounce you husband and wife."

We all jumped up and cheered as Steven pulled Vera into his arms. They kissed twice, then faced the crowd. I can't put into words the amount of happiness on their faces. They held hands as they ran down the aisle. The fairies began flying frantically around us. It took me a moment to realize they wanted us to move.

"We need to get things ready for the banquet," I heard one say.

Chapter Twenty-Four: The Banquet

The fairies were working tirelessly turning the seating area into a banquet area. The aroma of food began to get stronger and stronger.

"I know that smell," Rapoza said, taking a whiff of air. "I just can't put my finger on it."

"What are we having for dinner?" Moe asked. "I can't imagine what type of meals they prepare in a place like this."

"I don't know," I answered. "No one knows what Fish picked for a menu."

"*Fish* picked it?" Netiri asked.

I told him yes and watched the fairies working their magic. They covered the tables with moss and flowers, then set gold plates all around it. Each table was set for a party of ten. They placed the same trunk-like seats around the table. The centerpieces were tall, clear vases, with moving objects inside. When we took our seats, I was able to see some of Magia's fish, swimming inside the vases.

"I've never seen fish like that before," Sean said, admiring the vases. "Are they changing color?"

"Yes, they do that often," I explained. "It usually depends on the time of day."

Everyone rose to their feet when the bride and groom walked back into the village. Vera had taken off the veil and modified the wedding dress she'd worn. It was now shorter, with a different tint of white. There were only a few snowflakes coming down the back of the dress.

The happy couple sat with William. My mother and father were with them. Cory and his wife were at a table next to them. I scanned around for Viola. I didn't like that she was sitting with that young wizard. Renee and Cheryl were about two tables away from her. Netiri and I were sitting with the Rapoza and his men, but I had a perfect view of Viola.

"She talk to you yet?" Netiri asked.

"She has no reason to," I answered.

I rose to my feet when Vera and Steven got to our table. We all congratulated them and wished them a lifetime of happiness. Vera showed us her ring, kissed Steven, and they walked to the next table. As I was sitting down, I caught the young wizard that was sitting with Viola, whispering into her ear. She giggled, leaned closer to him, and whispered something back.

"Calm down, kid," Netiri said, when I wouldn't stop looking at them.

I didn't want to tell him that I was hurt because Viola hadn't glanced at me once. I didn't miss a chance to look her way. No matter who was talking to me, I never looked away from her. I felt broken-hearted as she flirted with the young wizard. The worst thing about it was, I knew that wizard. He was a genuinely nice and polite kid. He was also very handsome, and had a way of making people laugh.

I turned away from them when I felt myself wanting to go punch him. I wasn't going to do something foolish to ruin Vera's big day.

"I'll be right back," I said, getting up from the table.

"Where are you going?" Netiri quickly asked.

"Don't worry," I said, looking toward Viola. "I just need a minute alone. I won't be gone long."

Netiri sat back down as I walked out of the village. I pulled out my staff, made it hover, and took to the sky. What I really wanted to do was rip that wizard's head off. I wanted to look into his eyes as I held his head in my hands. I was better than that now. I had to conduct myself like the future wizard king I was. No more skinning people alive. No more tearing their teeth out. I had to put that kind of fighting behind me. Much like William, I had to learn how to use my wisdom, instead of my magic. I just wish someone would tell that to my heart.

I flew to a place I went to as a child. Attor and I would spend hours there, exploring the area. It was the only place in Magia that grew what humans would call pine trees. Here, the *pine trees* grew much taller and fuller than in the human world.

I threw my staff aside when I arrived there. I wanted to clear my head before I went back. I didn't know if I could hold myself back if that wizard kept flirting with Viola. She didn't seem to mind all the attention he was giving her. Who could blame him? Viola was a very beautiful woman. I only wished the wizard would wait until I left for Salem.

I was looking out into the trees when I heard someone arrive. I could hear their footsteps behind me.

"Ethan? Are you okay, son?"

It was my father. He was putting his staff down as I turned and faced him. He kept looking all around, with amazement in his eyes.

"What is this place?" he asked.

"Oh, this?" I said, looking toward the trees. "Just a place to come and think."

My father kept looking all around.

"This isn't the spot you made for the newlyweds, is it?"

"No. That's about two miles from here. I made this place that same day."

"It's amazing, Ethan."

"Thank you," I said, admiring my handy work.

I loved hearing the stories my mother told me about Santa Claus and the North Pole. Her adventures with him kept me captivated every time. She called the North Pole the most magical place on earth.

"Why Christmas?" he asked.

"Mother's stories," I answered. "I tried to remember every detail she told me about the North Pole. I wanted it to look like the magical wonderland she spoke of. I know the snow feels funny, but I've never seen snow before. I just wanted it to feel like magic."

"And so, it does," he said, gazing around.

I covered the pine trees with as much snow as possible. My mother always said that snow looked like ice cream on a tree. I had lights, blinking everywhere, in every color and every tree. I used berries to make strands of garland and hung them on the pines. There was subtle snow falling all around us. I placed a cottage, decorated with lights, which sat snuggled in the woods.

I made sure that Christmas was everywhere. Ornaments of all sizes made the forest come alive. Living in the human world certainly helped me create this place. Humans started decorating weeks ago. I watched carefully and took it all in. But nothing compared to my mother's stories of the North Pole. I only wished I had done it justice.

"Just a place to think, huh?" my father said, with suspicious eyes.

"The truth is Father; I was going to marry Viola here. When I created the newlywed's area, I created this place. I was going to surprise her and bring her here after the wedding. I know you didn't want me to get married, but I had to follow my heart. I even created a place for us to stay," I said, looking toward the cottage. "But none of that matters anymore."

My father kept looking into my eyes. I sensed he felt bad for not standing with me on my decision to marry Viola.

"You really love this girl, don't you?"

"I always did, Father."

"Yes, I see that now," he said, looking at our surroundings.

"I don't blame her for ending things with me. I took her for granted. I didn't appreciate what I had with her. She was always understanding and kind. I should have put her first. It was never my intention to hurt her the way I did."

"Fight for her," my father said. "Don't give up and try to work things out."

I looked down.

"She doesn't want me, anymore."

"All couples fight, Ethan. Your mother and I are not immune to that. Look at Fish and Delia, they fight all the time. Delia may yell at Fish a lot, but she would stand in front of the devil himself if it meant saving him. That's what love is, son. It's a bond that no one can break. We forgive, then we forget. The love between us is unbreakable. You must see that and fight for it."

When I began to tear up, my father pulled me into his arms. I wrapped my arms around him as I allowed myself to mourn her love.

"You're a good, decent man, Ethan," he whispered. "You deserve to be happy. It's no fault of your own that you fell in love so young. I'm sorry for not understanding that."

He pulled away.

"Come on, let's go help Vera and Steven celebrate their big day."

I wiped away my tears.

"Did they start serving dinner yet?" I asked.

"Fish didn't want to say what the meal would be."

My father began laughing.

"That kid has not stopped messing with the dragons and guards. Did you see what he made them wear?"

We both laughed.

"I think William may kill him," I warned. "He's still not happy about that *bow* Attor was wearing."

"Wait till you see what he requested some of the wizards wear."

"What? I didn't see anything unusual about what they were wearing."

"You don't understand; the wedding is one thing, but the reception is another."

"Oh no," I laughed.

"Come on, let's get back."

By the time we got back, it appeared they were serving dinner. We spotted Delia stomping around the village. She would go into one cottage, then another. What was she looking for? It didn't take long to figure that out.

"Fish!" she shouted. "Where are you?"

"James, over here," my mother called.

She was sitting with Sean and the warlocks. Netiri was in the middle of a laughing fit. I didn't see William anywhere.

"What happened?" my father asked, as we took a seat.

"I'm not sure," my mother answered. "But Delia was not happy when the fairies started bringing out the food."

"Where *is* the food?" my father asked, looking at the table.

"Fish!" Delia shouted. "Chow mein? At your daughter's wedding, you picked chow mein?"

Fish was holding a plate in his hand, his mouth full of food, or should I say, chow mein.

"What's wrong with chow mein, Dells? It's my favorite."

This isn't *your* wedding, you idiot!"

William came walking out from one of the cottages. Vera and Steven were with him. He gave Vera a kiss on the cheek and told them to take their seat. I thought I heard Vera thanking him for saving the day.

As Vera and Steven walked away, William gave Fish the evil eye. I could see he was truly angry with him. With one swift wave of William's hand, he made gourmet meals appear at every table. There was seared duck, filet of beef, roasted vegetables, and many other dishes. The bread alone was enough to satisfy me. The cinnamon butter went perfectly with it.

Everyone began to feast as Delia gave William a huge hug. She must have thanked him about a million times that night. Fish, on the other hand, kept his distance from William and stayed near my father. Once we finished dinner, and Fish was put in his place by Delia, Steven began dancing with Vera. William made sure her favorite song was playing. He took all the decision-making away from Fish.

I decided to warn William about the wizards, and the crazy scheme Fish was up to. I didn't want the wizards to be humiliated after being so helpful to Fish and his family. There were no more surprises for the rest of the night. William kept a watchful eye on Fish the whole time. I felt bad about that. William couldn't enjoy himself because of it. My father tried to tell Fish to ease up, but as usual, Fish acted like he'd done nothing wrong. It was starting to get a little annoying.

When another song began to play, I thought of asking Viola if she wanted to dance with me. It was a slow song, and I thought perhaps it would be a good opportunity to speak with her. I rose to my feet, determined to beg for her forgiveness. I slowly sat back down when I saw her dancing with the young wizard. It was irritating to me that he would stay close to her between songs. He wouldn't give anyone an opportunity to have a dance with her.

I decided it was time for me to go. I told William about the area I had created for the newlyweds and took my leave. Netiri and the warlocks left with me back to Salem. Once home, I asked if anyone wanted some coffee.

"Yes, but I want to get out of these clothes," Netiri answered.

We all decided to put on normal clothes and meet back in the kitchen for coffee. I was brewing coffee when Rapoza walked in.

"I can already smell it," he said, pulling out a small bottle.

"What's that?" I asked.

"It's just some brandy," he said, taking a seat.

I reached for some cups as the coffee brewed. Sean, Moe and Lima were next to walk in.

"I brought some, too," Sean said, showing Rapoza his bottle. "A little night cap doesn't sound too bad."

"Pour me a double," Moe said, pushing his cup forward.

"Not waiting on the coffee?" I asked.

They all laughed. What was so funny?

"Coffee is like cream," Moe explained. "Just a little goes a long way. But this stuff, it's like sugar, the more the better," he said, taking a drink from his cup.

"You having one with us?" Sean asked.

I said no and poured myself some coffee. I took a seat with them as they talked about Magia.

"I still can't get over the fact that dragons are real," Lima was saying. "They can talk, can you believe that?"

"I think everything in that place can talk," Sean answered.

As they chatted about Magia, I couldn't help but notice the scratches on their arms. I didn't see it before because they had on long sleeve shirts. The scratches were deep, and recent. I began to look them over as they finished off one of the bottles. Two of Lima's nails were black, as if he had smashed them. Rapoza had bruises along his ear. I looked at Moe, I hadn't noticed his bald head had a scab.

"May I ask you something?" I said to them. "You don't have to answer if you don't want."

"Shoot," Sean replied.

"Why are you here? I mean, I know *why* you're here, but why did you say yes?"

They all looked at each other. Moe downed his drink and asked for a refill. Sean pulled out another small bottle and filled Moe's cup. After filling his cup again, Rapoza leaned back in his chair and let out a sigh.

"The wizard showed me the future," he began. "The day he placed his hands over my head to break the spell, he also showed me the things to come. I knew there would not be a world to come back to if we didn't help him."

"William approached me years ago," Sean chimed in. "Showed me the same thing. I didn't need convincing. I wanted to help."

Sean was the one that didn't make sense to me. I knew for a fact that he had killed someone before. William said no life had to of been taken. What was Sean's role in all of this?

Lima took a drink of his brandy and shook his head. "You know what I don't understand? What makes us so noble? Why does that place *not* do to us, what it does to him?" he said, pointing to me. "I see no woman there, no fire, and no devil. What do you all see?" he asked the group.

Sean shrugged his shoulders.

"I saw a wet, damp place. The only thing that seemed real to me were those beasts we fought. I didn't even feel the heat William said we may experience, or the sadness."

"But your sword?" I said, leaning forward. "You put it between me and the woman. How did you *not* see her?"

"No, I put it in front of your face, to snap you out of it. I thought that's what the light was for. William put some kind of spell on our swords that made them radiate like that. He got the spell out of a white book of spells he was holding. Those guards brought it to him."

"What about that strand of hair William gave us?" Rapoza asked. "What do you suppose that's for?"

"Strand of hair?" I asked.

They all took another drink. I wanted to know more, so I decided to keep talking to them.

"Do you gentlemen drink scotch?" I asked.

"Hey, now you're talking," Sean answered.

"I believe my father has some in his study," I said, pushing my chair out.

I went into my father's study, retrieved the scotch, and headed back into the kitchen.

"It's not much of a wedding until someone breaks out the scotch," Moe laughed.

I grabbed four glasses, poured them a stiff drink, and slid the glasses to them.

"You were saying?" I said, taking a seat. "Something about a strand of hair?"

Rapoza was the first to speak.

"Yes, the wizard gave it to us. He gave us the strand of hair, and a tooth. Well, he didn't give it to me, he gave it all to Sean."

I looked at Sean.

"Why you?"

He took another drink.

"Apparently, we're waking up some White Witch to take that black book of spells back. William needed a descendant of the deceased to hold those items. I guess I'm related in some way."

It was making sense now. I had forgotten all about the White Witch. I was the one who found the thread of hair and tooth. William took it from me when Netiri and I came out of Vera's house. He said two virgins were required to find it, and that was us.

"I'll tell you what impressed me about all of this,' Lima said, pointing to himself.

"What's that?" I asked.

"The way all those wizards killed those things. They were waiting, expecting us to take them there. The dragons came in very handy, too. That's some kind of magic you all have."

"Killed *those* things? What do you mean? When did that happen?"

"When we went into Magia," Moe answered. "Hey, did you know that Magia means magic, in Spanish? What are the odds? How fitting is that word for that place?"

"What did you mean by *those things*?" I pushed.

Moe downed his drink and asked for another. I was quick to refill his glass.

"There's a witch using a black book of spells," he explained. "She's casting spells on animals. William figured that out when we killed the first animal. We take them to Magia where they can be disposed of and not multiply. Fire seems to be the easiest way to destroy them."

"Animals?"

"Yes. Dead ones," Rapoza answered. "The witch has been going to locations where animals have been killed or euthanized. William thinks the carcasses have to be fresh for the spell to work. The ones we can't kill, the wizards and dragons take care of."

"The wizards? Have they been coming here?"

"I don't think they can," Lima answered. "Something about unbalancing the fabric of time, whatever that means."

I found all of this every interesting. I had to be careful about what questions I asked. I didn't want to change anything because they were talking.

"Have you been going into Magia a lot?" I asked.

"Three or four times a day," Rapoza answered. "The animals have been trying to enter this house for days. It's mostly when *you're* home," he said, pointing to me with his glass. "They want you in the worse way. William said that time was running out and the darkness was getting desperate."

"How does William know that time is running out?" I asked.

"That white book of spells, it told him."

"The white book of spells, speaks?" I asked surprised.

"It does to him," Moe said. "We all saw it when the guard brought it to him. He opened it up and he went into some coma or something. He kept mumbling that time was running out."

Lima poured himself another drink.

"I'm just glad we didn't have to kill this kid," he said, motioning to me. "After what the wizard warned us about, I thought we would be cutting him into pieces."

"At least you get to kill," Sean said. "My job is to push those animals to you. Nothing I do hurts them, but at least I can make sure you can."

"What do you mean?" I quickly asked.

"They don't see him," Rapoza answered. "It's the weirdest thing. They run right past him and straight to us. It's like he's not even there. William said they only see us because we've never killed anything before."

"So, they can't see someone that has taken a life before?" I asked.

"Guess not," Moe answered. "What do you think that means?"

"It means you're letting my glass get empty," Rapoza said, sliding his glass over.

I was about to ask another question when William stormed in, holding Fish by the neck.

"Don't kill me, William," Fish screamed.

Chapter Twenty-Five: Howl

We all jumped up when William lifted Fish up and threw him over the table. Glasses flew everywhere as the table collapsed. Fish quickly tried to drag himself away.

"Ethan, help me!" he shouted.

William waved his hand, making Fish come right back to him. He grabbed him by the neck again, then slammed him against the refrigerator.

"William," I said, trying to pull Fish away from him.

"Leave us!" William said, waving his hand at me.

I wasn't thrown far, but far enough to know he was serious. Sean and the warlocks didn't know what to do. I put my hand up, stopping them from trying to help. William glared at Fish as he put his face right up against his.

"I went out of my way to make you feel welcomed," William growled. "I gave you every tool needed so you wouldn't miss your home. I tolerated your *ridiculous* pranks on the dragons and guards. But you crossed the line when you tried to make fools out of the wizards."

Fish had such a terrified expression on his face as William leaned in even closer.

"Those wizards have done nothing but be at your beck and call. I am *disgusted* at what you tried to do to them."

"I…I'm sorry, William," Fish cried. "It was only a joke."

"A joke!" William shouted, as he slammed Fish against the refrigerator again. "Does my home seem like a joke to you? You have no respect, no honor. There isn't a single redeeming quality about you that is worth saving."

He tossed Fish across the kitchen and straight into a cabinet. I never saw William so angry in my life. I thought he would kill Fish as he scowled down at him.

"You are no longer welcomed in Magia. And that is not a joke."

I was absolutely shocked when William turned to leave, and Fish threw a coffee cup at him. The cup missed William, and it was shattered on the wall. William slowly turned and faced Fish.

"What do you expect from me?" Fish shouted. "You want me to be miserable all the time, huh? Look what you've put us through. We've spent our whole lives guarding your daughter and risking everything. We lost Sammy, Javier *and* Joshua because we stayed by Thea's side, *and yours*! Do you really think all this doesn't affect me? You think I don't get nightmares?"

Fish had tears, streaming down his face.

"Excuse me if I try to find humor in my life. Sorry if I don't like thinking about how much I've truly lost. My daughter can't even live a normal life without being in some kind of danger all the time. Delia and I stopped having kids because of that. Who wants to bring a child into a life like this? It's always something, isn't it? A Black Witch, Wendell, and now hell? When does it end for *us?* When will it end for *them?*" he said, pointing at the warlocks. "Doesn't our happiness count? How many more people are you going to pluck out of their lives so they can help you?"

You could hear a pin dropped as Fish stormed out of the kitchen and up the stairs. William stood frozen, looking into space. I wanted to know what Fish had done, but knew it wasn't the time. Moments later, Netiri walked in.

"Hey, there is something going on in Ethan's room. Fish is in there."

"He's just upset," William answered. "We both are."

"No, I'm saying, there's something wrong with him. I heard glass breaking in the room. I tried to kick the door down, but something was holding it closed."

In an instant, we all ran out of the kitchen and up the stairs. Before even getting to Fish's room, William waved his hand at the door, ripping it off its hinges. When we ran in, the window was broken, and it had a piece of Fish's robe still on it.

"Quick, outside!" William shouted.

I pulled out my wand as it instantly grew into my staff. I mounted it and flew right out the window in search of Fish. Netiri was right behind me.

"Over there!" he pointed. "On the street!"

There was something big dragging Fish away. I couldn't make out what it was, but it had a tail. We both flew faster as the beast-like thing began to maul Fish. The creature put its head up and began to howl. The howling sent echoes into the sky. You could actually see the pulsations in the wind. We flew down as the beast began to rip away his robe with its mouth.

"He's going to kill him!" Netiri shouted.

"The hell he is," I heard from behind us.

It was my father, and he flew past us like a bullet. My father flew over and kicked whatever that thing was right in the head. He jumped off his staff and pulled out his whip. Netiri and I landed right next to him, our swords held tightly in our hands. I've never seen anything so ugly in my life. The thing was about eight feet tall. It had what I could describe as rotted skin. It was covered in warts and puss. The puss oozed from its skin and sent an odor I can't even describe. If vomit could spoil, it would smell like that.

I noticed the puss was dripping all over Fish's body. Wherever the puss fell, it would sound like dripping water on a hot surface. My father raised his whip, cracked it and lashed out at the beast. The whip made contact, but it didn't seem to hurt the beast.

"James, I think the puss is acid," Netiri said, pointing at Fish.

Fish's skin was slowly melting away. My father cracked his whip again, trying to move the beast away from Fish. I tried waving my hand at it, but my magic only bounced off its skin. I quickly jumped back on my staff. I thought maybe I could fly by quickly and grab Fish. Before I could attempt it, William beat me to the punch. He flew by so fast that he seemed like a flash of light. Fish looked like a kite when William snatched him away by his ankle.

The beast began to howl again. This time, his howls were answered. We began to attack it, trying to cut it down with our swords. My father swung his whip high, aiming for the beast's head. The beast wouldn't look at us, wouldn't fight back. It was like we weren't even there.

I spun around when I heard what sounded like a herd of cattle.

"Oh shit," I said, when I saw about twenty more beasts, running our way.

Netiri was facing the other way.

"Oh shit, is right," he said, tapping me on the shoulder.

I looked over my shoulder. There were about fifty more beasts, headed our way.

"Good luck," I said to Netiri, as I braced myself.

"Nice knowing you, kid."

My father began to crack his whip on the ground. I knew he did that to give it more power. The more he cracked it, the more damage it would do. I didn't know if we would be able to kill them. After what the warlocks told me, it wasn't likely.

"I'll take the left, you both take the right," my father instructed.

"Leave some for us," Sean said, spinning his two swords around.

Rapoza and his men stood next to Sean, their swords beaming with light. The beast began to howl the moment the warlocks got there. We braced ourselves for the battle. When the stampede of beasts got to us, they ran right past us and straight to Sean and the warlocks. I swung my sword at one creature about to attack Rapoza. I was shocked when my sword did nothing but bounce back.

"What the hell?" my father said, when he, too, couldn't kill them.

The warlocks began to attack one beast after another. With every strike they made, the beast would cry out like a wounded dog.

"Get out of our way!" Rapoza shouted, when we kept trying to help.

I began to hear sirens a good distance away. The neighbors all around us began coming out of their homes. The sound of wounded dogs was loud. You would have thought we were slaughtering hundreds of them.

"Now! Sean shouted.

Rapoza pulled something from his pocket, slammed it on the ground, and continued fighting. A white cloud soon formed around them. I could no longer see them, but I could hear the battle. Police cars, with sirens blaring, began to pull up all around us. My father quickly put his whip away.

"Ethan, Netiri, your swords."

We both quickly shrunk our swords back into our wands. We placed them in our pockets as we put our hands in the air. The officers already had their guns pointed right at us.

"Get on the ground, now!" one shouted.

We followed instructions as the officers moved closer to us.

"Put your hands behind your back!"

"What do we do?" Netiri asked.

I looked towards the battle; the white cloud was still there. It had become unusually silent. I no longer heard the sound of wounded dogs. I couldn't hear Sean or the warlocks. Were they dead?

"I don't know," I answered.

My father noticed the same thing I had.

"What the hell is going on?" he said, as he placed his hands behind his back.

The officers began to search us.

"Any weapons or needles I should know about?" one of them asked.

"No officer," my father answered.

We kept our eyes on the white cloud. It looked more like mist now. The warlocks were gone, so were the animals. My father and I looked at each other.

"Magia," he mouthed to me.

I already knew that's where they had gone. The dragons were probably setting the animals on fire by now.

"What is this about, officer?" my father asked.

"We'll get to that," one of the offers answered.

They put handcuffs on us, then pulled us to our feet. I kept looking around for William. This would be a good time for him to work his magic. I had no idea what to do. There were humans around, and I didn't want to make a mistake.

"Where are the dogs?" one officer asked.

"Dogs?" my father answered. "I'm afraid I don't know what you're talking about."

The second officer flashed a light on our faces.

"Neighbors called; said they heard dogs being hurt. What did you do with them?"

"We didn't see any dogs," my father said.

When the two officers got a glazed look in their eyes, I knew William was close by.

"Took you long enough," my father said.

One by one, the neighbors began going back into their homes. The handcuffs opened up and dropped to the ground. The lights from the police cars stopped flashing. The officers simply started walking back to their cars. I looked back to where the mist had been. There was still nothing there.

When William came out from the darkness, I saw something strange about the way he looked. He was like a statue, pale and stone-faced. I looked down as his hands that were shaking.

"How is Fish doing?" my father asked, as he picked up the handcuffs.

William didn't answer and put his head down; something he *never* did. I knew the news was bad.

"William?" my father said.

"I think you'd better get back to the house," William said softly. "We'll need to pick up Delia and bring her here."

"William, how is Fish?" my father asked again.

William wouldn't look up.

"I am truly sorry, James. I did everything I possibly could."

"Oh no," Netiri whispered.

"Fish!" my father shouted, as he ran toward the mansion.

Chapter Twenty-Six: Idiot

I could hear my father sobbing as I ran up the stairs. He kept yelling and telling Fish to wake up. William stayed in the hallway, a blank look in his eyes as he stared into space.

"Fish, wake up!" my father was saying, when I walked in. "Wake up!"

He had Fish in his arms, rocking him back and forth. You could see Fish's bones in the areas the acid had hit him. There were deep bite marks, all over his body. I was thankful his suffering had ended.

"I'm so sorry, Fish. I'm so sorry," my father cried.

I knew how much my father loved Fish. He always called him his brother. My father always said that he and Fish shared the greatest friendship he had ever known and was proud to call him friend.

I decided to leave my father and give him a moment with Fish alone. I planned on asking Netiri to come with me to get Delia. I wasn't planning on giving her the news. It wasn't my place to do that. We also had to tell my mother. She loved Fish, too and was going to take the news badly. I thought of poor Vera. Who was going to tell her? Better yet, would they tell her right away?

I was about to walk out when something caught my eye. At first, I thought my father was causing Fish's fingers to move. When I got closer, I saw a small sign of life.

"He's not dead," I quickly said. "He just moved his finger."

"William!" my father shouted.

He picked Fish up in his arms and told me to put on my ring. I was about to slip it on when William came in and put his hand over mine.

"It's too late," he said. "He's already dead."

"William, he moved his finger," I pointed out.

William's face lit up.

"What?"

"His finger, he moved it," I said again.

"Put him down, James," William said, reaching for one of his many jars.

"We have to take him to Magia," my father said, with Fish still in his arms.

"There's no time to explain," William answered. "Put him on the bed, quickly."

William must have waved his hand at Fish about a million times. I knew he was sending healing magic to him. You could see his magic curving around Fish's body. William opened the jar, pulled out some leaves, and began placing them all the wounded areas.

"Take him to Magia!" my father shouted again. "The river will heal him much faster!"

"I can't!" William shouted back.

He took a deep breath, then continued working on Fish. William repeatedly cast spell after spell on him. Fish was laminating with streams of energy that were coming from William. About two hours had passed, and William was still working on him. I couldn't understand why William wouldn't take him to Magia. The River of Life would have already healed him.

"Why won't you take him to Magia?" my father kept pleading.

William ignored him every time. He just kept trying to heal Fish over and over again. When I tried using my own magic on Fish, William pushed me away.

"I will heal him!" William shouted. "Just leave the room, please."

Netiri and I cleaned up the mess in the kitchen. I had offered to make coffee for my father, but he wouldn't leave Fish's side. They decided to wait on bringing Delia. William said he didn't want her to see Fish this way. I didn't question Sean and the warlocks when they returned. I had already solved that puzzle. I told them what happened after they left. They were very sorry to hear about Fish.

Before I knew it, it was daylight. I hadn't got a moment of sleep. Then again, neither had William nor my father. I went upstairs to see how Fish was doing. When I walked in, my father was coming out of a vortex. He handed William some flowers, and went back in. I was about to question it, but my father came right back out with more flowers.

"Are these faster than the first batch?" he asked William.

The vortex disappeared as my father sat on the bed next to Fish. I could see dark circles under Williams's eyes. I don't think he stopped or sat down to rest once.

"We'll try more of the water next," William answered. "All we can do is sit and wait now."

"Is he suffering?" my father asked, looking down at Fish.

William looked away and didn't answer. I knew he felt bad about their fight. They both said horrible things to one another. It was in the heat of the moment. I know I wasn't blaming William for what happened to Fish. Although I think William was blaming himself.

"William, he moved his finger again," my father said, getting to his feet.

William quickly began looking Fish over. After checking his pulse, he seemed to breathe in a sigh of relief.

"I think he's going to make it, James."

"I'll stay with him, William. Why don't you go get some rest? At least I took a nap."

"No. I'm staying here, with him. Some coffee would be nice, though."

"I'll go get it," I said to him.

"Make that two," my father said.

I nodded and headed downstairs. Moments later, I was back with a pot of coffee and three cups.

"Would either one of you like something to eat?" I offered.

They both shook their heads. I placed the coffee on a table and poured the coffee.

"William, what was going on when you left with Fish?" my father asked. "That's why I came here last night. I saw you both leaving Magia."

William looked away and didn't answer. I knew he really didn't want to talk about it.

"Your coffee," I said, holding it out to my father.

"Thank you, Ethan."

William took a seat next to the bed as I held out his coffee. His hands were shaking when he took the cup from me.

"I can stay with him if either one of you want to get some rest?" I said, as I poured myself a cup.

"I'm staying here," William answered.

Two days passed and William never left the room. My father had to go tell Delia a lie about Fish so she wouldn't worry. William begged him not to mention the condition Fish was still in. In those two days, William didn't sleep, didn't eat. He didn't do anything but stay with Fish. William also told Viola's guardians to keep her there until he sent for them.

The warlocks had been waiting on William to tell him about the other night. But William wouldn't see or talk to anyone. By the fourth day, my concern for William grew. Netiri and I tried to get him to eat, but he would only shake his head and look the other way. Today, I was determined to help him. Whatever guilt he was feeling, he had to let it go.

I knocked on the door. He never answered. When I walked in, William was just staring into space. I looked at Fish, I could already see new skin growing. I closed the door behind me and took a seat.

"Can I make you something to eat?" I offered.

He only stared into space.

"William, he's going to be okay."

He looked straight ahead, still staring blankly.

"Do you know why I couldn't take him into Magia and heal him?" he asked.

He spoke, that was progress.

"I don't know," I answered.

"When I told him he was no longer welcomed in my kingdom, Magia closed its doors to him."

"You didn't mean that, William. You were both…"

"I meant it… then," he said, cutting me off. "I said horrible things to him. I told him he didn't have one quality that was worth saving."

"It was the heat of the mom…"

"Don't make excuses for me, Ethan. I'm the King of Magia, and I should have known better."

He looked at Fish.

"Even the flowers from my kingdom didn't want to help him. I was ashamed to tell James they were doing nothing for him. I allowed anger to fill my heart. Magia was not happy their king was upset."

He held Fish's hand.

"He's right you know, about what he said. I've taken so much from them and given so little in return. They've spent their lives standing by Thea's side. How can you repay something like that?"

"They did it out of love for her," I said. "Fish told me that he would do it all over again."

"And I said he had no honor," he said, shaking his head.

He went back to staring into space. I couldn't take seeing him like this anymore. He was blaming himself, and maybe even punishing himself.

"William, you have to let it go. This wasn't your fault. You just got angry. We all get angry, but we get over it. He's going to be fine."

"Will I still be allowed to be funny?" Fish mumbled.

William quickly rose to his feet.

"Fish, are you in pain?" he asked him.

Fish slowly opened his eyes and looked at William.

"I'm such an idiot," he said. "I'm sorry I embarrassed you. I felt bad the moment I left the kitchen. I never thought you would sic your dogs on me."

William smiled.

"You're lucky I didn't send the dragons."

"Yeah, that would have been worse," Fish answered.

His voice was weak, but at least he was awake and talking.

"How about some food?" William asked. "I can make all your favorites."

Fish's eyes spilled over as he looked into William's eyes.

"I'm sorry, William."

William nodded as huge tears welled up.

"Forgive me as well, Fish."

"We're not going to kiss or anything, are we?" William laughed a little.

"Would you settle for a kiss on the forehead?"

"As long as there's no tongue," Fish answered.

William asked me to get a message to my father that Fish was awake. He said to also tell Delia that she was needed here. He said he would be the one to tell her what happened.

"The warlocks have been waiting to speak with you," I told him, before leaving.

"One moment, Ethan."

"Yes?" I said, from the door.

William reached into his pocket, pulled out a small bottle, and handed it to me.

"What's this?" I asked, looking down at it.

"A little bit of cheer," he answered. "It is safe to drink."

I looked at the bottle. There wasn't anything written on it. I placed it in my pocket and turned to leave again.

"Ethan," William called.

"Yes."

His eyes were spilling over again.

"I have faith in you. I always have."

"I know," I smiled.

Netiri was downstairs when I walked into the kitchen. I gave him the good news about Fish and asked him if he would deliver the message to my father. He said yes and disappeared into a vortex. I would have gone myself, but I was in a lot of pain today. I knew I needed to see Doctor Crowley. I think the stress about Fish and William made my nerve pain flair up.

I grabbed a jacket, tucked my wand in my pocket, and headed out the door. I can't explain the feeling I got when I saw what was happening outside. The ground was covered in snow. When did that happen? I knew I hadn't been outside in a few days, but how did I not notice this?

I closed the door behind me and looked out in amazement. My mother's stories did not do the snow justice. It was far more beautiful than I ever imagined. Even the fake snow I used on my little Christmas village wasn't the same. This snow was fluffy and light. It came down like beautiful white crystals. It gently fell in my hand as I held it out. There was truly no comparison to real snow. No spell could even come close. There was a beautiful silence about it all. My footsteps sounded muffled as I took a few steps. The cars that drove by sounded as if they had driven over cotton.

"I just want to shovel this before it piles up," I heard someone say.

Rapoza was coming out from the side of the house. He was holding a large shovel in his hand. Lima and Moe soon joined him, both holding shovels.

"How's the kid?" Rapoza asked.
"He's going to be okay," I smiled.
"And the wizard?"
"Both doing better."

"Good. Hey, do you have any salt?" Rapoza asked me.

"Salt?"

"Yes, you now, to salt the driveway?"

I couldn't understand why they would need salt. I tried to think of my mother's stories but couldn't recall anything about salt.

"No worries," Rapoza said, spitting on the shovel.

Moe and Lima did the same. Their spells began to grow sharp looking teeth on the edge of the shovels. When they shoveled the snow, it came off the walkway like butter. I offered to help them, but Rapoza said it wouldn't take long.

I bent down to touch the snow. I grabbed a handful and made a ball. It was odd to the touch. I always thought ice was hard, but this was very soft.

"What's the matter?" Rapoza asked. "First time seeing snow?"

"Yes," I answered. "I can't imagine it being more beautiful in the North Pole."

"The North Pole?" Moe laughed. "What's next, you going to see Santa Claus?"

The others laughed and I wasn't sure why.

"I'm hoping he'll allow me to fly with him around the world," I said. "I want to see how he does it in one night."

They laughed again.

"My mother and he are very good friends," I informed them. "She's known him since she was a child. She says he smells like a warm cookie."

More laughter.

"Ethan, all mothers tell that to their children," Moe said. "They also tell them that Santa keeps a list of who is naughty and nice."

"Yes, my mother went through that list with him one year. He was very tired that day, so my mother helped him. She said it was her fault that he didn't get any sleep the day before."

Rapoza slowly stopped laughing when he saw I wasn't kidding. He looked at Moe and Lima, then back at me. I wasn't sure what he was thinking.

"Would you like to meet him?" I asked. "Now that I'm in the human world, I'm sure my mother will ask him to come here."

"Guys, I don't think he's kidding," Rapoza said.

Moe laughed some more.

"Ron, come on. Santa Claus?"

"Did you believe in dragons before?" Rapoza asked hm.

"Talking dragons," Lima added.

I smiled and looked at the beautiful scenery again. The snow was truly taking my breath away. Now that I knew what it looked and felt like, I would make some changes to my little Christmas village.

"Have a good day, gentlemen," I said, making my way down the driveway.

"Can it be true?" I heard Moe say.

Chapter Twenty-Seven: Nor'easter

    I took my time walking to Doctor Crowley's office. I wanted to enjoy this beautiful day. I think the snow was making my nerve pain feel worse. I didn't care. Walking in the snow was worth it. I knew I should have told someone where I was going. After what happened at Crowley's office, I should have taken precautions.

    I continued walking without care. I was enjoying this feeling the snow had given me. I was in a good mood. I had no bad thoughts, no desire to kill anyone, no feeling of despair. I would say the snow brought out the good in me. I wasn't feeling my broken heart, either. Nothing seemed to be bothering me today. I took a deep breath and took it all in.

    Salem was a picture-perfect postcard right now. The snow just made the town look even more magical. I looked for the biggest tree I could find. I wanted to see how snow truly looked when it filled the branches. I passed a small park filled with trees. I took a seat on a bench and just looked at the trees. My mother was right; the snow did look like ice cream when it filled the branches. I was going to miss this little town. I could see all the qualities my mother had fallen in love with. It was a certain feeling you got from this place. It was hard to explain, but it charmed you, just like Magia would.

The pain reminded me where I was supposed to be. I got up and continued walking to Crowley's office. My shoes were covered in snow when I arrived. I had to shake it off before going in. My feet felt numb and cold. The snow had picked up and was really coming down.

"You're too late," Erika said, when I walked in. "We're closing early because of the snow. Most of the staff went home already."

Erica was the front desk nurse. She was there the day I was pulled into hell. I was very glad William had erased that horrible memory.

"I'm sorry if I'm late," I said, stepping up to the counter. "I was admiring the snow."

"Admiring?" she said, making a face. "You haven't been in New England very long, have you?"

Erica was Puerto Rican and had light brown hair and brown eyes. She had a crooked smile and a rounded nose. She was very friendly and had a slight accent. It always surprised me how many witches held jobs in Salem.

"I suppose not," I laughed.

"Okay, let me go see if Doctor Crowley is still here. Just have a seat and I'll be right back."

There was a large waiting area just behind the front desk. I took a seat and looked out a big window. The snow was getting heavier by the minute. I still couldn't get over how beautiful it looked.

"Ethan, I didn't know you were here," a voice said.

It was Kelly. She was coming out of the office with a tall gentleman. I instantly knew the man was a warlock.

"Ethan, this is Steve Pimental. He's the director here at the clinic. We were just leaving."

"Nice to meet you," I said, shaking his hand.

"You look familiar," he said, squinting his eyes. "Haven't I seen you before?"

"I don't think so."

"Yes, I have seen you. It was at the Fall River Country Club. You got turned away because you were wearing jeans."

"Did we meet?" I asked.

I tried to think back and remember if he was sitting with Rapoza. He was a tall man, with dark, thinning hair that was starting to turn gray. I couldn't remember him from that day.

"No," he answered. "The only reason I remember you is because the waitresses wouldn't stop looking at you. I was at the bar and that made me look back and see who they were staring at."

"I see," I answered.

"Well, if you ever go back there, just don't wear jeans. The club is always looking for new members. The food is good, too. I know the chef. She calls me, Moses."

"Moses?"

Just then, Erika came back and said Crowley had already left. I said thank you and apologized for missing my appointment again.

"We are closing early today because of the snow," Kelly explained.

"The snow makes you close early?" I asked.

"It does if it's a nor'easter. Don't you watch the news?"

"I'm afraid I don't watch much television."

I didn't bother asking what a nor'easter was and thanked her for her time. I went back outside and decided to just enjoy the snow. It had really picked up quite a bit. I looked over at the nearby pier and noticed how the snow looked at it fell into it looked. I made my way over and found a bench. I wiped off the snow and took a seat.

I put my face up to the snow and smiled. How could anyone be upset because it was coming down so much? It was giving Magia a run for its money. Magia never looked this beautiful to me before. Why didn't we get snow? I was starting to realize that this realm had magic of its own.

I looked over my shoulder when I heard the sound of something scraping. I saw Kelly with some kind of stick in her hand. She was using the stick to push the snow off her car. She seemed to be having a hard time, so I decided to go help her.

"Need a hand?" I asked.

"Oh, you scared me," she said, putting her hand on her chest.

"I apologize."

"What are you still doing here?" she asked.

"Just enjoying the snow. Here, let me help you," I said, taking the stick from her.

"I would use a spell," she said, looking around. "But these days, there's cameras everywhere."

I agreed with her and tried to figure out how this thing worked. I saw the small, flat surface and quickly realized what to do with it. I began to scrape the snow from her windshield.

"I'm sorry you couldn't get the nerve blocks today," she said.

"I'm starting to think I wasn't meant to," I laughed.

I was walking around the car to get to the other side when I spotted something odd. It was Melanie, and she was placing hats on the edge of the pier. I couldn't understand why she kept leaving them near the water.

"Melanie at that again?" Kelly asked.

"You know her?"

"Yes, she comes in for nerve blocks."

"What did you mean by, *she's at that again*?"

Kelly stood next to me as we watched Melanie placing the hats.

"She's been doing that for days. I can see her from my office window. Then she sits there, waits on that old lady to come get them."

"You've seen her?"

"Yes. I think the old woman is wearing a costume, because she looks dreadful. I've been trying to figure out what the hats are for."

I remembered the map I'd found at Irene's house. I was right about the marking being water. Is this where the Black Witch was hiding now? Was she in the water, or near it?

I finished cleaning the snow off her car, I said goodbye to Kelly and ducked out of sight. I found a store that had an awning over the entrance and stood under it. Kelly was right; Melanie was waiting for her sister. I knew the old woman Kelly spoke of was Irene. Melanie kept looking out towards the water, then placing more hats down. When she put down the last hat, she got into a gold-colored truck and waited.

I was starting to get cold as the snow got thicker. I wasn't really dressed for this weather. I cast a warming spell on myself as I kept my eye on Melanie's truck. I moved closer when Melanie suddenly got out. Then I saw her, Irene was standing by the pier. She had already picked up one of the hats. When Melanie got to her, Irene threw the hat into the water. The seemed to be arguing.

I moved closer, hoping I would be able to hear them talking. I ducked behind a truck and watched Irene kick another hat into the water. She didn't seem happy that Melanie was leaving them for her. As I looked closer at Irene, I noticed she didn't look as bad as she did the last time I saw her. In fact, she looked stronger. Don't get me wrong, she still looked like death but wasn't weak and failing. It was obvious she had that black book of spells in her possession again.

"I don't understand, then why did you ask me to make them for you again?" I heard Melanie say.

"Why did you change the spell you put in them?" Irene shot back.

"It's the same spell," Melanie answered. "I don't know what you're talking about?"

"You're so useless," Irene hissed at her. "I should have never contacted you again."

Her voice was so raspy. She had truly lost herself to the darkness again. I had hopes that I had gotten through to her, but as far as I could see, she was the old Irene again.

"Irene, we want to help you," Melanie cried. "You have something to live for now. Think of your daughter."

Irene raised her hand and struck Melanie across the face. I could hear her crackling laughter as Melanie fell to the ground.

"It took you long enough to get here," Irene said.

"What?" Melanie said, looking up at her sister.

"I almost went inside and got you," her raspy voice rang out.

"What are you talking about?" Melanie asked, confused.

"It's a good thing, the snow," Irene said. "It makes it so easy to sneak up on wizards like you."

I instantly felt something bite down on my leg. I looked down as my instincts made me kick whatever was biting me, away. The beast rolled a few feet, then came back at me. I tried reaching for my wand, but another beast bit down on my hand and pulled me forward. I fell to the ground as more beasts began to attack me. I knew my magic was going to do nothing to help me.

I could feel their pus burning and melting away the areas where they would bite down. I was being mauled as I desperately tried to get to my feet. I knew my only hope would have been the warlocks, but I didn't tell them where I was going. An idea suddenly came to me. I didn't know if I could pull it off, but I had to try. I took my free hand and managed to pull out my phone.

"Call Netiri," I said into it.

Moments later.

"Hey, kid. You finally used it, huh?"

"Netiri, the beasts!"

"Where are you, Ethan?"

The phone was snatched away from me before I could answer him. One beast grabbed me by the neck and started dragging me through the snow. I was being dragged closer and closer to the water.

"Irene, don't do this!" Melanie screamed.

There must have been twenty beasts on me, each of them biting and scratching my skin away. I began to feel the intense heat the closer we got to the water. Not even the snow was helping to cool it off. I tried desperately to get my neck out of the beast's mouth. It dragged me away as if I were a feather. I waved my hand several times, but my magic did nothing but bounce off their pus-covered skin. The heat became more intense, and so did the pain. I would have sworn I was burning alive.

"Netiri," I cried.

Had Netiri heard me? Did he know where I was? I was losing hope as the beast began to drag me down a ramp. I inhaled as much air as I could when I realized they were about to jump into the water.

"Irene!" was the last thing I heard Melanie scream.

Chapter Twenty-Eight: Keeper of the Gates

    I was disappointed when the icy water did nothing to calm the heat inside me. I felt I had red, hot lava flowing through my veins. The more the beast swam down with me, the more intense the heat was getting. How much more of this could I take?
The beast swam deeper and deeper as I tried to pull myself free. I began to see the ocean floor splitting open. Soon after, fire began rising up from the cracks.
    A yellow mist began mixing with the water. I intuitively knew it was sulfur. My nose began to bleed as my lungs begged me for air. I was drowning and living through my last moments of life. If this was the way I was going to die, then I would die thinking of Viola. I allowed the thought of her to take me away. I wasn't looking forward to the suffering I knew was awaiting me. My body felt tired and drained. It was time to let go and find my peace.
    As the beast swam through the cracks, I finally felt warm air hitting my face. The beast dropped me

on the ground as I filled my lungs with air. They began to circle me as they howled at their mistress. I knew she was here. What was she waiting for?

I rose to my feet when that crackling laughter filled my head. The beasts kept circling me as I looked around.

"Where are you?" I shouted.

Huge, red flames roared and burned all around me. The smell of mildew and sulfur made me want to vomit. I spun around when I heard the sound of a cage being rattled. A dark dragon-like beast began moving closer to the iron gates. It looked angry and wanted out. It would slap the gates with its tail before turning.

"No one is going to find you here," a raspy voice said.

"Show your face, Irene!"

"That's not going to work this time, wizard boy. I'm not falling for your tricks."

I was thrust hard against a wall. Skeleton-like hands came out and grabbed my arms and legs. I felt something piercing my back and side. The hands pulled me repeatedly, and again I felt something piercing me. I could feel warm blood running down my leg.

"There, that's better," Irene said, coming out of the darkness.

I was trying not to let this place get to me, but I was having a challenging time holding back my sobs. It seemed as if the sadness of this place had been doubled. I felt despair like never before. Then, an overwhelming heat began spreading throughout my body again. I even checked under my feet to see if I had been set ablaze. The rattling became louder as the dark beast put its face closer to the gates. I saw two sharp talons, taking hold of the gates. When the image put its face against bars I thought I would die of fright.

Its dragon-like eyes were made of pure evil. Their red glare was penetrating right into my soul. Its teeth dripped lava and drops of fire. The skin was red and oozing with pus. It looked demonic, a true and real monster. It shook the gates as it hissed and glared my way. My whole body was shaking from the fear that shook me.

"Irene," I cried. "Please help me. I'm bleeding."

"Help *you*?" she said, moving closer. "Why would I help you? You left me here, remember?"

She was holding the black book of spells. She seemed to be getting stronger the closer she held it to her body. The skull faces on the cover were moving. They were lost souls that Satan had claimed for his own.

"Irene, please."

"Even my sister didn't help me," she continued. "She thought those stupid hats she left near the water were going to change me."

"Irene, I'm dying," I pleaded.

"You can't die yet, wizard boy. You haven't opened the gates yet."

"I will never open them," I sobbed.

"You will when your mother gets here."

"What?"

"Your life, for hers," she said, looking toward the gates.

I looked at the book of spells again. If I could just free one hand, I could take it from her. Maybe being away from it would snap her out of it?

"Irene, you have to help me."

"Stop saying that name!" she shouted. "That witch died when she killed her children. She will burn in hell for what she's done."

"I can get you out of here," I said, trying to convince her. "You just have to be strong and fight your way out with me."

She laughed that stupid laugh of hers. I was becoming irritated when she began to laugh even louder. My mood was changing, and I wasn't sure if I liked it. I started to get angrier when the heat became unbearable. That stupid beast was making it hotter. Irene's laughter started piercing through me like needles. My blood began to boil with fury.

"Shut up!" I shouted at her. "You're right, you do deserve to burn in hell for what you've done. What was I thinking when I thought I could help you? You deserve to rot in this demonic place."

Her laughter abruptly stopped. She smiled and walked over to me. She reached around me and pulled my wand from my pocket. I didn't like the evil look on her face when she looked down at a wolf-beast. One beast came forward, almost kneeling before her.

"You know what to do," she said, placing my wand in its mouth. "Go find her and bring her to me."

I knew she was giving the beast my wand to show my mother they had taken me. I sobbed at the thought of them bringing her here.

Irene faced me again.

"We *all* win today," she said, in her raspy voice. "I'll get to walk the earth again, but I won't be walking alone," she said, looking toward the gates.

The beast slammed the gates with its tail. It seemed to be sending Irene a message when it blew fire our way. Irene nodded and opened the book of spells. A loud ticking sound was coming from its pages. I noticed with every ticking sound the book made, the bars to the gates would get thicker.

Irene slammed the book shut but it didn't stop the ticking. She was angry about something. I think it was something about the book. Irene jumped back when the beast sent fire at her again. This time, Irene fell to the ground.

"Forgive me, Master," she said, holding her hands up. "I will find it, I swear."

I tried not to think of the heat as I looked down at Irene. Something wasn't right. Something about the book had angered the beast. It wasn't just the ticking sound, either. She told the dragon beast she would find it; what was Irene trying to find? She also said she would walk the earth again. There was only one person I knew that wanted that more than anything. It was the Black Witch.

"Where is Irene?" I asked.

That evil smile was unmistakable as she glared my way. She picked up the book, walked over to me, and hit me across the face with it. She hit me again when I began to laugh.

"You can't control her anymore, can you? She is fighting you. She's getting stronger, isn't she?"

"Silence!" she shouted.

"Irene," I yelled. "I know you can hear me. You can fight her. You can cast her out and not let her back in. Just think of Viola!"

The Black Witch began to strike me over and over again with the book. Apparently, that wasn't enough for her. She threw the book down and commanded two of the wolf-beasts to attack me. The Black Witch began grabbing her head. She tried reaching for the book of spells again but fell to the ground as she grabbed at her chest.

A dark cloud began coming out of her. An old, wrinkled woman fell to the ground as the dark cloud floated above her. I turned away when the dark cloud began coming toward me. Would I be strong enough to fight it? Would my heart remember who I loved? I feared the answer to those questions as the cloud engulfed me. I began to get the feeling of utter love. My heart began racing as a soft hand touched my face. The wolf-beast slowly retreated.

"My lord," a raspy voice said.

"No," I said, keeping my eyes shut.

"Ethan, it wasn't me," Irene cried. "I didn't cast those spells on animals."

I opened my eyes and looked toward Irene. The dragon-beast sent a ball of fire to her. It must have been lava because when it hit Irene, she did nothing but gasp from the pain. It began to choke her and caused her to vomit.

"Leave her alone!!" I shouted at the beast.

I paid dearly for my bravery. The beast sent a single flame dancing its way to me. When it hit me, I thought my whole body exploded. I had never felt that kind of pain before, and I had felt pain many times. A loud, agonizing cry came from my soul and out my lips.

"I can make it stop," the raspy voice said.

I was trying not to look at her. I knew that beautiful woman would be standing in front of me. I was too weak to fight off her magic. I was certain that if I looked into her red eyes, the world would be over.

"Please, no," I sobbed.

"My lord," she said again.

Her voice was like a symphony of angels singing love songs in my ear. My heart began to ache for her. The more she touched my face, the more I wanted her. It was a feeling of love that made me feel like dying rather than be without her. The pain began to subside as she placed both hands on my face.

"Open your eyes," she sang.

Her request was like an order, one I couldn't refuse. I slowly opened my eyes, finding hers looking back at me. Her porcelain skin was more beautiful than I remembered. Her fiery, black hair was more dazzling than ever. She was the beauty of my dreams; the hopes that lived deep inside me. Her love took away my pain and gave me strength. I wanted to feel her, tell her how much I loved her.

"My Queen," I whispered.

"No," Irene cried.

Her red eyes sparkled like the stars. I got chills

every time her fingers touched my face. I looked down at her lips, angry because they seemed too far away.

"Kiss me," I said, leaning toward her.

Our beautiful moment was ruined when we heard someone screaming. I could hear something growling as it clawed its way through the earth. My queen stepped aside as her beast returned with a prize. There was not only one, but two prizes. My queen smiled as the beast dropped my mother and Viola on the ground.

"Well done," she said to them.

"Ethan," my mother said, trying to run at me.

The beast behind the gates blew fire at her. My mother screamed out in pain as she fell to the ground. Viola was curled up in a corner, frightened out of her mind. My queen lifted my mother up by the hair, then threw her body next to Viola. They both had marks from where the acid had fallen on them. My empress looked at my mother like she was something to eat. She had done what she never thought she could; she got my mother back in hell with her.

My queen walked over to Irene, then held out her hand. Irene wouldn't take her eyes off Viola.

"Give it to me," my queen growled at her.

Irene glance my way.

"I don't have it, mistress," she answered.

"It's not going to help you, witch. Nothing will change. Give it back to me now."

Again, Irene glanced at me.

"I don't have it."

"Liar!" my queen shouted.

I wanted to kill Irene for angering my queen. I began to fight and pull away at the hands that held me. How dare she speak to my queen that way?

"Respect your queen!" I shouted.

"Ethan, no," Viola cried.

The beast behind the gates seemed pleased by my reaction. He made the heat inside me die down and extinguish. Irene cried as my queen walked back to me. Her eyes were like ruby gems as she reached for my face.

"Kiss me," I said, again.

When the skeleton hands released me, I quickly took my empress into my arms. She felt like life itself. She filled every dream, every desire I ever had. She was the perfect woman, and now she was mine.

"Get away from him, you bitch!"

My queen was thrown to the ground as my mother ran and slapped me across the face.

"Wake up!" she screamed at me.

She turned and glared at my queen.

"You were no match for me the first time, and you're no match for me now, witch."

She waved her hand at my empress, sending her crashing into the gates of hell. The wolf-beasts tried to attack my mother, but my mother waved her hand and sent them crashing into my queen.

"You can't have him!" my mother shouted.

She looked down at Irene.

"Fight her. Pull out her heart!" she ordered.

Irene only rolled into a ball and looked at Viola. She wept as my mother tried to pull me away.

"No!" I said, pulling my hand out of hers.

"I wasn't asking!" she said, grabbing my hand again.

I pushed her to the ground, but was met with a boot, right to the face. It was Rapoza and his men. Netiri was with them, so was Sean. The warlocks began killing the wolf-like beasts. The gates began to rattle harder and harder.

"William said not to look at it," Rapoza said, as he swung at a beast.

It was my dream all over again. I knew I was about to kill these men. I looked at Netiri as he pointed his sword at me. It was then I knew it would be his sword that I would use to decapitate him. All the characters of my dream were here, all ready to die at my hand.

When my mother tried pulling me away again, the dragon-beast behind the gates became enraged. It began sending pearls of fire directly at all of them. I heard their screams of agony as they were thrust against a wall. They were paralyzed with pain; squirming and crying out. Their deaths would be an easy kill for me now. I saw Netiri's sword lying a few feet from me. I reached down to grab it.

"No, Ethan" Irene cried, wrapping her arms around my ankles. "Think of Viola."

I could hear more wolf-beasts being called into the room. It was the sound of cattle again, coming to help me and my queen. They entered the room by the hundreds. The dragon-like beast rattled the gates even harder. I locked eyes with him. I can't explain it, but I saw death itself in its eyes. I moved closer to the gates as my queen took her place behind me.

"Ethan, don't," Irene cried.

I leaned down and began to pry her fingers off my ankles. I leaned down even closer and placed my hand over her mouth. My queen was behind us, trying to see what I was doing. I could hear my mother's cries of agony, begging me to come back to her.

When I rose back up, I looked at the gates in front of me. I heard the ticking of the black book of spells. It was almost running out of time. The beast raised its talons, directing me toward the gates. A tall wall of fire began rising up behind him. You could see hundreds of demons within the fire, all waiting to be set free. They wore armor and carried weapons, their eyes red and demonic. I was the keeper of the gates, and I was about to fill the world with terror.

I looked over my shoulder at my queen. I held my hand out so she would join me. This was a moment I wanted to share with her.

"Ethan, no!" my mother cried.

My empress smiled and made her way to me. I knew the dragon-beast would reward her for her labor. We would both find a reward when this was over. Too bad William couldn't be here to witness this. It would be the only regret I would live with.

My queen picked up the black book of spells and joined me. I looked at the dragon beast, smiled, and put one of my hands in my pocket.

"Hey, did you know you had maggots all over your face?" Irene asked, the Black Witch. "You should really try some make-up. A shower wouldn't hurt, either."

The Black Witch looked at Irene, then at me. I smiled and showed her what I was holding. It was the small bottle of morphine William had given me. I emptied its contents into Irene's mouth when I placed my hands over it. I know William intended that bottle for me, but Irene needed it more than I did.

Before the Black Witch could react, I pulled out the ring the Tree of Life had given me. The dragon-beast blew fire to me, but it was too late. I waved my hand at the ring, shattering it and sending sparkles of light, all over the room. Magia's magic made a wall between me and the dragon-beast. Its fire bounced off it and was sent back to him and his demons. The wind picked up and began to spin around us. Irene got sucked in right before it turned and headed to us. The Black Witch tried running from me, but I held her back as we were pulled into a vortex.

Chapter Twenty-Nine: Dragon's Fire

The Black Witch screamed and scratched at me like a wild animal. I had my arm wrapped around her boney neck so she wouldn't pull away. I finally allowed myself to breathe in a sigh of relief. I didn't know how much longer I could keep up the charade. It hadn't been easy. I knew, even in my mind, I had to think evil thoughts. The dragon beast was watching me and I knew he would be looking for signs of deceit. When I locked eyes with it, I sensed he could see right into my soul. It was convinced that I had really become terrified of it.

"Wow, she's being so mean," I heard Irene say. "I think it's the maggots on her face."

I never saw the beautiful woman when I was in hell. I knew the whole time what the Black Witch looked like. I could see her skull crawling with maggots; her rotted flesh that was still hanging off her bones. It took everything I had to look into those red eyes and make her think I loved her. As William would put it, I put on quite the performance.

I began to sense another vortex, and it was spinning right next to us. The Black Witch was latched onto my arm by her teeth when the vortex spit us out. I pushed her aside and grabbed my throbbing arm. It felt like poison was going through it. I dragged the Black Witch out of the way when I heard the vortex forming. It began to spit everyone out. First it was Rapoza and the warlocks, then my mother, Viola and Netiri.

Attor and the dragons had formed a circle around the area. The wizards were hovering above on their staffs. It was Magia's army, ready to battle the evil that was here.

"Get out of the way!" William shouted.

I dragged the Black Witch back even further. The dragons glared at the area and primed themselves. My mother was limping when she took hold of Irene and moved her out of the way. Then the vortex began spitting out the wolf-beasts. There were hundreds of them, growling and howling at us. Their red eyes searching the area for their mistress.

"Help me!" the Black Witch shouted at them.

It was a sea of fire as the dragons blew an inferno at the beast. The smell of rotting flesh began to fill the air. Attor looked at a group of beasts, smiled, and sent blue flames of fire at them. Some tried to outrun the fire, but the wizards quickly evaporated them. There was no protection from hell to help them. Here in Magia, hell didn't stand a chance.

When all the beasts were gone, everyone looked at the Black Witch. She was still clutching the black book of spells. There were so many maggots on her skeletal body now, that they would drip down to the ground. My mother limped her way over and threw her in the middle of the circle. I wanted to laugh when the Black Witch tried making the earth open up.

"Abrir," she kept chanting.

"There is no escape," William said to her.

He began to slowly walk into the middle of the circle. The dragons moved closer to protect their king. William held his hand up to them.

"All is well."

The Black Witch was still trying to get the earth to open up for her. She kept casting the spell over and over again. When she saw William's feet, she looked up at him. Her red eyes were full of fury. She hissed at William and clutched the book of spells tighter. William leaned down in front of her, looking straight into her eyes. His appearance began to change. His grey hair turned brown; his body more muscular. A much younger William was looking back at her.

"You," the Black Witch gasped.

William smiled.

"It's been a long time, Agatha. I see you are still trying to find your king."

She clutched the book of spells even tighter.

"I killed you," she said, dragging herself back.

"Yes, that was the point," he answered. "I wanted you to think that your secrets died with me. I would have never been able to warn the next king of your treacherous ways if not for fooling you. I always knew you and your master would never change how you lure them in. As far as you knew, I've been dead for hundreds of years."

"Impossible!" she shouted.

It was then I realized why William couldn't go into hell to help me. Hell thought he was dead and gone. William knew too many secrets about hell. He knew how it would try to fool the next king and weaken him. I have to say, I was truly in awe of him.

"I am going to make you the same offer every king before me has," William said to her. "It's the same offer I was never able to offer you."

"Save your offers," she hissed back. "You will never offer me what my master has."

Her bones would make a funny sound every time she moved. It sounded like rattling stones.

"Very well," William answered. "I do, however, need to know how you got your hands on that black book of spells?"

She began to laugh that crackling noise of hers.

"What do we have here?" she teased. "I know something the great wizard doesn't?"

"Not for long," William answered.

He lunged forward and placed his hands over her skull. A horrible, terrified look washed across William's face. I don't know what he was seeing, but I was sure it was the deepest part of hell. When William was done, he began to change back to his current age. He let go of the Black Witch and took his place next to the dragons. William looked at Sean and gave him a nod.

The Black Witch began to dig at the ground, never letting go of that book of spells. Sean ran to William and handed him a white orb. The Black

Witch began hissing when she saw it. She kept trying to cast spells at herself, but nothing was working.

"Oh, she's trying to turn herself into black smoke," Irene said, pointing at her.

"Her powers are useless here," William answered.

William looked at the wizards and gave a signal. They quickly pulled out their wands and nodded at him. William pulled out his own wand and tossed the orb up high in the air. All the wizards, including William, pointed their wands and sent streams of magic right into the orb.

A white, billowing cloud began streaming out of the orb. I began to see the face of a woman forming inside it. Her eyes were like two shooting stars. They shined bright as streams of energy flowed through them. It was the White Witch. William had done it, he pulled off what I thought he never could. The Black Witch hissed and screamed at the cloud. She tightly held her grip on the book of spells as she tried to run away.

The wizards sent their magic around the dragons, blocking her way out.

"She looks angry," Irene said, in a drunken-like voice.

The woman in the cloud began to float out if it. She spread her arms and looked down at the Black Witch.

"You'll never take it from me!" she shouted.

The White Witch pointed at the book, sending a lightning strike right at it. The black book of spells began to turn to ashes and burn. The moment the book was sent back to hell, the White Witch was gone. Her purpose was complete.

"Guard yourselves," William warned.

The Black Witch began running into one wizard after another. She would only bounce off them and try another. I knew what she was doing. She was trying to get inside of anyone that was weak. When none of the wizards fell victim to her magic, she turned and looked at Irene.

No!" Viola screamed, when she realized she was going after Irene next.

Viola ran and threw herself in front of her mother; her arms spread in a protective way. Irene had tears in her eyes when Viola did that. She got to her feet and slowly pushed Viola aside. The Black Witch came at her, but Irene was ready.

"Her heart," my mother shouted.

Irene thrust her arm inside the Black Witch's chest. She let out a scream as she pulled out the heart, still beating in her hand. The Black Witch turned to smoke and just drifted into the air. We all cheered as Irene fell to the ground. My mother ran and waved her hand at the heart, sending it back to hell.

"Mother," Viola said, trying to help her up.

My mother held her back and told her to wait. Irene's body began to change. The wrinkles in her skin began to fade away. Her hair turned brown and got thicker. There were no more bald spots or threads of grey. When Irene looked up, a beautiful pair of green eyes were filled with tears.

My mother let Viola go. She ran into her mother's arms and started crying. The dragons began breathing fire into the air. William gave my mother some kind of signal.

"Irene," my mother said, leaning down. "There is someone else here to see you."

The dragons began spreading apart. When they cleared a path, Melanie was standing behind them. Melanie held her hand over her mouth, unable to stop her choking sobs. Irene looked at her sister with those emerald, green eyes.

"Sister," she cried.

Melanie broke into a run, choking on her sobs the whole way. It was a moment Melanie had worked so hard and so long for. She never lost hope, never gave up on her sister. I think that's what made me try so hard for her. It was that hope in her eyes that showed me how powerful love really was. Everyone had tears in their eyes as the two sisters embraced. I smiled as I slowly fell to my knees.

"Ethan!" my mother shouted.

I fell over and closed my eyes. My work was done. It was time for me to finally rest. I was tired of all the pain. Tired of the heartbreak and sorrow. I just wanted to drift away and sleep for days.

"He's full of blood," I heard Sean say.

"There's something in his back," Rapoza pointed out.

I began to get the sensation of floating in the air. I knew William had me in his arms. I was still disappointed that he wasn't there to witness what I'd done. I fooled the devil himself and pulled off the impossible. I never had to take one single life. I refused to allow my dream to play itself out. When

Netiri was pointing his sword at me, I allowed the love I have for him to flow through me. I thought of our friendship and the times we spent together. It made me realize that evil could never make me kill him.

"The most powerful spell I know," I heard William whisper.

I was grateful I didn't pick Viola to think about. I was still heartbroken over our shattered romance. Evil would have taken advantage of that and turned me against her. Netiri was the perfect vessel. He was the one I had been around the most. He was my brother and friend. There was nothing I wouldn't do for him. In the end, it really was love that kept me strong.

"Almost there," I heard William say.

I soon felt the calmness of the River of Life. I could feel the current taking all my pain away. I felt proud of myself. I proved everyone wrong and never became the monster they expected I would be. Not one person was skinned alive or tortured by me. Although my mood changed on a daily basis, I never allowed my soul to get dark again. I couldn't change the way I killed in the past, but I knew moving forward, I would never take another life. I would be the king this land expected me to be. I would show the Tree of Life that it had chosen the right person to rule.

I drifted into a space in my head, one where I could find solace. I didn't want to think anymore. My mind was weak from exhaustion. I didn't want to hear any voices. I felt my mind needed a long break. I felt when William took hold of me, wrapping his arms tightly around me.

"Well done, my son," he whispered in my ear as I slowly awakened.

I could hear the roar of a waterfall as I opened my eyes. I was lying in bed in our old cottage. I couldn't remember the last time I felt so rested. I began to scan the room. My mother was the first person I saw. My father was standing next to her. They both had big smiles on their faces. My mother quickly sat on the bed with me when she realized I was awake.

"Ethan how are you feeling?" she asked.

I sat up. "Actually, I'm feeling rested, Mother."

She smiled. "Everyone has been waiting for you. There is somewhat of a celebration going on."

"Celebration?" I asked.

My father laughed.

"You'll see," he said, tapping my feet.

I jumped out of bed and stretched my arms. There was such a feeling of calmness in my soul. It was over. There was no longer a need to fear the unknown. At least for now, I could finally seek out my happiness. I knew I had a lot of work to do. I would first make things right with Viola. Even if it took a hundred years to win her back, I was prepared to wait for her.

My parents said they would be waiting outside and left the room. I changed into a robe and put on my shoes. I couldn't wait to see what the celebration was all about. I mean, I knew I had fooled evil and defeated it, but I wasn't expecting anyone to celebrate it.

I shook my head and smiled when I walked outside. Fish was there, and he looked completely healed. I couldn't believe Charles was still following him around. I was happy to see that Magia had forgiven him for the jokes. I still didn't know what he had done to the wizards. They didn't seem bothered by it. They were talking to Fish and not showing any signs of a grudge.

"Is this what we're celebrating?" I asked. "The return of Fish?"

Everyone turned and cheered as I made my way out. Cory and his wife were there. Renee, Cheryl, and Delia were also there. I assumed Vera and Steven were still on their honeymoon. I searched the crowd for Viola, but she was nowhere to be found.

"Where is Netiri?" I asked.

"He's with William," Cory answered. "William said they would be right back."

I looked for Viola again. I couldn't help but wonder where she was. Then I remembered about Irene. Had she gone back to Salem with her already? I wanted to throw myself at her feet, beg her a million times to forgive me. I could only hope that I wasn't too late.

"Someone has been waiting to see you," my mother said.

My heart began racing. I began to look around for Viola again. I think my mother realized I assumed she was talking about Viola.

"She went home, Ethan. She left two days ago with Irene and Melanie."

"I see," I said, looking down.

As everyone celebrated Fish's return, I went back inside to get my wand. When I came back out, I asked my mother where Viola was staying.

"I think at Melanie's house," she answered. "But you can't leave yet. William will be disappointed if you miss the celebration."

"I won't be long, Mother."

"Attor has been waiting to see you," she informed me.

"Please, tell him I won't be long," I said, removing my ring.

I disappeared into a vortex within seconds. I was back in Salem, back in the kitchen of the mansion. I quickly made my way out in search of Viola. Melanie's house wasn't far from here. I ran as fast as my feet could carry me. I was out of breath when I reached Melanie's house. I knocked on the door and stepped back. When Melanie opened the door, she threw herself into my arms.

"Thank you," she cried. "Thank you for giving me back my sister."

"How is she doing?" I asked, as Melanie pulled away.

Melanie hugged me again. She sobbed as she thanked me over and over again.

"You'll never know how much you truly gave back to me," she said, going into another sob.

"How is she?" I asked again.

She pulled away from me.

"She's still in Magia. William said he needed to help her with a few things before she could come back and resume her life."

"My mother said she had left with you? She said both her and Viola came with you."

"Ethan, Viola is gone. She left two days ago."

"Gone? What do you mean?"

"When William said it would take a few months to help Irene, Viola decided to leave Salem. She said she would come back when her mother returned. She said something about not wanting to feel heartbreak anymore."

"Do you know where she went?"

"I do, but she didn't want me to tell you."

I didn't insist and walked away. I deserved this and more. It was my fault she wanted to forget all about me. I never treated her like someone I loved. I took advantage of her love for me and neglected our relationship. What did I expect would happen? I remembered what Renee and Cheryl had said to me. They said I had never done anything to deserve Viola's love. They threw in my face that Viola already loved me when I arrived in Salem; reminded me that things had already been laid out for me. All these things were true. I never lifted a finger to earn Viola's love.

Viola had put herself in so much danger to help me. She never questioned the things William asked her to do. If the requests had anything to do with me, Viola was always on board. I thought of the horrible things I've said to her in the past. Those were my dark days, and still, she never stopped loving me.

I decided to return to Magia. I would beg Renee and Cheryl to tell me where she was. I didn't care if it took me years to find her, I was going to win her back. I ran back to the mansion, grabbed a few things, and disappeared into a vortex.

Chapter Thirty: Black Witch

    I was rather shocked when I returned to Magia. The celebration seemed to have grown. There was a large crowd standing near the waterfall. All of Magia's wizards were there. The fairies circled the area, spreading sparkles of light into the water. There must have been about fifty guards, all holding up their swords. Around the crowd were the dragons. Attor was standing in the middle, looking down at someone.

    I was starting to think the celebration wasn't about Fish. As I got closer, I saw Renee and Cheryl kneeling down. They both had their heads bowed, and William was standing over them. I was surprised to see that William was wearing his crown. He held his crystal sword over the two women.

    "Magia owes you a mountain of gratitude for what you've done," William was saying. "You have shown bravery and honor when protecting this kingdom. Let it be written in stone that no woman will ever be passed over again. You are true wizards and will always be known as such. Magia had learned its lesson. Women have shown they can be as strong as a man, if not stronger. You will walk this land with heads held high. All wizards will bow before you and show their respects. I bestow upon you the title of knighthood. May all kings to come, see your worth."

William lowered his crystal sword and tapped each of their heads. Bright, gold sparkles of light came streaming out of the sword. I smiled when beautiful gold and silver armor began forming on Renee and Cheryl. Attor blew fire down in front of them. When the fire burned out, two large swords were laying before them.

"You may rise," William said to them.

"Thank you, Your Majesty," they both answered.

The dragons began blowing fire as Renee and Cheryl picked up their swords. The guards lowered their swords and took a knee. William glanced at the wizards, then nodded. When they too, took a knee, everyone began to cheer. I knew this was a big deal. There was only one magical being in Magia with that honor, and that was Attor.

I made my way to Renee and Cheryl and took a knee. "Congratulations," I said, to the knights.

"Thank you," Your Majesty," they said bowing.

I knew this honor and moment was too big to ruin. I decided not to ask them about Viola and let them enjoy the moment. One by one, the wizards stepped forward to congratulate them. I began looking around for Netiri. There was something I needed to ask him. William approached me as I was about to go look for my friend.

"A word, if I may?" he said to me.

William removed his crown, handed it to one of the wizards, and waved his hand at himself. I couldn't understand why William chose human clothes for himself.

"Have you seen Netiri?" I asked.

"He's at Thea's Lake, waiting with the others. I told them to wait at the village until we got back."

"Got back?"

"We have a few stops to make before we speak to them," William answered. "A few loose ends we must take care of."

William waved his hand at me. Soon after, I had human clothes on my frame.

"Shall we?" William asked.

We both disappeared into a vortex. When we came out, we were at the Fall River Country Club.

"The warlocks?" I asked.

"Yes. They should be along very soon."

Just then, three cars began coming down the long path. William and I stood aside as the warlocks parked. The wives got out first, then the warlocks. Rapoza got a worried look on his face when he saw us. William quickly assured him that everything was fine. We were introduced to the wives before the women headed inside the club.

"Glad to see you are doing well, Ethan," Rapoza said to me.

"Yes, I'm much rested," I answered.

"How can I help you both?" Rapoza asked.

William looked at Lima, Moc and Rapoza. I knew he was trying to find the words to thank them. How could you thank them for something so huge? These men put their lives on the line, even when they knew it was possible that I would kill them.

"You seem to be having trouble finding your voice," Rapoza said to William. "Why don't you join us for lunch, and we can talk after?"

"Another time," William answered. "I'm afraid we have other matters to attend to."

"Of course you do," Moe laughed.

"The reason we came here," William began, "I wanted to thank all of you for standing by us. When I began my search for men of honor, your names were the first to be revealed to me. I spent years observing you, watching you all live honest lives. You were fair to your enemies, kind to your friends, and protective of your families."

I suddenly realized that the Tree of Life had given William the names of these warlocks.

"You never allowed Simon to taint your character," William continued. "You saw right through his evil and stood your ground. It is men like you that make this world a better place. I can see how much family matters to you. Because of that, your offspring will continue your legacy."

He reached into his pocket and pulled out three rings. I smiled when I realized what he was about to do.

"If there is ever anything I can help you with, these rings will show you the way. Because you are men of honor, you will always be welcomed in my kingdom. Know that you will always find a friend in us."

He gave them each a ring.

"Use them wisely," William said.

Rapoza looked down at his ring.

"This is quite the gift, William," he said, looking back at him. "I once told you that you were never my enemy, but that you were also never my friend. I cannot say those words to you anymore. You will always be more than a friend to us. If ever you need us, we will always be waiting."

William glanced at me.

"That day may come, Ron."

We shook hands with them then turned to leave.

"You know, Wizard," Rapoza said. "You should come and play some golf with us some day. I think you will find it very relaxing."

William smiled. "I will take you up on that, Ron. I see that I will have more than enough time now," William said, glancing at me…again.

We thanked them again and left for our next stop. We were back in Salem and headed to the deli. I have to say, I really missed working there. Most of all, I missed those delicious grinders. It's hard to believe that just a few months ago I tried one for the first time. So many things were new to me then. I remember my first day in Salem, I couldn't understand why the humans covered the ground in cement. Of course it was pavement, something I understood now. I understood a lot of things that didn't make sense to me then. I was really going to miss it all.

"May I ask you something?" I said to William, as we walked down the snow-covered street.

"You may."

"When did the Tree of Life give you those names?"

He chuckled. "Five hundred years ago. Do you know how frustrating it was trying to figure out why the tree had given me those names?"

"It didn't tell you?"

"Unfortunately, no. I memorized those names and tried putting the puzzle together for years. I asked myself; are they names of enemies or friends? It took me so many years to finally discover the answer."

"I think I'm starting to understand the Tree of Life," I laughed.

"Yes. It gives you the answers, but not the way you would hope."

As we neared the deli, I looked at Viola's empty bench. It was covered in snow and salt from where Sean had cleaned the sidewalk. It made me sad to think she would never sit there again. I looked through the window of the deli, thinking of all the good times I spent here.

"You'll have time to make new memories," William said. "Sean will be an especially important part of your life. Susan will play a vital role in your future."

"My future? Here?" I asked surprised. "I thought I was staying in Magia?"

"You will, but not for long."

"What do you mean?"

He gave a sideways glance.

"Why don't you ask the tree?"

He was chuckling as we walked into the deli. Sean and Susan were busy cleaning. Sean had taken all the racks apart and was scrubbing them down. I quickly offered to help.

"Pedro and Wayne are here," Sean said. "They're cleaning the walk-in and freezer. I think we've got this."

I went to the back of the deli to say hello to them. Wayne was scrubbing the slicer when I walked in.

"Hello, Wayne," I greeted him.

Wayne was Sean's delivery driver. He was a good guy and a hard worker. As I approached him, I began to get flashes of his life. I was there, fighting by his side. I instantly knew he would also play a part in my future.

"Hey, Ethan. What's up?" he said, extending his hand out. "Haven't seen you in a while. How have you been?"

I shook it and glanced around for Pedro.

"I've been good," I answered. "I'll be coming back to work soon. Where is Pedro?"

"He stepped out to grab us some lunch. The walk-in is empty right now, so we had to order food."

The moment I said Pedro's name, I knew he would also be part of my future. I said goodbye and walked out. I said hello to Susan then helped her move one of the display cases. I thanked her for helping my mother and gave her a hug.

"You sound like you're leaving Salem," she said.

I glanced at William.

"Just for a brief time. I'll be needing a job when I come back," I smiled.

"It will be waiting," Sean answered.

William thanked Sean and told him he would see him soon. I noticed he didn't give Sean the speech he had given the warlocks. That only meant one thing; Sean knew I was coming back.

"Consider this your vacation," Sean said to me. "I bought the bakery next door. Cory made me an offer I couldn't refuse. I'll be expanding the deli, so get some rest."

When we left the deli, I asked William about what he'd said to me. I had no idea I was coming back to Salem. What changed?

"I didn't sense my return to Salem, William. Are you sure I'm supposed to come back? Why did I just see Wayne and Pedro in my future?"

He only gave me another sideways glance.

"I know, ask the tree," I said, rolling my eyes.

When we approached Doctor Crowley's office, I asked William what we were doing here. I could see Kelly through the big window from where we stood. She was talking to Erika. William wouldn't look away from her.

"Why are we here?" I asked again.

William looked towards the water, then back at Kelly. His eyes followed every move she made.

"You saved one tortured soul from hell," he said. "Now it's time to save another one."

"Kelly? Is she in danger?"

"I wasn't talking about Kelly," he answered.

I had to give his words some thought. Then it hit me. Was he serious?

"You want me to save the Black Witch?"

"Her name is Agatha, and the answer is yes."

"Wait, you said she's been down there for thousands of years. How am I supposed to help her when no one else has been able to?"

"That is a good question, Ethan. I hope you find the answer."

"William, won't hell just look for another Black Witch to replace her?"

He was still looking at Kelly.

"Perhaps hell has already found her." he said, looking back at me.

I looked into his eyes, hoping I was wrong about what I was thinking.

"No," I said, looking toward Kelly. "Not her."

"What have I done?" William said, in a sarcastic tone. "I just told you the future. Oh no, now things will change."

I looked at Kelly, then toward the water. I remembered that map Irene had left me. Was it a clue? Was she trying to warn me about that? Then it hit me; hell had been watching Kelly this whole time. She was the perfect candidate, too. Not because she was evil, but because she was strong. I always knew Kelly was a sassy witch. What she did at the bank showed me she was brave as well. Would evil flood her with problems now? I knew it was the only way to change her.

"Not her, William. I can't let that happen."

"Let what happen? I don't know what you're talking about?"

"Here we go again," I said, throwing up my hands. "You said Kelly was the next Black Witch, remember?"

"You know, Ethan. Sometimes I think it would be easier to just hit you over the head."

He pulled out his ring.

"Can we go now? Or are you still figuring things out?"

When I didn't answer him, he rolled his eyes.

"I just moved the branch, Ethan. It can't happen that way anymore."

"But you said it would happen regardless," I reminded him.

"I also said you were supposed to kill the warlocks. Are they dead? What happened at Doctor Crowley's office changed everything, Ethan. Neither one of us ever lifted a finger to change the future. When they gave you the morphine, things changed organically. That's when I realized a different outcome was possible."

I looked toward Kelly again. She was talking to one of the patients. I couldn't see how it was possible that hell was going to change her. I understood *why* it wanted her. Kelly was fearless. Not caring about what people thought about her was one of her best qualities. She didn't think twice about speaking up for herself or helping someone in need.

As I watched her, I knew I would keep a watchful eye and protect her. I wasn't about to let hell change her into something she wasn't. If William had moved the branch, then I was going to cut down the tree. I know; I don't know what I meant by that either.

William took off his ring and we disappeared into a vortex.

Epilogue

When we returned to Magia, the celebration had ended. My parents were sitting near the waterfall with Fish, Delia and Cory. This part of the story I knew. My parents were about to tell them they had decided to move back to Salem. I wasn't sure if my parents were ready to hear what *they* were about to tell *them*.

William and I made our way over to the group. I noticed Fish and the others no longer had an orb following them around. Delia already had tears streaming down her face. Had they told my parents already? William and I stayed a few feet back as they continued their conversation.

"We're going back to Salem today," Cory was saying. "But we have something to tell you both. We all agreed that we would tell you before we left."

My mother smiled and looked at my father. He nodded and reached for her hand.

"Thea and I, well, we have something to tell you as well."

"We're moving back to Salem," my mother announced.

Cory, Delia and Fish just looked at each other. Delia started crying into her hands.

"Is something wrong?" my mother asked. "I thought you would be happy to hear the news?"

Cory cleared his throat.

"Thing is, Thea. We've been talking, and we've made a very important decision."

"Oh?" my father said.

Fish kept his head down. Delia only sobbed into her hands.

"You're scaring me," my mother said.

"It's nothing bad," Cory answered. "I mean, you may take it hard, but for us, it's a long time coming."

"What is it that you want to tell us?" my father asked.

Cory took a deep breath.

"Well, we will never regret helping you both. I would do it all over again if I had to. But to be honest with you, I feel it's time we all get on with our lives. I have a wife now, and hope to one day have kids. Helena and I have talked about adopting. Point is, I want to live a normal life with my family. I don't want to be dragged away because there's danger around the corner. I want to have grandchildren and watch them grow up."

"Delia and I want more kids, too," Fish added. "I'm sure Vera and Steven will give us plenty of grandchildren. I don't want my daughter or her children going through what we did. Again, we have no regrets about that. It's just time, Thea. No more danger, no more killing, and no more fearing a vision you may have."

"But you can have all those things," my mother said. "Salem will be peaceful when we all go home."

"For how long? Until the next time someone comes pounding on our door?" Delia shot back. "Don't you see, Thea? We're done. I think what we're all trying to tell you is; we're not going to take the aging potion anymore. We want to grow old and never worry about being in danger again."

"We've talked about it a lot," Cory said. "It's time to let us go, Thea. I want to travel the world. Helena was never the same after what Simon did to her. I think a trip around the world will do her well. We've been in Salem for so long that I can't remember the last time we left that place. I mean, I still love Salem. It's where I want to grow old with my family. But for now, it's time for us to leave and search for our happiness. You know we'll always love you, Thea. Nothing can ever change that. I have no regrets about the past.

My mother's tears spilled over as she looked at her friends. They were her greatest loves, besides my father and I, that is. They shared a special bond, one that couldn't be broken. I knew my mother would have a hard time letting them go.

Even if my mother decided to age with them, it was well known that wizards aged very slowly. Our lives ended when the Tree of Life said it would. Some wizards hadn't aged a single day in hundreds of years. Each wizard had a purpose, and until that purpose was fulfilled, their lives could last forever. There were some wizards that were killed; poisoned in the human world.

"I don't know what to say," my mother cried.

"Say that you'll stay with us until our end," Delia cried. "Say you'll watch us grow old and be by our side. I want you to be there when we play with our grandchildren. I want them to know you and love you the same way we do. Say you'll do all those things with us, Thea."

"I will," my mother said, throwing her arms around Delia.

Soon, they were all crying in each other's arms. My mother kept kissing and throwing her arms around them. Something told me she would try to find a way to grow old with them. I would make it a point to ask the Tree of Life to help her.

"I also have a bit of news," William said, stepping forward.

They all looked at him.

"What is it, father?"

"What I'm about to say is directed at your friends," William said, looking at them. "Many years ago, when you all were kids, I had to take something away from you. It was not a choice I made lightly. I knew your lives would be in danger if I didn't step in."

"You took something from us?" Cory said. "I don't remember knowing you when I was a kid."

"Aww, but you did, Cory. You lived next door with Sharron."

"I remember Sharron," he answered. "But Thea lived next door, alone."

William smiled.

"Your part of the story has reached its end. It's time to live your lives and move on. What I took from you, I took out of concern for you all. I knew it would be too dangerous to remember who I was. But now, there is no reason for me to hold what is yours."

William waved his hand, sending his magic at the group. Streams of energy flowed into their ears and mouth. They seemed dazed for several long moments. When the streams of energy faded away, they all gasped. I knew William had given them back their childhood memories. Even though they remembered being kids, William erased himself from their memories. Every adventure they shared, William had played a role in. He watched over them, making sure they wanted for nothing.

My mother told me the stories she lived through with them. Her trips to the North Pole, meeting Santa Claus, riding a pumpkin she had turned into a carriage, and so many other adventures. William was there for everyone; always saving the day and bringing them back home.

William's eyes began to spill over as they took it all in. His voice was cracking as he tried to get his words out.

"How can you thank someone for their sacrifices," he began. "You have been, and continue to be, Thea's loves. You stood by her when I could not. You never abandoned her in her time of need. You have been faithful and loving to her. I cannot explain the amount of gratitude I feel. I know I can never give you what you've lost, but I hope this gift will help you find your happiness," he said, holding up a box.

He placed the box in front of them and stood back. Delia reached for it and looked up at William.

"What is it?" she asked.

"In that box are three rings, one for each of you. If ever you have a need for anything, simply place the ring on your finger and it shall be granted."

"Are these so we can come visit Magia?" Fish asked.

"No," William answered. "Think of it as, Charles."

They all gave William a hug. My father had tears in his eyes when he threw his arms around Fish. William and I walked away as they all cried in each other's arms. William noticed I was looking around for Netiri. Where had he gone?

"He's sitting just outside the Tree of Life" he informed me.

"How about Irene?" I asked.

"She's with the wizards. It's going to take some time for her to forgive herself for the past. I'm sure Magia will help her. She has a lot of traumas from being down there. The trauma of killing one of her children will take the longest to heal. I will help her understand that evil made her to that."

I nodded and pulled out my wand.

"I have one more stop to make," I said, mounting my staff. "It's time someone else forgives himself for the past."

I took to the sky and headed toward the Tree of Life. When I got there, Netiri was leaning against one of the big oak trees. He sat motionless, just staring at the Tree of Life.

"There you are," I said, landing a few feet away. "What are you doing here?"

I leaned my staff on the tree and took a seat next to him. There was such a sad look on his face.

"What's going on?" I asked.

He was still looking at the Tree of Life.

"That's some tree, huh?" he said, in a soft voice. "I don't think I've ever seen a more beautiful tree in my life."

"William calls it the Tree of Life. I like to call it the Tree of Wisdom."

"I think you're both right," Netiri said, never taking his eyes off the tree.

"What troubles you, Netiri?"

He swallowed thickly.

"You don't want to know, Ethan. You would probably never talk to me again. Couldn't say I would blame you. I deserve that and more."

There was only one word I could think of right now. *Remorse.* Netiri had plenty of it. It was that remorse that told me he never meant to hurt the girl. I knew if he could have switched places with her, he would have.

"Is it about the girl you almost raped?"

He spun his head to look at me.

"How do you know about that?"

He placed his hands over his head. "I never wanted to do that to her. It wasn't me who dragged her into the woods. I wanted to help her, Ethan. I swear it. The warlocks kept saying to rape her or they would kill me. I'm not making excuses. I deserve everything that comes to me. I should have killed them and taken the girl back home. I wanted to; I really did. I will never forgive myself for what happened to her. Why don't you just kill me, Ethan? Just kill me, please," he cried.

His eyes began to change color. They went from blue to green, and now brown. In that moment, I finally figured out why they did that. It was his conscience. William's eyes changed color like that once, and it confused me. Now I understood that they both had things they felt bad about. William felt bad for all the lies, and Netiri felt bad about his past. I could see that Netiri was never going to forgive himself for what he did to that girl. It was time to free him from his torture.

"Answer me, Ethan!"

I ignored him and placed my hands over his head. I didn't erase his past, just the events from that day. His past is what made him who he was today, but I didn't want him to continue blaming himself for the girl. He'd already paid a heavy price for it. He spent hundreds of years alone because of his remorse. He punished himself on a daily basis. He thought himself undeserving of happiness and joy. He never lifted a finger to make his life easier in any way. He had been his own judge and jury and gave himself a life sentence. I had to help him. If he was going to be an important part of my future, I couldn't let him continue to think this way.

When I was done, I got up and reached for my staff. It took Netiri a few moments to shake off my magic. I made it seem like I had just gotten there.

"Oh, Ethan. When did you get here?" he asked.

"Sorry I snuck up on you. I just needed to ask you a question."

He jumped to his feet.

"Sure, what is it, kid?"

There was a different kind of smile on his face. That sad look he always had was gone. I can't explain it, but he looked happy. It only made me realize that I had done the right thing.

"I was wondering what you were doing for the next few hundred years?"

"What?" he laughed.

"I'm going back to Salem. I'll be needing a partner who's got my back. I figured since you're my best friend, who better than you?"

"Kid, I wouldn't have it any other way. We can share my apartment again."

"That won't be necessary. Fish and Delia gave my parents back the mansion. They don't want it. I'll let you have first pick of the bedrooms. That sound fair?"

He smiled. "I love you, kid."

"I will always love you, Netiri."

"I was about to give him one of those, bro hugs when...

"Am I interrupting?"

It was my father.

"No. I was just telling Netiri that we'll be staying in the mansion. He's coming back to Salem with me."

I noticed my father was holding something round and shiny. He saw me looking down at it.

"Oh, this is why I came to find you," he said, holding it up. "It's my contribution to your little Christmas Village. It's an ornament I made for you. I told your mother about the village, and she couldn't wait to see it."

He gave the ornament to me. It had small dragons inside, flying around Magia.

"It's lovely, Father. Thank you."

"Why don't we go show your mother the village? I know she's going to fall in love with it."

I asked Netiri if he wanted to come. He said yes and we all took flight. My mother soon joined us as we flew over her lake. When we arrived at my Christmas Village, my mother had tears in her eyes.

"Oh, Ethan. It's beautiful."

"I had to fix the snow," I explained. "It looks much better now."

"It's perfect," she replied.

"Nice going, kid," Netiri said, from behind me.

"It is nice, isn't it?"

"Where are you going to hang the ornament?" my father asked.

"I'm not sure," I said, looking for a good spot.

"Why don't you put it over there?" he said, pointing toward the cottage.

When I looked that way, my heart almost stopped beating. There, standing in the snow, was Viola. She was wearing a yellow sweater with butterflies on it. Her hair was a knotted, tangled mess.

I think I forgot to breathe as I took in her beauty.

"Go find your happiness," my father whispered in my ear.

Netiri gave me a small pat on the back, then left. My mother kissed my cheek and left with my father.

I slowly made my way to her. The closer I got, the more my heart would pound. There were so many words I wanted to say to her, but for some reason, I couldn't think of a single one. All I wanted was to take her in my arms; beg her to forgive the fool I had been. I loved her. I truly and fully loved her.

"Hello, Viola," I said, taking in her scent.

She looked around the village, then back at me.

"You made this, *for me?*"

"For us," I answered. "I thought it would be our forever place."

"It's beautiful, Ethan."

I wanted to beg her for forgiveness; show her how much she meant to me. I wasn't expecting her to jump into my arms. It was time to earn her love. I reached into my pocket, got on one knee, and opened the box I had.

"Viola, if you choose to forgive me, I will spend my life earning your love. I know my life would be nothing without you. I was a fool to think that you would always be there, no matter what. But I learned that love would die without nourishment. Forgive my ignorance and stupidity. Allow me to show you how much you mean to me. Viola, would you do me the great honor of being my wife? Will you marry me?"

Her eyes were telling me yes, but her mouth hadn't caught up yet. Why wasn't she answering me?

"I can't, Ethan."

This time, I think my heart really stopped.

"I understand," I said, bowing my head.

"No, it's not what you think."

"Unless *I can't*, has a new meaning, I think your answer was no."

I rose to my feet and began to close the box. I looked at her when she placed her hand over it.

"May I say something now?" she asked.

Her liquid brown eyes were melting my heart.

"Of course."

"I love you, Ethan Wade. I want to spend the rest of my life with you. I realized that we both took things very fast. We never gave ourselves a chance to discover who the other truly is. I don't know what your favorite food is, or how late you sleep, or if you like the things I do. I want us to discover all those things together. I want to know everything about you, Ethan. And I need you to know everything about me. I'm not going anywhere. You are my one true love. I just can't marry you right now. Not until you can't live a single day without thinking of me."

I ran my fingers along her face. She was right; I didn't know much about her. I did know this; I didn't want to live without her. I also knew I had done nothing to earn her love. That would always be in the back of my head. Had she fallen in love with me because of *me*, or because she was *told* she would? The answer was staring back at me right now. Her own words told me the truth. She knew nothing about me. Would she still fall in love with me if she got to know me? Would I be man enough to win her over on my own?

Renee said I never had to lift a finger to earn her love. She said Viola already loved me. That always stuck with me. I wanted Viola to experience what I had when I first met her. She was the shy girl who sat in front of the deli. I fell in love with her smile, her personality and her charm. If she hadn't known about me, would she have fallen in love with my *qualities*? There was only one way to find out.

"I love you, Viola."

She smiled. "I love you, too."

I leaned in as if I was about to kiss her. When she closed her eyes, I waved my hand. I took any memory she had of me from her head. I took a step back and let my magic take me out of her heart. She deserved to be courted. If I had to spend the rest of my life earning her love, so be it. I was determined to win her love by my actions, nothing else. She would love me because of me, not because she saw it in her future.

"I love you, Viola," I said again, just before taking her back to Salem.

Made in the USA
Middletown, DE
19 October 2024

62853840R00222